Bound by Light

Demi Warrik

Demi Warrik
Bound by Light: Fates Mark 2
Copyright © Demi Warrik 2021 All rights reserved
First published in 2021

No part of this book may be reproduced, stored in a retrieval system, or transmitted in any form or by any means whatsoever without written permission except in the case of brief quotations embodied in reviews or articles. All characters in this publication other than those clearly in the public domain are fictitious, and any resemblance to real persons, living or dead, is purely coincidental. The unauthorized reproduction or distribution of a copyrighted work is illegal. Criminal copyright infringement without monetary gain is investigated by the FBI and is punishable by fines and federal imprisonment.

Editing: Proofs By Polly
Proofreader: Raven Quill Editing, LLC
Cover: Ryn Katryn Digital Art

AUTHOR'S NOTE

Well, hello there, dear reader! I see you made it back for more torture. I mean, uh, book two! As with Marked by Night, this book will contain themes some readers may find triggering. It also includes detailed sex scenes, fighting, and lots of cursing. But y'all already knew that by now, didn't you? *waggles eyebrows*

Take care, my loves. You're in for a ride with this one.

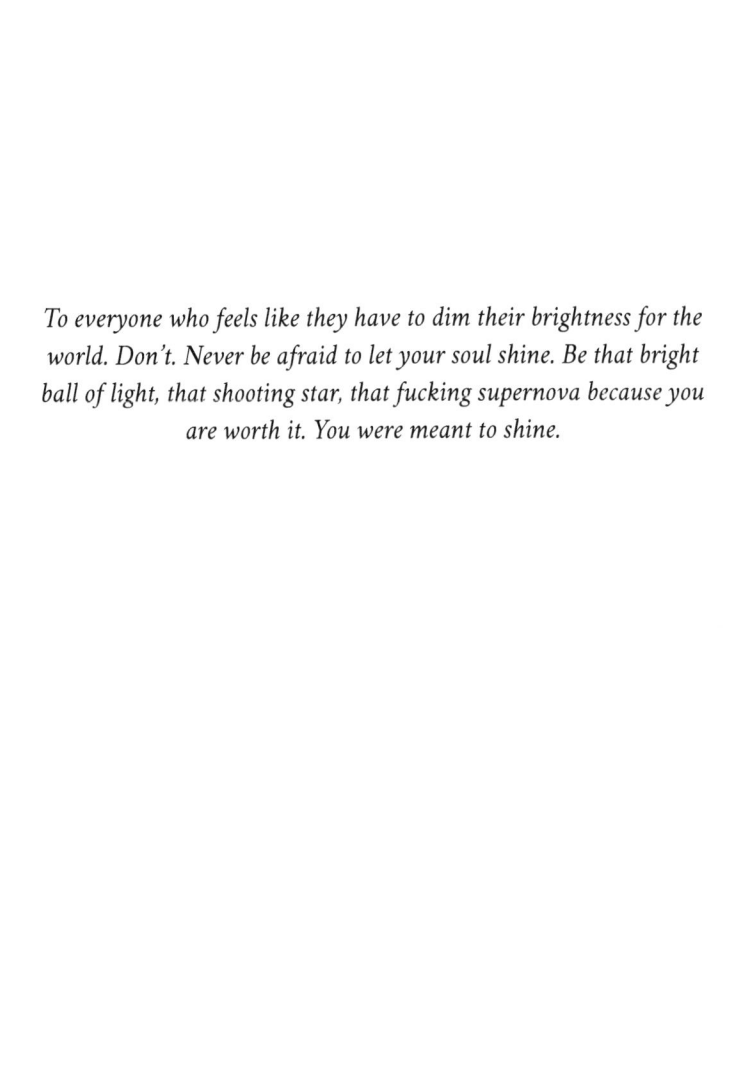

To everyone who feels like they have to dim their brightness for the world. Don't. Never be afraid to let your soul shine. Be that bright ball of light, that shooting star, that fucking supernova because you are worth it. You were meant to shine.

1

SADIE

They say killing takes a chip out of your soul, leaves a crack in your essence, yet all I feel is numb as blood drips down my arm in heavy rivulets. It splatters across my face as I yank the dagger free from the man's lifeless body and let him slump to the ground at my feet. I don't spare him another glance as I continue the search for my next target.

Sometimes in life, you have to make bad decisions to right the wrongs of others. An eye for an eye, of sorts. I don't care about the trail I'm leaving behind and I sure as hell don't care about the despicable lives I'm ending. I haven't cared much about anything since Elian dropped those three little words.

Ashley is missing.

That statement was like a bomb going off in my life, shattering a piece inside of me. I wasn't good enough, strong enough, or even powerful enough to keep my best friend safe. I failed her.

The shadows haven't left my side since the battle with my shitty ex-boyfriend, Tyler. They've chosen to envelop my body like a protective blanket, like they know I need them. Sometimes I feel like they're more sentient than even I know, but the guys don't get the same vibes from them as I do. They seem to think they're only a mass of darkness while I believe there's more to them than that.

We've used the three days since Ash's disappearance to relentlessly scour for leads on where she might have been taken and we finally found a small outpost, hidden amongst the trees, long forgotten by anyone other than the cruel Elites. One of Elian's connections led us here and I'm convinced the Night Weavers are the ones who have her. The Light Weavers may have attacked us at the concert, but I don't think I was their true target. The other Night Weavers were and in my opinion, Kaos and I got caught in the crossfire, but that's probably something I need to ask Reed to be certain.

Speaking of the Elites, the one at the entrance of the dilapidated building spots me and readies his blade, but I'm quicker. I pounce on him, forcing us both down to the dirt as we battle for dominance. He writhes beneath me as I center my weight and settle over him before driving the dagger straight into his chest. I stand, wiping the blood on my jeans as I continue the search for Ash by throwing open the door to the building and running inside. No alarm bells sound at my intrusion, so I'm considering that a win.

Though, a different Elite on the inside spots me and attacks, but I'm able to render him useless as quickly as the first. Another faceless Elite down, who knows how many more to go. They're all the same at this point, blending together like one big blight on this earth. I refuse to feel guilty over their deaths. Especially when they deserve to die.

Kaos rounds the corner from the opposite direction at the same time as me and I barely avoid stabbing him in the chest, deep in the bloodlust keeping my limbs moving and my mind numb. If it weren't for that, I'd likely have collapsed by now. I'm exhausted but I can't stop. If I let myself settle, I'll certainly succumb to my fatigue and I can't.

Kaos takes in my wild hair and blood splattered appearance in a smooth glance. "Moons above, Little Flame. I know you're hurting and angry, but we can't keep dropping bodies. We will do everything in our power to find her, but we're supposed to be in and out, silent as the night." He tries to take the dagger from my hand while reprimanding me, but I snatch it away from him and hold it to my chest. It angers me that he doesn't think I can handle myself with it.

I'm not the greatest with the longer blade yet, considering it's three times the width of my switchblade and a lot heavier. I haven't had much practice with it either, but he told me I couldn't come in here without a *proper* weapon. The thought almost makes me chuckle. Almost.

When are they going to learn? I *am* a weapon.

As if to prove my point the inky black shadows crawling around my body flare, fluttering to life with the onslaught of my tumultuous emotions.

"The men back there were rapists and deserved to die." How I know that about them though, I've no clue. Another talent I've acquired from my intuition as of late. With a lot of things in life, my intuition gives me a leg up that others don't have, but now it's so much more. With certain people, mainly bad ones, it gives me a play-by-play or sometimes a rundown on their life, which does come in handy.

I side-step Kaos and head toward the stairs that lead to the underground basement. According to Elian's schematics, anyway. I poured over those on the way here, making sure I marked each and every hidey hole these bastards might stick her in.

"That may be so but you're only going to enrage the

Elders further," Kaos says cautiously, making my lip curl at the mention of those assholes.

"At this point, I don't care."

The stench of dried blood hits my nostrils as I descend the steps. Gods, this place is essentially a concrete tomb for anyone trapped inside. I kick the stairway door open and steady myself as Kaos' pounding footsteps echo behind me. He stops me before I can burst through the degrading double doors labeled 'dungeons.' Like this is the freaking eighteenth century.

"Please, stop for a second, mate," he pleads, grabbing onto my wrist and tugging me into his chest. He pulls my eyes to his with his fingers gently touching my chin, lifting my head as I wrap my arms around him.

Being in such close proximity to him makes me yearn for his touch. He's downright delicious in a black leather jacket, tight black cargo pants, and combat boots. Yet, I find no peace in his embrace because I can't. If I allow myself even the smallest of his comforts, I'll break down and I don't know if I could get back up.

He sighs, rubbing his hands up and down my arms. "You can't keep burning the candle at both ends. You're going to burn yourself out. Besides, we still have the matter of the challenge issued—"

"Screw the challenge," I interrupt. "Savannah will get what's coming to her, but Ash needs me, Kaos. We have to find her." I stare into his eyes, desperately urging him to understand my need to find my best friend.

He leans his forehead against mine. "And we will, of that I'm certain."

"She might not even be here," I admit, hating that my intuition isn't telling me anything about Ash right now. "It's my fault for letting her go."

"Don't blame yourself, Little Flame. Everything's going to

be all right, okay? There are more compounds to search I'm sure, we just have to find them."

I shake my head. "I'm going to own my mistake even if I have to burn every one of these wretched places down. Every. Single. One. Until I find her, Kaos," I say through clenched teeth, and wrench away from his arms before I lose myself in them, racing through the doors.

To my surprise, Dante, Elian, and Hemsworth are already in the basement, the former two cutting the spelled ropes that bind the shivering shifters' hands. They're hardly wearing anything at all, only thin scraps that you can barely call clothes. My heart squeezes for them.

Apparently, the ropes binding them are called bane ropes and they nullify any supernatural's power while wearing them. The guys were shocked I was able to get mine off to defeat Tyler when he bound me at our last standoff—after I told them the whole story. Yet another thing showcasing my differences from the normal Night Weavers.

The shifters are skittish and shaking, covered in scars, but I know that's the least of their worries. It's the mental stains that will last. Some of them flinch at the sight of me as I step toward them, likely because of the blood covering me, or maybe it's the fact that I'm a Weaver.

At least it isn't innocent blood, I tell myself, maybe to appease my conscience, I'm not entirely certain.

"Are these all of the prisoners?" I ask, and Dante gives me a grim nod.

After surveying the whole room once more, my eyes connect with Elian's. He's dressed similarly to Kaos and Dante, but danger and destruction leak from his very pores, giving him an edge that the other two don't have. Well, they do, but in completely different ways. He runs a hand through his tuft of hair before giving me a slight head shake, indicating that Ash's not here like I suspected.

Without thinking and utterly frustrated, I waltz over and punch the concrete wall as hard as possible. There's an audible crack as the skin of my knuckle splits open and the bone shatters. Before the pain can fully register, Kaos is there with those glowing black hands and his healing magic. "But I want to feel the pain. I shouldn't feel anything less while she's being held hostage."

He levels those bright blue eyes on me and his magic brushes up against my senses, threatening to make the careful control I have over my emotions slip. "Sadie, I want you to listen to me. This is not your fault. You can't keep beating yourself up over it." He grips my hand a touch harder, as if stressing his point.

"But it is!" I shout as tears spring to my eyes. I take a deep breath and try to rein in my emotions, glancing away from the comfort in his gaze. I need to stay calm and in control if I'm ever going to find Ash. She may not have the luxury of time to wait on me to sort my shit out.

He places his thumb and forefinger on my chin, bringing my eyes back to his. "Ultimately, she left to go visit her parent's graves." I start to object but his eyes implore me to listen. "Despite your wishes, she left. You are *not* at fault for that." A small part of my brain recognizes that he's right, but it doesn't ease the guilt gnawing away at me. He puts his arm around my shoulder, not seeming to care about the blood in the slightest. "Come on, let's get you home, Little Flame."

And for some reason, I let him guide me outside. Past the cages stained red, past the chairs with heavy metal chains, past the dead shifters still in their wolf form splayed out on tables, sans their vital bits with empty eyes. Nausea pools in my gut, threatening to make me expel its measly contents at the sight.

Moons, I don't think I'll ever be able to rid my mind of the atrocities I've witnessed in this prison, because once this adrenaline wears off... Once that is gone, all I'll be left with is sorrow, exhaustion, and the images of what they've done to these prisoners. I try not to picture Ash as one of them.

I shove all of the spiraling thoughts out of my mind, locking them up tight in my mental box; the one where I place any desperate memories I don't want to examine too closely or else I might fall apart. Instead, I focus on Kaos' hand on my back while he leads me outside. The sound of Hemsworth's paws clicking on the floor trails along behind us, lending me his silent support. Much like the shadows, he hasn't left my side in days. I don't mind either of them, really. Some days, I like them being around. It's like a constant reminder that I have someone in my corner, helping me in everything I do.

After my fight with Tyler, the Elders and the Elites have backed off a bit and have stopped sending forces after us. Though, I'm not naïve enough to think they've given up completely, but at least I don't have to worry about running headfirst into an all-out brawl every time I leave the wards anymore. For now.

Apparently, after the fight at the concert, and the ambush outside Bedi's, they learned they can't come at me directly without incurring a lot of casualties. Even if most of it was purely coincidental. They don't need to know that though. As far as they're concerned, I'm a total badass.

When we emerge from the compound, I take a deep breath, inhaling the fresh night air. The crickets chirp and an animal rustles in the nearby trees as a coyote lets out a lone howl. The stars are out in full force without light pollution blocking them out. Even the moon sitting high in the sky is brighter, winking at me from above, like it's telling me everything is going to be okay, but will it really?

"Can you think of anywhere she might go? If she did manage to escape?" Kaos asks, his blue eyes softening.

Frankly, the thought never crossed my mind that she might've actually managed to escape. She's scrappy when she has to be but she's not a fighter like I am, and against Weavers who have magic? The score isn't good.

But still, I take a moment to sort through everything I do know, instead of focusing on what I don't. The biggest thing that stuck out to me about the scene of her disappearance, was that there didn't seem to be any kind of struggle. Their car was parked on the side of the road, and there was a bullet hole through the windshield—likely magic bullets according to Kaos, and a ton of blood on the driver's side like the shifter bled out, but no body. There was nothing on the passenger side, but Ash's door was open like she tried to make a run for it.

Think, Sadie. Where would Ash go?

Both of our families were dirt poor, so we never really had a lot… but Ash did have a home before her parents died and it was condemned due to no one living in it and the foundation starting to crumble. *That has to be it, right?*

After Skylar died, Ash became my only family and by extension—her family. They never treated me like an outsider and welcomed me with open arms at one of the lowest points in my life. I felt their loss like they were my own parents, and I was right there with Ash through it all. After that, we decided not to let anyone else in. We became each other's only friends, leaning on one another instead of the outside world. Occasionally, Ash fucked around or had boyfriends that kept her attention but never for long. It was mainly the two of us against the world.

"My gut is telling me we need to check her old family home," I say, turning it over in my mind. "If she did manage to escape, it's familiar territory for her. She knows that would be the first place I'd check, a place that the enemies wouldn't likely know about."

Kaos watches me from under his thick black lashes, assessing the pros and cons in a millisecond as he rubs my arms. Finally, he gives me a nod. "I'm learning to trust your gut as much as my own."

"Maybe I should be learning how to do that also," I respond with a sigh. "But when you've been on your own for as long as I have, it's hard to let others in, to trust that someone else might know what's best for me. Ash has always been my person. The one constant presence in my life. Now I have all of you and… it's been challenging to say the least."

"You don't have to explain yourself to me, Little Flame. I'm your mate, I'll always stand behind you, or if you'll let me, at your side."

Tears spring to my eyes but for an entirely different reason. How did I manage to get so lucky? Sometimes I wonder if my life is even real anymore or if I died that night with my brother.

Hemsworth nudges my hand comfortingly as I back away from Kaos and wait for the others to emerge. He has been quiet lately, but I know he's hurting seeing me in pain.

The outside guard lies at the door where I killed him. I feel like I should care, but I don't have any remorse. He deserved to die. Though, I do have to wonder about their security here. Either they didn't expect us to find this place or they don't care about the lives here. Both ways you look at it, it's fucked up.

When Dante and Elian emerge, coming to a stop before me, I give each of them a look, waiting until I have their full attention before speaking. "Get the shifters loaded up. Tomorrow we're heading back to Hale Springs."

My hometown.

No one argues with me. Not even Elian. I think they know I'm hurting and need to call the shots right now.

It takes us a while, but we finally get everyone, all ten

shifters included, loaded into the cars to head back to the estate, and then we're ready to go.

Dante gives me a lopsided grin from his position in the driver's seat and when we're far enough away, he snaps his fingers. I catch the bright orange head of the explosion over the tops of the trees as the compound explodes in a fiery wreck.

Fitting, I think.

2

SADIE

Dante and Elian accompany me to Ash's family house the following day. According to the latter, he drew the short stick.

Meanwhile, Kaos and Hemsworth went to check another lead regarding a different prison we found out about from Elian's connection at the main compound. I don't like being so far away from them. My mate bond and familiar bond aren't happy about it either, judging by the faint pull I sense coming from their direction.

There's also the matter of Reed. My fourth mate. My Light Weaver. Technically, my sworn enemy if you go by the culture norms. Not that I give a shit about any of that. I make my own decisions. If he is meant to be with me, he will be. Even if the prospect of having four mates intimidates the hell out of me. He stayed behind at the estate, ensuring us he would keep an eye on things, like the new shifters we took in yesterday. I have to wonder if being sidelined bugs him or if he's glad for the extra time to heal. I make a mental note to ask him about it when I get back.

My thoughts drift as the movement of the car lulls me

into a calm sort of complacency, and for some reason Vinson pops into my mind. The blackness creeping through his veins is getting worse and we're running out of methods to heal him. The mere thought of him dying for protecting me makes me physically sick, even if I barely know him. Sometimes you meet people in your life, and you know they're important without knowing how or why.

On the flip side, Reed seems to be doing much better. But between looking for Ash, killing the bastards that might be behind her disappearance, plotting ways to find her, and him staying back at the estate, we haven't had a chance to talk. Another thing that's piling up on the to-do list. One I know I'm going to have to deal with sooner rather than later. I don't like leaving things so open-ended with him, and I don't want to cause a rift between him and the others.

As soon as Elian turns the car onto Ashley's street, I know something is wrong. Really wrong. If Elian's white knuckles on the steering wheel are any indication, he feels it too. It's like the air itself is tainted and the feeling of unease washes over me like a wave. I almost choke as I open the door and the foul air assaults my nostrils, burying itself in my senses like a deadly smog I can't escape. My shadows seem to recoil in on themselves, sensing things aren't quite right, even if I can't place exactly what yet.

Something bad happened here. Recently, if I had to guess. Swinging the car door shut, I make my way around the side of the car, eyes connecting with Dante and Elian as they stand at the hood. We all give each other a silent look of understanding before we head to the front door. I slip my dagger out of its holster on my thigh, palming the grip with determination. If anyone magical is already here, they'd better run because I'm in the mindset to decimate anyone hostile in my path.

Dante's Illusion magic tingles across my skin, settling my

anxiety. His presence is so calming. He must be casting a spell to provide us some cover. I mean, considering a woman with black swirling shadows encasing her and a dagger in hand isn't exactly inconspicuous. Ask me if I care.

Spoiler alert, I don't.

Not right now, anyway. Maybe if something hadn't happened to my best friend and there wasn't a snake after the men who are also my mates.

Kaos tried to explain more about the logistics of how their magic works, but between the stabbings and the raging, there hasn't been much time to talk about the Weaver world either. We've all been focused on so many other things.

Though, they did manage to give me the basics. Some Weavers, like my Sworn, have an affinity for more than one type of magic. While all Weavers' powers differ from person to person, they're split up into two categories: offensive and defensive.

Kaos' arsenal is mainly defensive, while Dante's more offensive. Elian's still a mystery because he's tight-lipped about it, and so is Reed, but only because we haven't had the chance to talk about it.

My spine prickles and my gaze flicks over to the direction I know my uncle's trailer—or the pit of hell as I used to call it—rests. If we were to take a left out of here and drive down that road a few miles, we'd stop dead center in that wretched place. Gods, everything that happened to me there feels like a lifetime ago.

Being back in the area where my life was changed in so many ways gives me a chill that runs bone-deep, and walking past the decrepit flower bed that leads to the sunken in front porch is disheartening. This place has always been a bit of a dump, but it's gone completely downhill with no one living in it. Not that anyone would even want to live in it now. Especially since part of the kitchen has collapsed in. I'm surprised it hasn't been torn down yet, but the thought of that upsets me.

For Ash and I, this place used to be a safe haven. She had one of those picture-perfect families that you only see in movies, and while they barely had two pennies to rub together, they loved each other. They had these amazing family nights where we would gather around and play Monopoly all night. Ash would flip the board if she lost so we all got to the point where we silently let her win. They were tragically killed in a car accident a few years ago. Hit head-on by a drunk driver and killed instantly.

Shaking myself from those thoughts, I concentrate on my footfalls as they creak across the dilapidated wooden steps. For a moment, I'm afraid we're going to fall right through the boards, but they hold.

My fingers wrap around the doorknob, and I have to take a deep, steadying breath before I twist it open and step inside the worn entryway.

Nostalgia hits me square in the chest as I take in the interior. The picture frames are still meticulously placed down the hallway by Ash's mother, but without most of the pictures in them. Ash took them with her when we found out we couldn't afford to keep up with the mortgage.

Their metal dining room table sits empty in the middle of the kitchen, and even their end tables are still adorned with the crystal bowls they used to ash their cigarettes in. If it weren't for the layer of dust collecting on everything, the stench of mildew, and bits of the ceiling laying on the ground in the kitchen, I'd think they never left. Letting this place go was one of the hardest things for Ash, but we couldn't afford the upkeep.

My gaze snags on one picture in particular and my heart squeezes when I see their three smiling faces. I've always been envious of Ash's relationship with her family. Jealous, even. The hardest time for me to cope with their happy go lucky relationship was after Skylar died and I was bitter, but they were good people and they tried to fill that void for me even though nothing could replace my own family.

I clench and unclench my hand around my dagger in an attempt to bring myself to the present. I'm not here for a trip down memory lane. I'm here to find my best friend, the closest thing I have to a sister.

My shadows trail alongside me, sensing my need for them. "Ash, are you here?" I call out into the empty shell of a home that used to house such laughter and life.

There's no answer.

Fuck, this is another dead end. My teeth grind together, and I reach up to finger Skylar's necklace, trying to find solace in the cool metal but it only gives me a small amount of comfort.

To be certain there are no monsters lurking in the bedrooms, I make my way down the hallway. Elian steps in front of me, cutting me off to take the lead. The action stuns me for a moment because he's such a jerk I don't expect it. It's not until Dante places his hand on my shoulder and gives me a slight squeeze that I start moving again. I'm silently grateful for their support, even though I don't voice it aloud. Especially in front of Elian.

The tiny bathroom Ash and I spent so many hours getting ready in is vacant. Thankfully. I don't think I could handle it if there really were monsters hiding in the shower, waiting to strike. The next room is Ash's old bedroom and it's also undisturbed. Disappointment swirls in my gut like an angry ocean swell.

Yet, the phantom strings of fate guide me onwards. Even if we don't find Ash, I know I'm supposed to be here, in this moment. Everything is leading up to something, but I haven't figured out exactly *what* that is yet.

16 | BOUND BY LIGHT

I find myself holding my breath as Elian pushes open the door to her parents' room. At first, I don't spot anything out of the ordinary. It looks exactly like it did when they were still alive, but as the door swings open further, my heart jumps to my throat.

Written in scrawling handwriting with a substance that looks suspiciously like blood, is a note on the wall, and it's most definitely for me.

"Have you missed me?"

My feet carry me closer as my gaze snags on an odd symbol toward the bottom. It looks vaguely familiar, but I can't force my brain to focus on anything other than the color and Dante's arms as he pulls me back.

Another splotch further down the wall captures my attention, still dripping like the culprit only left moments ago.

"I'm back and I'm coming for you. -M.S."

"M.S. as in Mickey Sinclair, my fucking uncle," I whisper, thinking about how he used to sign all his letters. Never his full signature, only his initials. Icy chills explode down my spine and every single hair on my body stands on end. The coppery tang of fresh blood assaults my nostrils. *Is it Ashley's blood?*

Distantly, I hear footsteps and the front door slamming closed as Elian's demanding presence fades while he presumably goes after my uncle, but I already know Mickey's gone. The bastard is as slippery as an eel. He's been evading me since the night he killed Skylar.

My hands clench into fists and my side. "What if it's hers, Dante?" I eventually ask into the silence, staring at the red splotches on the wall. My vision starts to go wonky as everything around me fades in and out. "I would know if my best friend was dead, right?" I choke on a sob and sink to my knees.

The rest of the shadows slink from the corners of the house to join me as my powers churn inside me. Much like the night of Tyler's ambush and Ashley's disappearance, a black haze descends on my vision, but before things can escalate too far, I'm plucked from the floor and pressed into a hard, lithe chest and the haze evaporates.

Tears stream down my cheeks as I collapse into Dante's arms. For a long time, he doesn't do anything but hold me while I fall apart in his embrace. It's been so long since the last time I cried... Now that the dam is broken, it's going to take a miracle to staunch the flow.

When I realize what I'm doing, Mickey's words swirl through my mind, bringing back the memory of the first time I cried around him. It was right after social services dropped my brother and I off there. I hadn't seen the monster lurking beneath his empty, glassy eyes yet.

That particular day, I scraped my knee on the concrete while playing with the other kids in the trailer park. The first thing I did was run back to his house, crying as my little feet bounded up the steps. Mickey was sitting on the couch, drinking, which should've been my first clue to run, but I was a child and I was hurt. My only thought was my uncle would bandage me up like my dad. As soon as he saw my tears he cracked me across the face, sending my tiny body flying backward. *"Tears are a sign of weakness, Mercedes. And us Sinclair's are not weak. Do you understand me?"*

My lip trembled as much as the rest of my body. *"But—but I scraped my knee."*

The smile on his face sent shivers down my spine. The next thing I knew, he was standing over me. He stuck his thumbnail into the scrape, making me cry out in pain. That was also the second time he slapped me. *"You bear the pain on the inside, girl. You hear me? Not another peep."*

Even then, I looked up at him with defiance I didn't truly understand.

Skylar appeared a moment later, scooping me into his arms. I remember the look of hatred he shot our uncle's way before carrying me to our bedroom. He was my very first knight in shining armor. He doctored me up and kissed my forehead, then kept me distracted the rest of the night. From that moment on he made sure to always be around to take the brunt of Mickey's rage.

I let out a deep breath and try to bring my focus away from the past, to be strong, and not let it suck me under. I reach up to wipe my tears away, but before I can, Dante snatches my wrist and intertwines our fingers, allowing my tears to fall freely. My watery gaze connects with his fiery one as the shadows twirl and dance around us, feeding off my emotions.

"Lean on me, Angel. Let me see those gorgeous tears. You don't have to be strong in front of me."

"What if he comes back?"

I warily glance behind us, but Dante brings my eyes back to his. "Don't worry. We can handle him. Elian's one tough motherfucker. Tell me what's bothering you."

"I can't take my mind off Ash," I admit. "I wouldn't be able to live with myself if something happened to her because I dragged her into this world. Especially at the hands of *him.*" My tears continue to fall and I suck in a ragged breath. "This is all my fault. I should've killed him. I should've—"

"Shh, it's okay. I've got you," Dante murmurs, cutting me off while he squeezes his arms around me, letting me borrow his strength. "We're going to get to the bottom of this, I promise. We don't know for sure he did anything to her yet. This could be a coincidence."

Too bad I don't believe in coincidences.

I turn my head away from him, ashamed for losing my

composure and crying, but he doesn't let me for long. With a firm, but gentle hand, Dante brings my face back toward his, searing me with his amber eyes. "Do you trust me, Angel?"

I don't even have to think about the answer, which should scare me, or at the very least, surprise me, but it doesn't. I give him a head nod and he raises our joined hands into the air. He places his other hand low on my hip, making my breath hitch as his fingers work their way under my shirt. Then, as if he was born to do this, he starts to move, expertly navigating my body alongside his.

Time seems to slow down and speed up at the same time while Dante dances with me. He lets me warm up to the motions, but once I'm comfortable the room blurs around us, making me forget everything, if only for a moment.

Elian returns a little while later, looking pissed as hell he didn't find my uncle. I catch his eyes on us when Dante twirls me, watching me from the corner of the room, his eyes ablaze.

I let it go, silencing my emotions, my thoughts, and everything other than the feel of my feet on the floor, and Dante's hands on my back as he guides me around the room.

3

DANTE

I can't stand seeing the hurt in Sadie's eyes a moment longer while she relives her past, standing in a room that should hold good memories, but is tainted instead.

My heart broke for her a bit watching that memory even though she wouldn't want my pity. Honestly, I don't think she meant to do it, or even knew she was doing it, but she managed to project the memory of her uncle into our heads and now I want nothing more than to murder the bastard myself.

Elian used our connections to look into her records and we knew it wasn't good, but we didn't know how bad it was until she inadvertently showed us this tiny glimpse of it.

My fingers shift on her back as I lead her into another dance move. Dancing is something else that's slightly complicated for me. When I was younger, I loved watching my biological father spin my mother around the kitchen while she was cooking. My other fathers could never hold a candle to them while they danced, but she loved them all the same.

And I loved the easy way he could control a room with

his graceful precision. As a child, I assumed it was harmless, the easy way he could command anyone's attention with movement. It wasn't until much later I learned the truth behind his actions and what he could truly do.

"Would you like to hear a story?" I ask while continuing to lead her around the room. We stick to the open space at the end of the bed, expertly navigating the small area. Thankfully, she finally seems to be relaxing, but I know she's still hurting. We've been worried about her these past few days.

Elian stays against the doorframe to give us extra room. He may be a huge fucking asshole, but he's considerate, even if he tries to hide it under all that heartache. Though, he definitely has the best reason to be the way he is. He's probably the most scarred out of all of us. Especially with who his father is and with what he can do.

Sadie nods, looking up at me with eyes full of pain. She's struggling to stay afloat at the moment, and I'm going to do my best to keep her above water. The last thing we need is for her to go on another killing rampage.

Word of her actions is spreading fast and the whole Weaver community is buzzing about her. There's even talk about a rebellion by the Night Weavers, which is treasonous in and of itself. I try not to let the thought give me hope. The Elders are extremely good at snuffing out those kinds of dark desires. The last time someone was brave enough to go against them, well, let's just say it did not end happily.

I stumble slightly, and my cheeks heat with embarrassment, but I keep moving instead of dwelling on my fumble. "My father was what's called a Mood Weaver. They're incredibly rare, but they can control emotion through dance or movement."

"Really? That sounds—"

"Amazing?" I supply with a small smirk. "It was. It was a

beautiful gift." I pause my story to throw her into a spin which she executes perfectly. It also gives me a moment to swallow past the lump in my throat for the next part.

"When I was younger, I thought it was normal to always be happy. To always have a smile on my face. It wasn't until I was much older that I realized what my father was doing to me.

"My family life was rough. Hell, Weavers in general have a rough life. We lived out from under the Elders' radar for many years, escaping their notice, but eventually, they found out about what my father could do. The Elite came, killed my mother's other mates since none of them were as powerful and therefore, not essential in their eyes. Then they took my father and mother with them."

She gasps, fumbling her steps. "Oh, Dante. No." Her face is blotchy from crying, but she's still one of the most beautiful things I've ever laid eyes on.

"Sadly, yes." Our movements slow as Sadie rests her head on my shoulder, soaking my black t-shirt with her tears, but it doesn't bother me. Besides, black is a multipurpose color. Not only does it hide the blood of my enemies, but it also hides the tears of my woman.

She glances up at me with sad green eyes that look so much brighter from her crying. "I'm so sorry, Dante. What happened?" I can almost feel her mentally slap herself as soon as the words leave her mouth. "I'm sorry, it's rude of me to pry. You don't have to tell me if you don't want to."

My throat feels like sandpaper, but I manage to swallow through the onslaught of emotions battering at me. I haven't talked about this to anyone really. What makes Sadie so utterly and completely different?

Why do I feel comfortable telling her this truth about me and my life? Is it because she understands pain? Probably more so than others?

Either way, it feels good to finally open up to someone. "When the Elders learned what he could do, they forced him to help keep the masses under control. He performed daily during their interrogations and during their monthly dinner parties—pretty much anytime they wanted to sway the public's opinion. He was one of their greatest assets. And yes, an asset because that's all he was to them. Don't get me wrong though, the Elders are powerful and twisted in their own right."

A shiver racks down my spine thinking about their seemingly endless capabilities. I've seen them behead Weavers for the tiniest slip ups. One wrong word out of line and you're dead. It doesn't matter that our numbers are already dwindling. We were once an overpopulated warrior race or that's what my mother used to tell me. The stories have been twisted by the Elders over time. No one knows what to believe anymore.

"That's awful." She kisses my chest and squeezes me tighter. "I noticed you said was?" Her softly spoken question brings me back to the present.

I have to take several deep breaths—in through my nose, out through my mouth—before I can answer her. "He killed himself. He hated manipulating people like that. With me, it's because he loved me and he wanted me to be happy. He didn't want life to taint me. With the Elders... they made him manipulate people into doing awful, twisted things. He couldn't–he couldn't take it anymore."

Her shadows flare around us before one tendril reaches out to stroke me, like it's comforting me. Maybe there is something more to them.

"I'm so sorry, Dante," she tells me while rubbing her arms up and down my back, keeping me grounded to the moment while we slow dance. Moons above, I'm supposed to be the one comforting her. "What about your mom?"

I know she means well but her question is like a jab to my heart. "They dangled her in front of my father to keep him pliant. When she passed away from a freak accident at their mansion… Well, I don't think he had the will to live anymore."

"I don't even know how to express the depth of my sorrow for you, Dante."

"It's okay, Angel." I take another deep breath. "You know, sometimes I resent dancing, but I know if I let it get to me then the Elders win, and I refuse to live like that. Sometimes I wish I could change things because I never learned how to cope with the hardships life throws my way. When something bad happens, I lash out or I throw a smile on my face and push onwards, because being happy is the only emotion I truly know." My voice is raw, and I'm sure my eyes betray the depth of my emotions, but maybe with Sadie around, I'll finally be able to deal with my repressed past.

It's a step in the right direction, anyway.

Sadie

My heart breaks for Dante after learning all he's been through in life. Gods, I've been such an asshole. I never stopped to think that my mates might be working through their own problems. "I'm so sorry for your loss," I say again because I don't know what else to say. Hell, what can you say to someone in this kind of situation? Still, sorry doesn't seem like enough. It never will be.

"Thank you, Angel." He gives me another twirl, spinning me several times before bringing me back in. The first time he did it made my stomach flip and having to rely on someone else to lead me is strange, but I'm starting to like the sensation. He clears his throat. "Now, I say we leave the sad shit alone for a while and just dance. What do you think?"

With a grateful nod, I let myself go, turning off my brain. Or trying my best to, anyway. Sweat clings to our skin dripping down our bodies onto the carpet and still, we dance. Still, we show each other our deepest secrets through our locked gazes and our meticulous show is for our eyes only. And for Elian who is like our stoic sentinel in the background.

I needed this. He needed this.

After a while, the thoughts start creeping in again and I can't seem to shove them down anymore. "What if she *is* dead, Dante? I don't think I can live in a world without her."

Ash and I practically came out of the womb together, and when we met... well, it was a done deal from there. We never left each other's sides and here I've gone and let her get kidnapped.

"We won't let you sink, Angel. We'll be your life rafts." His words are kind of ironic considering when I first met Elian, I knew he was the storm heading my way. They all are, really. The difference is, we're all in the lifeboat, getting ready to weather the shitstorm together.

"Are you ready to talk about what the fuck this means?" Elian interjects. Our eyes connect and his mask must've slipped because he looks absolutely broken watching Dante and I dance. Dante spins me once more and when I find Elian again, his emotions are gone—replaced by that simmering indifference he normally displays as we come to a halt.

"It means my uncle is back," I respond because I don't have the energy to fight with him. "It means he's coming for me. Yet another bad guy to add to my ever-growing list."

Elian sighs, rubbing his temple as he leaves his spot against the wall to get a closer look at the bloodstained wall. "I meant the symbol. It looks like a version of the Elder's, but different." He points to it, and I move to his side to study it further.

Underneath the blood is a four point star that looks like it was burned into the wall. I bend over, doing my best to ignore the red words scrawled above. Elian leans his head toward mine to get a closer look.

"There's another point that's never been there before. They're known for their tri-point star."

"What would my uncle have to do with the Elders?" I ask, confused.

He seems to mull it over in his mind before speaking. "Likely nothing. Unless they've been here too, and it was a warning."

Great. Either way, I'm done being lenient when it comes to the bastard who abused me. Dealing with work and having to struggle to make ends meet, I'd become complacent in my old life. I'd done what I needed to survive day in and day out and I'd let it go, let him go. Let him get away with murder. But now?

Now that I'm strong enough, relatively safe, and smart enough to outmaneuver him, I want him dead. I want to find him and take my pound of flesh from him, and I'm not going to stop until I do.

Dante speaks up from behind us, interrupting my bloodthirsty thoughts. "I think it's time we gathered pictures for evidence and then head home. We can go over everything with the others later. What do you say, Angel?"

This time, I don't argue.

4

SADIE

After we're finished collecting evidence, a thought strikes me. We're in my hometown… where my father is buried, and this may be one of the last times I'll be able to visit him. I absolutely adored the man, but this area taints my soul. I'd rather honor his memory every day by living my life like he'd want than be forced to relive these things by visiting his corpse.

He's no longer here and he'd want me to be happy, but I think I should at least say goodbye.

Ashley's parents are also buried there, and it would give me the peace of mind to make sure she's not there for some reason. Our thoughts about death differ a bit. She hasn't missed a single month visiting hers since they died while I've only visited my dad a handful of times. I'm a firm believer that graveyards are for the dead, not the living.

Elian starts to turn in the direction to take us back to the estate, but I stop him. "I need to make one last stop while we're here." He brakes the car and flicks his gaze over to me. "Don't fight me on this, Elian. Just drive."

Surprisingly, he follows my directions all the way to the

cemetery without bitching, even if his jaw is clenched the entire time. He parks the car and I open my door to get out when Dante stops me. "Uh, Angel. Why are we here?"

"I want to say goodbye to my father and check on Ash's parents' graves."

He doesn't say anything else and instead follows me with a curious look on his face. Elian trails along further behind, his posture tense. The gravel crunches under my converse as I make my way down the little walkway. Once I find our family plot, I step off the path, making sure to avoid stepping on anyone else. A raven squawks in the distance, making me jump.

Sheesh, why are graveyards so creepy?

A chill skates down my spine and it has nothing to do with the weather. My inner alarm bells ring louder the closer we get to my dad's stone, which is quite a ways off the main path toward the back of the graveyard. Our plot is underneath a beautiful tree, but much like my brother, I don't want to be buried here, despite its beauty.

Something out of the ordinary catches my eye in the direction of Ash's parents' headstones and I make the decision to visit them first. I skirt the edges of the graves and scan each of the headstones for their names. When I reach Nicole and Jimmy Campbell, my heart sinks to my toes. The dirt is disturbed, and their flowers are strewn across the ground like someone messed with it recently.

With a glance around, I don't find anyone but Elian and Dante. But I also know this is a known hangout for teens, so I chalk it up to a few assholes and start trying to fix everything, starting with picking up the flowers. "Why would this, of all places, be a cool hangout spot for teenagers? Is the idea of possibly finding a ghost that exciting?" I grumble. It's creepy and a good way to get murdered, if you ask me.

Dante shudders. "The idea of ghosts gives me the creeps."

"Me too." I place the last flower in the holder. "Ash would be so upset to find their graves like this, but there's really not much that can be done for the dirt."

"Don't worry, Angel. It'll go back to normal after it rains a few times." I give him a look and he puts his hands up. "Maybe we can find the groundskeeper and ask him what's going on."

"Yeah, maybe." I sigh and retrace my steps until I find my dad's headstone. Another tremor works its way down my spine when I look up to find an empty whiskey bottle sitting atop his grave—my freaking weakness. My heart starts to beat faster, pounding in time to the roar in my ears.

It's an omen and a sign of foreboding if I've ever seen one. I suck in a sharp breath, pull my switchblade from my pocket, and scan the perimeter, listening for anything out of the ordinary. My sudden shift in demeanor sets Dante and Elian on alert. "He's been here too," I tell them.

"He's not here now, but it seems like he knew you would come," Elian says, eyes scanning the distance for any threats, and the trees around us seem much more ominous than they did before. "Either that or he's following us. I don't like it."

Dante eyes the whiskey bottle and pulls me into his side. He knows what happened to me with Ben and Tyler at the concert when I froze and what that particular substance does to me. "It's going to be okay, Angel. Don't let him get to your head."

"He already has."

Disappointment and anger at not finding Ash war in my gut. With Mickey visiting my dad, it's like losing him all over again, and the shitty icing on the cake is not finding my best friend.

A single tear drips down my cheek and I let it fall to the ground, soaking into the soil above him. I reach for the whiskey bottle and as soon as my hand wraps around the neck of it, I chuck it at the tree. It shatters into a million pieces much like how they would when Mickey was around.

"I'm coming for you, Uncle." I cast one last glance at my dad's grave. *"Goodbye, Dad. I love you,"* I whisper into the silence around us and then I turn around, blocking out the memory of that lone whiskey bottle atop his grave, and it shattering into tiny little pieces.

I can't stand being here a moment longer and walk back to the vehicle, leaving Elian who is casting a ward around his grave behind. I leave because there's nothing left for me here anymore but tainted memories and broken dreams.

5

SADIE

After the longest ride of my life, we finally make it back to the estate. The guys and Hemsworth decide to have a meeting to discuss everything that's happening, but I can't handle any more information today. I'm at my limit and overloaded. I tell them all good night and escape to my bedroom.

The glow under Reed's door catches my attention as I walk past, and I choose to check in on my fourth mate before I pass out. The first sight to greet me when I open the door is his bare chest. Naked, wet with little streams of water dripping down his abs, soaking into the towel slung low around his waist. His silver eyes slowly rise to meet mine. If that's the sight I'm greeted with when I open doors around here, I'm going to do it more often.

I clear my throat and start to back out of the room, eyes cast anywhere but his junk on full display. "Uh, hey, Red! Sorry, I didn't mean to disturb you. I'll come back when you're, uh, dressed."

"Wait! Please, Love," he says, reaching out to stop me with his hand. Ah hell, it melts me when he calls me that. No, dammit, I don't melt. Okay, that's also a lie. My vagina melts but I sure as hell don't.

Reed's grip goes no further than my wrist and I notice he's extremely careful to avoid my palm. It doesn't matter though. As soon as our skin connects, tingles explode across my body like little jolts of lightning. Much like with the others.

He pulls me into his arms, enveloping me in his warmth, and I wrap mine around him back. I'm powerless to stop the tug I feel toward him, and I'd be lying if I said I wanted to stop it. Without our palms connecting, no mate bond snaps into place, and I can't decide if that disappoints me or not.

"Red," I say breathlessly with a touch of reproach as the lightning continues to assault my synapses.

"I know," he responds and lifts my head from his chest with two carefully placed fingers. He leans in until our lips are mere inches away from each other. "I just need you close, if only for a moment." He cups my face as he looks into my eyes with such desolation and pleading.

Instantly, I want to wipe it all away from him and give him purpose again, but I don't. More importantly, I can't. I have no idea how my other mates would react, and I refuse to jeopardize anything with them until we all have a chance to talk it out.

I standing there, staring into his silver eyes as they darken with pain. He's been through so much and my heart breaks for him.

Our lips touch in the barest of ways, and I want nothing more than to close the distance and see what they would feel like against mine. But the minute that thought enters my mind, he turns away, resting the side of his head against mine, much to my disappointment and relief. The energy between us is intense and pulls me toward him in such an all-encompassing way. I'm not sure how much longer we will be able to deny our connection.

"We need to talk about this prophecy you started to tell us about before everything went to shit."

He sighs. "I know, and we will. But Suns blaze, has anyone ever told you how amazing you smell?" He inhales deeply, like he's trying to imprint my scent into my memory.

My faces scrunches in confusion and I lean back to look up at him. "Uh, thanks? I think." A yawn breaks free from my lips, making Reed smile. He runs a hand through his red hair, tousling the strands.

Red.

Blood.

For some reason, the image of the wall from Ash's house pops into my mind. Thinking about the message from my uncle makes me shiver. The last thing I want is to be alone tonight. The exhaustion from hunting nonstop the past few days is slowly settling into my bones, creeping up on me like a predator ready for its next kill. I know I need to leave and head back to my room, but I don't think I'll make it. My eyelids are too heavy, my tiredness too great.

"Hey, are you okay?" Reed asks, rubbing his hands up and down my arms, looking at me with concern in his eyes.

"No," I respond as I climb into his bed, fully clothed. "Cover your dick and come cuddle me. I can't stand to be alone tonight, and I don't know how long my other mates are going to be."

Reed seems stunned and doesn't move for a second, but hastily drops the towel where he stands when I open my mouth to speak again.

Thankfully, he doesn't need to be told twice. I should probably be worried about my boldness, but I'm too drained to care. He scrambles over to the dresser to grab a pair of boxer briefs and some gray sweatpants. His bare ass is on display for me while he grabs the items needed, and it's absolutely perfect, sculpted by the Gods themselves.

I do my best to ignore how lean and muscular his body is. Pretty sure I catch a glimpse of his enormous manhood before I turn away from him and let him dress in peace.

Once he's finished getting dressed, he comes back over and crawls into the bed. He wraps his arms around me, being the big spoon and holding me until I fall into a blissful sleep cradled in the arms of the mate I know the least about with a warm need low in my belly.

6

REED

Light filters in through the curtains, highlighting the soft curves of Sadie's face. She looks so beautiful and serene in her sleep. When she's awake, she's always fighting—always sticking up for herself and others. When she's asleep, she's finally at peace. She looks like an angel. I definitely understand why Dante calls her that.

I didn't bother closing the door last night because I knew her other mates would come looking for her, and they did. But once they learned that she was sleeping peacefully, they left, albeit reluctantly. I can't say I blame them. I'm still an outsider here, but I plan on rectifying that as soon as I can. Sadie is my one true mate, and unlike Night Weavers, we only have one. Light Weavers are usually monogamous, although it's starting to look like the Gods want to change that.

Sadie slowly starts to wake, pressing her back directly into my hard-on. I groan a bit when the little minx starts to rub up against me. I shouldn't take so much pleasure in it, not when she's not mine yet, but Gods, her ass is divine.

"Rise and shine, Love," I say, biting my lip to keep from

groaning out loud as I try to rouse her from her half-asleep state. My greeting makes things worse and she starts grinding even harder into my erection. My hands grip her sides to try and stop her, but it doesn't help. "Sadie, *shit.*"

"Are you making moves on my mate, Light Weaver?" Kaos asks as he walks through the open doorway looking between us. He takes in our closeness in a single glance. Thankfully, he doesn't seem upset, but I can tell he still doesn't know what to think about me by the dip in his brow.

Sadie startles and shoots into a sitting position. Her hair is mussed from sleep, and she looks more than a little groggy. I guess running on a few hours of sleep for four days straight will do that to a person. She's absolutely perfect to me though.

She looks down at where she is, back to me, and then over to Kaos with wide eyes. *"How did I end up in bed with Reed?"*

"It's not what it looks like!" she blurts and my lips twitch. "Isn't that what people say when it is what they think?"

He lets Sadie stew for a moment before cracking a smile. "I'm kidding, I know it's not."

"Wait. You know?"

"Of course I do. You weren't in your room last night, so I went looking for you. Reed offered to watch over you and I stayed outside the door to be certain."

"You watched over us last night?"

His eyes blaze with the depth of his feelings for her. Mate bonds are serious. They make you fall faster and harder than anything because they're a piece of you. "I'd do anything for you, Little Flame," he confirms.

I know the feeling and she's not fully mine yet. I guess, technically, she never will be *fully* mine. I'll always have to share her and I'm slowly coming to terms with that, especially as I've laid in this bed recovering with nothing to do but think about her and the others.

The room falls into an awkward silence. Only to be broken by Sadie's voice a few minutes later. "We're going to have to chat about the elephant in the room eventually."

Kaos nods. "Yes, and we will, but there are so many things we need to consider besides the mate aspect of it. The biggest one being privacy. No one can know Reed is here, or they'll kill him in a heartbeat. As it stands, we have no idea if any of the other Light Weavers from his community managed to make it out alive. Reed could be all that's left from his faction. There's no way to determine whether his story about being your mate is true or at least, not without testing the theory, and I don't think any of us are ready for that yet."

I am. I was the moment I learned I had a mate out there, but I don't voice those thoughts aloud. His mention of my people—my family—threatens to shatter my heart again. I've been so wrapped up in Sadie and comforting her, and my recovery, that the memory of their screams and all their blood hasn't yet seeped into my thoughts today.

Until now.

"That's fair, but my intuition is telling me he's the real deal, Kaos." Sadie's words make my heart swell. He looks slightly conflicted, but also accepting. He and I have had quite a bit of bonding time while he healed me. Apparently, we both share a love of fairy porn books.

Sadie turns to me and touches my arm. Her face pinches with sorrow as she asks, "Can you tell us more about what happened that day, Red?" I automatically know what day she means.

"There's not much more to tell. I'd been sent out on a recon mission when I found you that day. Some rogue Light Weavers were in the area, and I was supposed to tail them and detain them. They were already dead by the time I got there but my father wanted me to stay and scope out the area. Find out why they were there."

"Did you figure out why?" Kaos inquires gently.

Reed shakes his head." No. And when I got the distress signal from home, it was already too late. Elder Vald was waiting for me when I appeared. He slit my father's throat and laughed while they beat the hell out of me. I only managed to make it out because I thought of you, of getting to meet my mate. The Sun God showed me mercy."

"A mercy of which I'm glad for," she murmurs, wrapping her arms around me. She squeezes like she's trying to patch me up with a hug and I fall for her even more. When she pulls back, she asks, "What about the prophecy you spoke of?"

"It's something all Light Weavers have passed down to their children but hardly anyone actually believes in it anymore. Most think it's a bedtime story to tell their kids to make them hold out hope for a better future."

"I'm guessing you don't think so?" she asks.

"No, I don't think that. Not anymore."

"Well, spit it out," Kaos says, watching me from across the room.

I take a deep breath and then start to recite it, recalling it from a memory long ago.

> *"Born from the night,*
> *Into the shadows and darkness alike,*
> *One who will bring them to their knees,*
> *A force to reckon she shall be.*
> *To right their wrongs,*
> *And mete justice with ease.*
> *She will be fate's guiding light,*
> *She will be night's enforcing might.*
> *Her heart so pure,*

With the strength to endure,
Only she can unite us,
Only she can save us from them all."

The weight of the prophecy ricochets throughout the room. Sadie stares at me warily, turning over my words in her mind. "And you think this is about me? You think I am the one the prophecy is speaking of?"

I give her a small nod. "Night's enforcing might and fate's guiding light? You're the only Weaver in recorded history to have a mate from both sides." I can tell she's not convinced by the wary look in her eye but that's okay. It'll click into place eventually. Exactly the way it's meant to. That, I'm certain.

Suddenly, Hemsworth bounds into the room, immediately going to Sadie to lick her cheek and comfort her. He interjects before anything else can be said. "Let's go grab some breakfast and get the day started, shall we? It's too early to be dealing with a prophecy on empty stomachs. We can talk more about this over food."

Each of our stomachs rumble in response, pulling an easy laugh from us. The world we live in might be brutal, unforgiving, and confusing as shit, but nothing can take these moments from us. Sometimes, this is all we'll have and that's okay, because we're stronger together. And together, we're going to get through this.

At least I hope we will.

7

KAOS

"You two go on ahead. We'll catch up to you in a bit," I call out as Sadie and Hemsworth trail out the door, on their way to have breakfast, leaving me and Reed alone. My hands glow black as I run them over the last of his injuries, searching for the source of his slight wince when he moves his arm. I noticed it earlier when he got out of bed and again when he waved goodbye to Sadie.

I will say that he's leaps and bounds better than when he fell through the roof. Even with our advanced healing though, he'll likely have a few scars.

As soon as I find the places still in need of healing, my magic enters him instantly with absolutely no resistance at all. So far, I've been pretty skeptical of him claiming to be Sadie's mate, but this practically proves it. It's not exactly pleasant to heal anyone outside of your Circle, and I don't even feel uncomfortable. There's no strain or pull. It's like my magic is a hot knife slipping through butter, as if Reed was always meant to be a part of our bond.

It's going to take a lot more than this to convince Dante and Elian of that though.

Over the past few days, I've been getting to know Reed little by little and he doesn't seem like such a bad dude. Maybe a bit shy but that's likely because of who his father is—was.

Reed never wanted the spotlight, but he was born a royal, which didn't leave him much of a choice. Most of the time he hides in the shadows until he's called forward. I feel for the guy. Our friendship came about in one of the most unlikely times and places, but I'm glad it did since it allowed us certain protections other Night Weavers didn't have.

"Hey, thanks for comforting Sadie last night. I know she really needed it and it's nice to know that she has someone else to lean on." My hands hover above his left arm, the glow starting to grow more faint as the injury slowly mends itself.

Reed pushes his glasses further up his nose, watching me do my work. "She's my mate," he says, like that's supposed to explain everything, and I guess it does considering I'd do the same. "I would do anything for her. Same as you."

True.

Still, I have to ask, if only for my burning curiosity. "How are you so certain about her?" Light and Night Weavers mixing is absolutely unheard of, which he knows, and the prophecy could mean anything.

He takes a moment to contemplate my question before responding. "Never in my life have I ever felt so desperate than I did in that moment when I knew I was going to die. They were absolutely going to kill me and all I could think about was a wild woman I'd only met one time. Once was enough with Sadie, honestly. I should've realized she was my mate sooner. The pull between us was too strong to be anything normal and then the boost to my powers... I should've known."

His eyes have a faraway look to them before he continues and since I'm finished healing him, I back away to give him some space. "As the killing blow was coming, I begged the Sun God to take me, to let me go to my mate, and he did. He transported me directly to her. Although, I wish my landing was a little better."

"You did make quite the entrance." His lip twitches. I clear my throat and decide to change the subject. "Do you want to go check on things today?" I ask, referring to the last conversation we had while I was healing him.

He told me he wants to go check on his people and his father, to bury them if there's anyone or anything even left to bury. At first, I wouldn't let him go because he was too injured, but now he's well enough. However, I don't think he wants to face the reality of what happened alone, and I don't blame him. I couldn't imagine watching my people be decimated or watching my father perish in front of my eyes, even if he was a bastard like Reed's.

My jaw clenches, but I hold my fury inside. I don't have to say it aloud for Reed to understand the direction of my dark thoughts, my eyes show it enough.

He shakes his head, confirming what I already know. "I'm not ready yet. I thought I was, but I'm not. As Sadie would say though, I know I'll have to buckle up and do it eventually."

"Whenever you're ready, let me know and I'll go with you."

He swallows thickly before saying, "Thank you. I appreciate that." There's a long pause before he sighs and speaks again. "You know we have to do something about *them,* right?"

He doesn't have to elaborate for me to know exactly who he means. "I know." It's been a long time coming and I can feel the change starting to stir in the air. I once said that Sadie threw a bomb into our world unknowingly, but I'm starting to think it's even larger than that. "We'll have to be smart about it. One wrong move—"

He gives me a head nod.

That's enough about that conversation. Talking about it gives me chills. The Elders have eyes and ears everywhere and even though I trust Elian's wards, the Elders' powers know no bounds.

"Have you read the new book I put on your nightstand yet?" I ask, giving us a distraction from those spiraling thoughts. As it turns out, we both like smutty romance novels. We bonded over a mutual love for ACOTAR but our most recent favorite is Chaotic by T.S. Snow.

"I'm up to chapter twenty-nine, and it's really starting to get, ah, interesting."

"Interesting isn't the word I'd use to describe that chapter. More like molten. Just wait until you reach that cliffhanger though. Brutal."

The corner of his lip turns up and he laughs. "Cliffy's are my favorite, man. They make waiting for the next book so much more fun. Come on, let's join the others, I'm starving."

8

SADIE

The dining room is buzzing with shifters when Hemsworth and I arrive. From the looks of it, they're the normal shifters milling about and not the ones we rescued from the compound.

I pause in the doorway with Hemsworth at my feet and collectively they turn, see us, and scatter, dropping whatever's in their hands onto the table and scurrying away like frightened mice.

It seems like chaos but once everyone is gone, the table is perfectly set and there's a mountain of food piled on it. I frown, opening my mouth to ask a question as the last shifter files out of the room, but the girl quickly shuffles down the hallway and disappears.

"Moons above, you'd think we have the plague," I say incredulously.

Hemsworth chuffs, trying and failing to hold back his grin. "Well, *you* have been on quite the warpath lately. Be patient, Sadie. Most of them have been through a lot and have suffered at the hands of the Weavers."

That deflates my sails and my frustration. Patient. I can

be patient. Hell, they probably see me as some brute like all the other Weavers. I need to *show* them I'm different and that I wasn't raised like all these other archaic assholes. They seem comfortable enough around my mates, so hopefully they'll warm up to me like Vinson did.

Speaking of which, I see his infamous biscuits sitting in the center of the table and my stomach grumbles. I place a hand over it, noticing the flatness of my abdomen and it makes me realize how much I've been neglecting myself lately. I love Ash and I want her back more than anything but Dante and Kaos are right… I can't keep burning the candle at both ends, running myself ragged trying to find her. It's not healthy.

With slightly more pep in my step than I've had in almost a week, I slide into my seat at the table, avoiding Elian's spot and opting for one of the seats on the side instead. "Let's dig in, Hems. We have the whole table to ourselves for once." And your girl can eat, as you well know. Sometimes, I think I can put more food down than even my familiar. I start piling breakfast on my plate as soon as my butt hits the chair. From eggs, to bacon, to sausage, and of course, Vinson's biscuits.

Dante swaggers through the door moments later, shirtless and dripping with sweat. He stops and does a double take when he sees me. "What a surprise, Angel. I'm glad to see you actually eating."

I wince. "Yeah, well, there are no new leads and I finally realized how unhealthy I was acting. Why are you all sweaty?"

"I went for a run this morning. Normally Kaos joins me but he was watching over you and Reed." He takes the seat directly across from me and his leg brushes against mine.

"I'm glad Kaos and Reed seem to be bonding."

Dante's nose wrinkles but his eyes are twinkling. "So, you

and the Light Weaver, huh? I didn't really peg him as your type."

"And I never foresaw myself with four mates but here we are," I jab back with a slight smile in my tone so he knows I'm messing with him and it makes him chuckle.

"Touché, Angel," he says around a mouthful of bacon. Once he swallows his bite, he continues. "Seriously though, the glasses?"

"I like them and that's what matters," I respond, my tone not leaving room for argument. Dante may be one of my mates, but I won't have him talking negatively about Reed, especially since we're all still learning our way around each other, even if it's in jest.

"He hasn't earned his place yet. I want to make sure he's worthy of you and not some Light Weaver trap."

"I'd expect nothing less from you guys. I know you'll vet him and make sure he's safe." I lean over and place a soft kiss on his cheek, knowing for all his ribbing and humor, he only wants what's best for me.

Hemsworth's head pops up from his own breakfast, which a hearty steak and probably something he bribed the shifters for. Spoiled, I tell you. "That really is a sign of a strong Circle, you know. With the fact that they're willing to make any outsiders prove themselves worthy of you, Sadie," he tells me.

"It's kind of hot too." I wiggle my eyebrows at him, making Hemsworth grimace from the mental image that likely conjures up. Kaos and I really must have scarred him for life.

A dark caress slithers up my spine seconds before Elian shadows in, taking his usual spot at the head of the table. My fork pauses halfway to my mouth, waiting, watching to see how he's going to react to all of us already seated and eating.

He doesn't even glance in our direction as he starts

picking out what he wants this morning. With a snap of his fingers, one of the shifters brings him a cup of coffee and from the looks of it, it's black just like his soul. *Where the hell did the shifter even come from?*

Guess I'll be the one to extend an olive branch today. "Good morning, Elian."

"Good morning, Mercedes," he says quietly, taking a sip of his coffee, shocking me. Some progress is better than none, right?

Reed and Kaos appear seconds later, saving me from having to make any more small talk. "It's nice to see everyone together like this," Kaos observes, taking the seat to my right while Reed takes the one to the left.

A large part of me still feels guilty for taking a moment to myself and my mates while Ash is still out there somewhere, but I know there's nothing I can do for her at this exact moment.

"Anyone have any luck tracking leads down?" I ask, even though I already know the answer.

"Not yet," Kaos responds gently. "Don't worry though, Little Flame. We'll find her."

"I know. What about the symbol from Ash's old family home?"

He shakes his head. "I've scoured the few books we have in the library and there's nothing in there on it, but I'll keep searching."

Something niggles at the back of my thoughts, and I pause. "You know, it reminds me of the symbol on the gag from the duplex. The one in Bedi's mouth. Could there be a correlation?" I ask.

Kaos' brow dips. "I'd forgotten about that… I think there are a few differences, but I'll keep an eye out for both."

Elian glances over at me. "Is there anything else you can tell us about Mickey that would help us track him down?"

So, he's still stuck on that too. I guess my uncle slipping away from us pisses him off as much as it has me over the years.

"If he doesn't want to be found, you're not going to find him, trust me. I've tried," I admit bitterly, thinking of all the internet searches I've done trying to get on his trail. I even scraped up enough money to hire a private investigator once but there wasn't a trace of him anywhere… until now.

"Tell us about him anyway, Angel. Maybe there's something we will pick up on that you didn't before," Dante prods, and my hackles rise.

"His full name is Mickey Sinclair. Social services dropped me and my brother off with him after our dad died because he was our only living relative. He fell off the face of the earth after he—" I pause, taking a deep breath to push back all the trauma swirling in my chest. "After he killed my brother." They wince at my words, knowing how much Skylar meant to me, probably through our bond, but honestly, I think anyone could tell how much I loved him.

"I hadn't seen nor heard from him since that night. Until yesterday. Now I know for certain he's still out there, polluting this earth with his darkness. He's out there hunting me, but little does he know that I'll be the one hunting him."

"We'll help you track him down, Little Flame, don't worry."

"There has to be a connection somewhere," Elian states, rubbing his jaw in thought, the food in front of him completely forgotten in favor of his coffee.

I nod. "Trust me, I don't think it's any coincidence that he chose this moment to reappear. Something is fishy, I just haven't been able to put my finger on what that is or why yet."

"We'll figure it out. You've got us now, Angel," Dante says, rubbing his calf against mine comfortingly.

"Was he your mom or dad's brother?" Elian interjects.

"Dad's."

"Is that where the Sinclair name comes from?"

"Yes."

"It's so interesting," he says casually, but his eyes tell a different story. "I've scoured the archives for that last name and haven't found it, but you had to have some family that were Weavers."

I snort. "That's not possible. My dad was definitely not a Weaver and even though I didn't know my mother, Skylar never talked like she had magical abilities." Everyone at the table tenses, making me suspicious. "What?"

"Weavers are born, not made, Sadie," Kaos says gently.

A scoff breaks free from my mouth. "No, there's absolutely no way. Besides, it doesn't make any sense. My father was my mother's only partner. From the way Skylar talked about them, they were over the moon with each other. There's no way my dad was sharing her with a Circle."

"The magic we possess has been known to skip a generation or two before," Elian rubs his chin with his thumb and forefinger. "Perhaps it's possible it skipped your father and your mother entirely, but somewhere down the line your family had magic."

I shake my head. "I'm done with this conversation. My parents were not Weavers, and my uncle may have been an awful bastard but he wasn't one either. Believe me, he would've used that to his advantage."

Thankfully, no one else prods me further. Kaos, moons bless him, changes the subject. "Back to the prophecy you were telling Sadie and I about earlier, Reed. Would you mind repeating it for the others?"

"Sure." Reed pushes his glasses up his nose and repeats the prophecy once more. By the time he's finished, Dante's mouth is hanging open and Elian looks physically confused.

Which is a first. I've never seen him display any emotion other than cold indifference and anger. Well, maybe some heat behind all that glacial ice, but never long enough to thaw it.

"Is there anything else you can tell us about it?" Kaos asks.

"Honestly, that's all I know. I've racked my brain but—" Elian suddenly shadows out of the room, interrupting Reed without an explanation, and his food left completely unfinished.

"Huh, I wonder what his deal is?" I ask.

"Who knows, Angel. But if he wanted our input, he would've asked. Finish your food." I stare after Elian and Dante's soft voice snaps me out of it. "Please, you need to eat."

He's not wrong, but I do wonder what was so important with Elian. He seemed spooked and that's not like him.

Elian

The prophecy sparks something in the back of my mind I haven't thought about in years. I shadow out of the room while the others are still talking, following my instincts. My skeptical side wants to reject his story, but there's something so familiar about it, and if my hunch is correct…

I pop out of the shadows into my room and immediately head toward my closet, pushing the clothes out of the way to find my old box of journals. Kaos' mother thought it would be a good idea for me to write my feelings down instead of bottling them up inside like I always tend to do. A habit that stuck with me, even now. I keep a journal on my bedside table that I use to write in every night.

Sometimes, I feel like the paper and pen know me more than I know myself. I can get lost for hours writing down what I'm feeling or experiencing. And after yesterday, watching Sadie with Dante…

Well, let's just say I had a lot to write about.

Using my fingers, I swipe the dust collecting on it away and pull open the lid, digging through the contents until I find the one I'm looking for. I hurriedly flip through the pages, trying to find it faster, to uncover the answers inside. With a frustrated huff, I decide to skip through everything and turn to the last entry.

Curses fly from my lips as I scan the page. Sure enough, the day after Kaos, Dante, and I bonded as a Circle, I wrote that exact same poem in my journal. Little did I know it was a fucking prophecy. Feelings of foreboding settle into my stomach like a ton of bricks. Hell is coming our way, that's for certain, but will we be able to manage it all?

That is the million-dollar question.

For my Circle and my mate, though?

I'll do anything, even if the latter hates me for what I'll do to protect them all.

9

SADIE

"Earth to Sadie?" Dante asks as he watches me zone out for the millionth time. My mind is on so many things; on Ash missing, on the shifters we've rescued, on the cruelty in Tyler's eyes as he tied me up with that bane rope. "Hey, are you okay?"

"Hmm?" I respond half-heartedly, still trapped in my thoughts. Everything is playing behind my eyes like my memories are a movie on repeat.

Today marks a week since Ashley's disappearance and we're still out of leads tracking her down. I can't seem to stop the dread churning in my stomach. Surely I would know if she were dead though, right? We're connected in ways that aren't supernatural—ways that defy the laws of nature.

Dante sighs and runs his hands through his hair. "I need you to pay attention, Angel. You need to learn this. Try again." He motions for me to ignite a flame into my palm, to call forth his fire, but it's being stubborn. His flames aren't coming to me as naturally as the shadows. Not after the exploded from me after they gave me the news. Honestly, I think that was pure instinct and rage.

Thankfully, Dante seems to have the patience of a saint. Him and Kaos both do. Elian is still, well—Elian. Not that I expect him to change any time soon, and Reed isn't involved with my training.

We're currently in the basement, which they've converted into a training room of sorts. On one side there's an assorted line of weapons and on the other there's various workout equipment. Treadmills, weight benches, the whole nine yards.

So far, Dante and Kaos both seem pleasantly surprised with everything I know about fighting. Occasionally, Dante will give me a correction, like my old trainer Ben, but I'm holding my own easily. Kaos is with Reed and Hemsworth today, bouncing ideas off one another about the prophecy and our people.

I blow out a breath when I realize I got lost in my own little world again and refocus on the moment. "I'm sorry, Dante. There's a lot on my mind."

His eyes soften. "I know, Angel. I can see the wheels in your brain turning from here. Let me help distract you." A devious smile appears on his lips seconds before he drops, attempting to kick my feet out from under me with a swipe of his leg. I'm forced to jump, barely evading his calculated kick.

Thank fuck for quick reflexes or I'd be flat on my ass.

He shoots me another daring smirk that makes my blood sing through my veins before he comes for me again. "C'mon. I know you can fight better than this," he taunts with a wild look in his eye. Almost feral. He's trying to rile me up and it's working. "Give it to me," he says and that's all it takes for me to snap out of it.

"Challenge accepted, Blondie."

Blow after blow rains down upon him from my fists. Muscle memory kicks in and I let myself go, letting my instincts take over. The burn in my muscles is a welcomed relief. I've missed the feeling of working my body to its breaking point.

When you can't think of anything beyond avoiding the next blow, your mind can't wander.

The hits get faster and faster until I feel like I'm blurring with the movement. Suddenly, Dante shifts his arm and opens his side to me. I take the advantage, ramming my shoulder into him. We go down to the padded floor, and I land on top with my legs straddling either side of him, feeling triumphant.

After he has a moment to catch his breath, he strikes, reaching behind me to grip me by the neck and yank my mouth to his. Our lips collide in a bruising blend of passion and fervor. He lifts me from the floor with his hands under my ass and backs us toward the nearest wall, but I'm not ready to stop fighting yet. I break out of his hold and start circling him again and my core clenches in protest.

"What are you up to, Angel?" he asks, watching me with amber eyes banked in desire. I've noticed whenever he's horny or angry, they twirl and dance, like little flames. His lips are swollen from our kiss and my nipples pebble under my sports bra, but I need this. I need the game of cat and mouse right now.

Instead of answering, I turn my back on him, undoing the gloves on my hands. He stalks closer to me and holds his hand out like he's going to grab me.

Without giving him a chance to react, I spin, yanking his outstretched arm and fling him over my shoulder. He sails over me like I intended, but I completely underestimate his strength and go down with him, landing with my ass directly in front of his face and his dick in mine. I chuckle, wiggling my glutes. "We're in the perfect position for a sixty-nine, eh, Blondie?"

"We are, aren't we?" The low rumble of his vibrato does delicious things to my lower region that's currently straddling his abdomen. I roll off of him and lay flat on the mat, panting with my arms over my head. Dante sits up and slides in between my still outstretched thighs.

"What're you doing?" I ask huskily, gasping when he grinds his hardened length against me. A shiver racks down my spine as the feeling sends little zings straight to my clit.

His smile, my oh my, his smile. "Distracting you," he responds, trailing a finger down my collarbone, and in between my breasts. He traces the little lines of sweat that run down my body, making me groan. I've so desperately needed this distraction.

Dante looks at me with questions in his eyes as he trails ever closer to my nipple across the top of my sports bra. I nod, giving him permission to continue. This mission is a go, the light is green, and we're ready for takeoff. Or, well, I'm ready for takeoff. He surprises me by shaking his head.

My heart sinks for a moment before he says, "I need you to say it, Angel."

"Say what?" My voice is barely more than a puff of air.

"You know what," he responds with a throaty chuckle. "Do you want this? Do you want me?"

"Yes, I do. Please."

"Please what?" he says, tone thick with desire.

I take a moment to contemplate what I want. What I truly want, as his knuckle skates by my nipple once more, but not close enough to make contact with the sensitive nub.

"Please, Dante. I want you. I *need* you," I reiterate.

"Good girl," he praises. "I needed to hear those words from your mouth." His hot breath puffs across the shell of my ear before he grazes it with his teeth.

And fuck if it doesn't turn me on further.

He moves to my chest, yanking my sports bra down to

bare my breasts to the cool air before taking my nipple into his mouth. Then he slowly circles it with his tongue. Unexpectedly, he tweaks the other one between his fingers, sending a jolt through my body. A moan tumbles from my lips as his fingers curl around the fabric of my shorts, but he halts before removing them. I glance up at him curiously, slightly peeved that he stopped.

"First things first, I want you to know that you have all the control here." My heart swells with his need to remind me of that fact. He may not think he's observant like Kaos, but he is in all the ways that matter. He always remembers the small things. "So, tell me, Angel... what is it you truly desire right now?"

Without hesitation, I say, "Taste me, Dante. I've been dreaming of that curly head of hair of yours between my thighs since I first met you and you had me over your shoulder at the festival." He smirks like the bastard he is as he ever so slowly tugs my gym shorts and panties down my legs.

These men. They love to tease me.

Dante halts suddenly, and his brow dips in confusion. *Fuck. I can't believe I forgot.* No one but Ash has ever really noticed the small scars that litter my body from the abuse I suffered at Mickey's hands. The largest one is on my upper thigh from a particularly nasty fight we had. Turns out a broken whiskey bottle makes for a nice weapon. Well, if you're the one wielding it, which I was not. It was dark when Kaos and I had sex for the first time, so he didn't see it and my shorts are normally long enough to cover it.

Dante traces the raised bump. "What is that?"

"It's a scar."

His eyes harden while he strokes some of them comfortingly. We lay there like that for a moment, reveling in each other's touch before he's calm enough to speak again. "Who?" He can barely contain the rage in his tone.

"My uncle," I finally say after the silence drags on for a while. "The man did not give a shit about breaking whiskey bottles above my head or throwing them directly at me. Amongst other things. He managed to stab me with that particular one. If I hadn't jumped out of the way, it would've gone through my stomach instead."

Dante's jaw clenches, and he looks away from me for a moment. His body thrums with tension and I feel him straining not to lose his shit. "Why?" he asks, raising those amber eyes to meet mine.

That one word from his lips makes me shiver. I know he'd never really hurt me, but fuck, Dante is menacing when he's angry over something he truly cares about. His eyes literally blaze like a raging bonfire.

I shrug. "I was his greatest burden."

"And you're sure that he's the one that left that note?"

"Positive. But no more of this sad bullshit right now. You're supposed to be distracting me, remember?" Dante looks unsure so I really drive it home. "Are you going to tongue fuck me or not, Blondie?"

I lift my hips, smirking when he rises to the challenge. He carefully tugs my converse and shorts the rest of the way off, then he cups my ass and yanks my heat to his face.

Not going to lie, the manhandling is really turning me on, and it makes all the bad thoughts float away, replaced by our dark desires. He spreads me open with his fingers and takes one long giant lick, groaning as my juices coat his tongue. He looks up through his lashes and licks his lips, tasting me. No, savoring me. The sight makes pure lust shoot through me.

Then he fucking ruins it. "You taste *heavenly*, *Angel*."

I can't help the small laugh that bubbles out, but it quickly turns into a moan as Dante buries his face in my pussy once more. He alternates between circling my clit with his devilish tongue and licking my slit. His hands shift their grip from my ass as he repositions my legs to put me at a better angle before dipping his tongue further into me.

Everywhere his touch skims, every lap of his tongue seems perfectly thought out to get the most reaction out of my body. The sensation is maddening, and I buck and squirm under the pressure. He lets go of my legs and pushes me back down with one hand on my stomach and the other reaches down to play with my nub since his tongue is otherwise occupied.

He works my body perfectly, doubling down on his effort to bring me to the brink. The sensations build and build until he suddenly stops, withdrawing his tongue from my molten core. I'm disappointed for all of two seconds before he lightly nips my clit with his teeth, and I reach my crescendo. I shatter, shouting my release as I grab a fist full of his hair, needing something to hold to ground me to reality. He laps me up greedily and doesn't stop until I'm squirming from the sensations. Every brush and lap send zings and zaps throughout my entire body.

"Too much. Too sensitive," I mumble.

He lifts his head, smirking up at me darkly. "Oh, Angel. I'm just getting started."

"Fuck yes," I breathe.

Dante rises, tearing his shirt clear off his body. *Show-off.* Then he proceeds to wrap the scraps of fabric from his shirt around his arms, dancing a bit as he teases me. He is actually taunting me, but you know what?

Two can play this game.

Besides, I've been wanting to get my hands on his lithe abs from the moment I met him at the lake. I rise to my knees and before he can even blink, I'm lifting my mouth to his lower region. I lick from the top of his shorts to the center of his chest, pulling a groan from his lips.

Said shorts are on the floor in the next instant, and his enormous dick springs free, standing at attention for me. I reach for it to place it in my mouth, but he stops me with a hand around my wrist. "Not this time. I need to be inside you. Now." Then Dante is on me again, but instead of going with the flow, I shift our positions, landing on top of him. He gives me a small smirk and doesn't argue with the turn of events. "All right, feisty. Tell me, what do you want? Say it."

My chest rises and falls rapidly from the anticipation. "I want to spear myself on your cock repeatedly until both of us are screaming each other's names."

He lets loose a long throaty growl at my choice of words. "Fucking hell. You're a dirty little Goddess, aren't you, Angel?"

I smile and give him a loose shrug. "I know how to adapt quickly." I line him up with my entrance, still soaked from my release, and gradually sink onto his cock. My head falls back with a groan the further I go. Having Dante finally inside me is a dream.

He lifts his hips, sinking all the way in. "Impatient, huh?" I tease, gasping when he grabs my hips and starts controlling my movements. "Ah, ah, ah," I say, bracing my hands on his chest to slow the momentum.

He growls his displeasure, but he should know better. I'm not one to have my power taken from me, and I can tell he's loving the banter by the way his eyes swirl with flames.

Lifting my hips, I slam back down, making him grunt from the force. I continue the motions, spearing myself on his cock continually. Over and over again. Like I said I would.

"Sadie!" he calls out like he's screaming to the universe the weight of my name. The total opposite of a whispered, reverent prayer. His shout is like a declaration of passion for the world to bear witness to, like he couldn't stand to hold all of that to himself.

Dante lifts his legs, putting me at a better angle to hit my g-spot with every thrust. His hips start moving in and out in time with mine while I bounce faster and faster.

"Yes! Dante!"

"Come for me, Angel," he murmurs while staring directly into my eyes.

And I do. I shatter for a second time, but there's not a moment for reprieve. Dante is relentless, chasing his own orgasm. I move my hips in time with his, drawing out my climax. He finishes with a shout, rocking against me a few more times while spilling his hot seed into me.

Breathing hard, I collapse into his open arms which he wraps around me. I tuck my hands into his chest, and the sight of our mate mark on my wrist draws his attention. He strokes it, making it turn silver and it sends another jolt of lust through me.

We stay connected, enjoying the feel of one another until Dante tenses and his eyes shoot over to the door where I spot a very pissed off Elian, but hell, when does he not look pissed off?

Oh, right. Never.

I catch his eyes banked in true unadulterated, raw desire before he quickly covers it up with a snarl. Though there's no denying what I saw. Elian the asshole wants me. *Me.*

Too bad he's going to have to earn it.

I don't bother to cover myself up. Judging by the tent in his jeans, he liked everything he saw. This begs the question though. What does it say about me, that I hope, even pray that he witnessed the entirety of me and Dante joining our two rough souls together?

I want the bastard to know exactly what he's missing out on. Because as much as I try to deny it, as much as he tries to push me away, I still want him. No matter how many times I try to tell myself that he'd be nothing but trouble for me, I *need* him.

Although, it seems like trouble is my middle name, so what's a little more?

ELIAN

My hands clench around my pocket watch as I slip it from the velvet pocket of my leather jacket, then curse myself. The habit is more of a tick than anything else. I take a deep breath and slide it back into its place.

I need to fucking move, to do something other than worry about the direction everything in my life is suddenly taking, to do something other than research Sadie's life and this damn prophecy. The energy pulsing through my veins is making me antsy.

I want nothing more than to go downstairs and exercise my muscles until everything else fades away. Until the pounding in my skull dulls with the ache and burn of my body contracting with each movement. Until my thoughts aren't plagued with a beautiful blonde haired female.

Goddess, if my father could see me right now, all pent up over a woman. He'd kill me. After all, he was the one who taught me how to block everything out, how to shove everything aside for my plans. Too bad it's going to backfire on him one of these days. Soon, he'll get his.

CHAPTER 10 | 63

Yes, I think a trip to the gym is in order.

The frigid air of the shadow realm smacks me in the face as soon as I step through, but I'm used to it by now. In a few quick steps, I land in the basement doorway and the scene before me makes the blood rush straight to my cock.

What is it about Sadie that makes me feel so *fiercely?*

I thought I had locked away my emotions a long time ago. Though I'd be lying if I said the little devil hasn't managed to surprise me lately. That woman is tougher than nails, and I'm begrudgingly coming to respect her tenacity. I'm still not convinced she will walk away from the Elders or my father unscathed though.

Especially with her mouth. *Fuck, that mouth.* They'd cut out her tongue in a heartbeat because of it. While *I* want nothing more than for it to be wrapped around my cock, sucking me into oblivion.

Mentally, I attempt to reach Dante, but he has thrown up a *do not disturb* sign, blocking anyone from his thoughts. I watch, enraptured as his mouth descends on her breasts and his tongue swirls around one nipple before swapping to the other.

For a moment, I consider barging in, interrupting their moment, but then Dante starts to tug her tight little gym shorts off, and their conversation stops me in my tracks. She proceeds to tell him about the scar, and how her uncle is the one who inflicted it. I had already made the assumption about him when I pulled her records and found a few notes from the hospital. Never more than she could heal—or hide though.

Everyone thinks Kaos is the most observant, but that's not exactly true. I'm quite handy with finding out the details. I have to be. And now I know everything there is to know that's public information about her, but I don't feel like I truly *know* her.

I miss part of their conversation, trapped in my thoughts. I open my mouth to call attention to myself when Sadie gives him the okay, and he starts devouring her relentlessly.

On second thought, what harm could it do to watch?

My shoulder rests against the doorframe as I settle in, crossing my arms over my chest. The longer I stand watch, the harder my dick strains against the fabric of my jeans. She writhes and moans under Dante's skilled mouth, and they're both so lost in their own worlds that they don't notice as I inch closer to get a better view of her glistening pussy. She screams her release with her head thrown back in pleasure, but Dante is nowhere near done with her.

And it seems Sadie isn't either.

She manages to flip their positions and that's when the action really starts. Her gorgeous tits bounce with each rise and fall of her hips as she spears herself on him continuously. She rides Dante like he's a fucking bucking stallion and she's determined to break him in, and he gives as good as he gets.

The largest part of me feels like an intruder, creeping in on their moment, but I can't bring myself to give a shit. I attempt to flee as they both climax, but can't seem to force my feet to move, to carry me away from her sweet sounds. A part of me wants to know what it's like for them to come together.

Their auras are almost blinding as they hold each other for what seems like an eternity. The sight is too gripping to walk away. Their combined passion is astounding, and it's in this moment I realize, I want to be a part of that. If it's not too late for a bastard like me. My meticulous plans were ruined the moment she and Kaos bonded in that park. Why not ruin everything further?

Dante's eyes find mine, and he smirks, the fucker smirks, making my lip curl at the exact moment Sadie's gorgeous eyes find mine. I scrub a hand down my face and leave, like the cowardly asshole I am.

Trust isn't built overnight, and I'd be a fool if I gave up on everything I've built for a moment with her. Because that's all it would be. A moment. I don't deserve her body or her soul.

I'm not built for loving someone.

Sadie

Elian disappears into his shadows, and I sigh as the last of his presence fades away. A part of me is surprised I didn't notice him beforehand. But I'm glad he saw us. He needs to *see* what he's missing out on and truly feel the repercussions of his asshole actions.

When Dante shifts, my attention returns to him. "I wonder how much of that he saw."

Dante shrugs, running a hand through his curly locks. "All of it, I assume. Or at least most of it. Why? Does it bother you?"

"No, I'm confused and maybe a little angry. Sometimes it seems like he wants me and other times it's like he doesn't, yet even he couldn't hide the desire in his eyes earlier."

"He'll come to his senses, I'm sure. Elian has been through a lot in his life and while that doesn't excuse the way he has treated you; I have a feeling it plays a big part in it. Kaos and I have dealt with the surly bastard for a long time, and he has never acted this way."

"Why? What has he been through?" I doubt Dante will tell me, but it doesn't hurt to ask, right? Something's got to give at some point. Or someone.

"It's not my story to tell, Angel, but you should know he doesn't trust anyone easily. I don't want to make excuses for him, because he needs to get his head on straight, but there are things you don't know."

"But I never asked him to trust me." I protest.

"I know," Dante responds softly, his lips scarcely a hairsbreadth from my own. He's trying to distract me and it's working.

"I merely wanted the benefit of the doubt from him and he can't even give me that." I take a deep breath before continuing. "He has fought me tooth and nail from the beginning and the worst part is, I don't even know why I fucking care anymore." So much for that deep breath. "I didn't mean to say that last part out loud and if you tell him I said I care, I'll deny it until my very last breath."

"Sadie—"

"Nope, I know how you men are. You say women are the gossips, but that's bullshit. Men are so much worse."

The devilish smile that lights up his face sends a shiver straight through my body. "I'll show you so much worse," he says with those amber eyes blazing and his length starts to harden inside me once more. And boy does he show me.

Over and over on their basement floor.

Thank the Night Goddess for supernatural libido.

11

SADIE

As Dante and I are reemerging from the gym a few hours later, Kaos comes rushing toward us out of breath. "We have a problem."

My body goes instantly on alert, ready to spring into action at a moment's notice. *So much for that post orgasmic bliss.* "What now?"

Kaos looks to Dante, giving him a look before he returns his attention to me. "The Elders' sons are here."

Those bastards have children? Sons no less?

My hands immediately find the dagger strapped to my thigh. The cool metal brings me a sense of comfort. *I'm not defenseless, I know how to fight, I have magic,* I repeat to myself like a mantra.

The fight with Tyler and losing Ash brought some of the painful memories in my mental repression box forward. Mainly the ones with my uncle where I was too weak to retaliate.

Not anymore.

"The Elders, of all people, managed to find their true mates?" I interject.

"No, they managed to find their true *mate,*" Kaos responds, putting emphasis on the last word.

My eyes widen as the realization hits me. "The Elders are a Circle?"

Kaos gives me a grim nod. "And their son's Circle is the only one in written existence to ever form a bond with family. Well, minus twins as they normally stay together. Everyone else is a ragtag bunch of kids who are thrown together when we come of age. We all hated them in our youth because they had years to get their kinks and dynamics worked out while the rest of us had weeks."

Dante scoffs. "You know those old bastards manipulated the system." Kaos smacks him in the stomach, making him wheeze in pain. Ugh, damn them. He barely even blinks when I do that.

"Careful, Dante. Watch your tongue." Kaos points to his ears and Dante nods.

My brain is still trying to process the fact that the Elders are a Circle. I wasn't expecting that. In my head, they're these ancient assholes banded together to wreak havoc throughout the Weaver community, and the fact they have children and actually procreated?

Blows my mind.

I can't seem to wrap my head around the Night Goddess having a hand in their pairing either, but I don't have time to question it any further because Dante speaks. "What do they want from us?"

Kaos' jaw ticks. "I'm not sure. Likely to see what all the fuss over Sadie is about." He lowers his voice, motioning for us to come in closer. "Whatever it is, I'm sure it's nothing good. Keep your guard up and watch what you say. They're inside the ward now. Elian's greeting them as we speak."

What about Hemsworth and Reed? We need to keep them safe, I project my thoughts into their minds. What do you know? Psychic communication does come in handy after all.

Dante chuckles, reaching over to grab a strand of my hair to twirl. *Don't worry about them, Angel. I have a feeling the sons are going to be so* enamored *with you, they won't be able to focus on anyone else, much less sense anything out of the ordinary.*

Mhm. What the hell is that supposed to mean, Dante? I ask, mentally giving him the middle finger.

Oh nothing. I just don't know how they wouldn't be struck by you... because you're so feisty and fiery and uh, so fucking gorgeous, he backtracks when I shoot him a look.

Yeah, nice save, asshole.

I readjust my sports bra, making Kaos glance at me. His nostrils flare and he looks at me fully for the first time since he announced the Elders' sons are here. My cheeks heat because I definitely smell like Dante. And Kaos knows. Will there be any issues? They say they're cool with it, but are they really?

"You should go get cleaned up, Little Flame. We can hold them off for you."

I nod and head in the direction of my bedroom, slightly embarrassed, but I'm stopped before I can make it two steps.

"Hell no, she doesn't need to get cleaned up," Dante scoffs, tugging me toward him. "She's going to go out there with my scent all over her so those dicks will know *exactly* who she belongs to."

Kaos doesn't give me the opportunity to object. "Good point, brother." He wraps his hand around the back of my neck and then slams his lips to mine, pushing his tongue into my mouth when I gasp from the sudden rush of *feeling*. I'm not used to Kaos being so assertive like this and I fucking like it. His kiss travels down my neck, nipping the dip in my shoulder, and back up to my lips again, leaving me utterly breathless.

"What was that for?" I pant when his lips finally leave mine.

He gives me a devious shrug. "If you're going out there with his scent all over you then you're going with mine too."

These. Two. Assholes. I swear.

"Let's go find out what they want," I grumble, trying not to let their heated stares affect me. If it were up to me, I'd be dragging them both upstairs for another round. Or two.

Just as we're opening the front door to step outside, Hemsworth bounds down the stairs. "Ah, there you are," he says.

I bend down and give him a few scratches on the head. "I'm assuming you heard?"

He bobs his head in a nod. "I smelled them as soon as they stepped inside Elian's ward."

My eyebrow crinkles. "Your sense of smell is that good?" I ask, thinking about my two asshole mates looking anywhere but at Hemsworth.

"Oh, how you wound me, Sadie. Of course it is. I've got the best sniffer in the entire western hemisphere." He sits on his butt and gives me a pointed look. You know, like a *listen up* face. What is it with everyone giving me that look today?

"You need to be careful. Watch what you do. Don't give them any ammo."

"For fuck's sake. What do you all take me for? An imbecile? I know how to keep my mouth shut, trust me." Everyone's eyes twinkle and Dante looks seconds away from cracking a smile.

"You, keep quiet?" Hemsworth scoffs. "Hell would freeze over before then, I think."

I roll my eyes. "Whatever. Let's get this over with. Stay quiet, Hems. I don't want to give you away yet, okay?" He gives me a nod as we walk down the steps.

Seconds later, Elian and three unknown men step into

view. Their sharp noses and defined jawlines are upturned as they strut toward us, carrying a conversation with Elian.

While they're distracted, I take a moment to study them fully. The one in the middle has strikingly blond hair that's cropped but longer on the top. Flanking him are what look like identical twins, from their high cheekbones to their short, tightly trimmed black hair. I'd say they're a few years older than us but not by much.

I'm not sure what I was expecting, but it wasn't *this*. Maybe gangly limbs and snouts instead of noses.

But no, they're stunning with their black cloaks billowing behind them in the breeze. What is it with everyone and sleeves when it's blue blazing hot outside?

Death wish, I tell you.

The man in the middle stops mid-sentence and his eyes travel to mine as the corner of his lip turns up faintly. Our gazes lock and hold, which makes his smirk widen even further and there's absolutely no way I'm losing this silent battle of wills happening between us right now. Of course, fate likes to test me.

Dante steps into my line of sight, cutting off our standoff. I give him a death glare, but that only makes him smile. *Sorry, Angel. I'm not letting you throw down a challenge with the son of an Elder when you don't know what it truly means.*

You know what I'm capable of, I project back.

He shakes his head and turns around to face our new visitors. *Be nice.*

My lips twitch. He should know me better by now. They all should.

I square my shoulders and level my gaze on the three amigos and Elian as they come to a stop in front of us with Hemsworth at my feet, Kaos on my left, and Dante on my right, mirroring their posture. "What the hell do you want from us?"

The middle one laughs, nudging his companions on either side. "She's quite feisty, don't you think?" The timbre of his voice is low and seductive, yet his charm does nothing for me, making me wonder if that may be a part of his power. Everyone in this society seems to be secretive about their abilities. And what is it with everyone calling me feisty?

Is it written across my forehead?

"More like bitchy," I mutter under my breath, recalling saying something similar to Dante when we first met. Kaos reaches out and squeezes my hand, giving me a silent cue to stay quiet but after a long moment of silence on both ends, my patience starts to wear thin. "Speak your peace or leave. I don't care for back-and-forth bullshit."

"Straight to the point, I like it," the same one says. Guess he's going to be doing all the talking. "We're here for several reasons. The first because we have heard you're harboring a Light Weaver. Is this true?" His statement makes my eyes widen, but that's the only outward sign I give him.

How do they know? I snarl, projecting my thoughts to my mates. Silence greets me in return. Judging by the confusion I sense down the bond, they don't know how either.

Something is fishy. Seeing as the only people who know Reed's here are standing next to me and the shifters, but I don't see them saying anything to their oppressors. I'd blame it on Savannah, but that snake hasn't been around since the day she issued the challenge.

"It's true." Reed steps out of the house with his head held high and comes to stand at my side. I want to snap at him and tell him he should've stayed inside, but I'd be pissed if one of my own did that to me, so I keep my mouth shut.

Besides, there's no way I'm giving these men the satisfaction of seeing us disagree. That would undermine Reed, and we need to present a united front. Even I have to admit that my other mates look proud of him with small amounts of respect dancing in their eyes.

I take the opportunity to draw our company's focus back to me and off of Reed. "You will not touch him, do you understand? Or you will make yourselves enemies of me and mine and that's not something you want."

"We're not going to harm him," the blond one says. He is definitely the ringleader out of the three since the other two have not yet spoken a word. "We are only curious about him. Although, I like your fire, girl. It's so refreshing and different from the docile women our fathers like to keep around."

"What's the other reason you are here?" Kaos interjects, bringing everyone back to the matter at hand.

"We'll get to the main reason in a minute. The second reason is to warn you. You've pissed the Elders off royally." I notice he says *the Elders* and not our fathers. Interesting. "From the fight at the concert, to Dante defying their orders not to bond with Sadie, to the men you killed a week ago, to the raid you conducted at their *special* compound..." He ticks off our infractions one by one.

My hands clench into fists and his gaze narrows in on the action.

"Ah, yes. You've been causing quite the stir. You're in for a world of pain when they finally get their hands on you, darling. Be cautious. They're extremely good at playing the long game and squashing you when you least expect it."

I'm not buying their nice guy bullshit one bit. I've always been guarded. Hell, I've been through enough in my life to understand how the world works, and people in their position of power don't stick their neck out for you without a motive. "Why are you telling us all of this?"

"Because..." He pauses for dramatic effect, a daring smile coming to his reddish lips. "We'd like to be allies."

My first reaction is to snort. I can't help it. "And what makes you think we would ever trust anything you say?"

"We have something of yours... You could call it a favor for a favor."

My dagger is out and against his throat before anyone can even react. My Sworn's shock brush against me in waves, but all I can think about are his words.

We have something of yours. There's only one thing—one person I give a shit about that's missing.

"Give her to me now, and you'll walk away with your life. Continue to hold out on me and you'll find out exactly how ruthless I can be."

A dark and dangerous voice has my blood turning to ice in my veins as I feel the cold metal of a knife pressed against my spine. "You can try, but you won't get very far, and you won't get your friend back. That would be quite a shame, wouldn't it?"

My gaze flickers over to see Dante, Kaos, Elian, and even Reed with their crotch knives out keeping the second twin at bay. Wait, when did Reed get a crotch knife?

Fucking magic, I swear.

My eyes flick back to the man behind me as I calculate the odds of winning and my options. To fight or not to fight, that is the question. Ash has to be somewhere fairly close, right? And we could take them on for certain, but do I really want to risk it without knowing what their abilities are?

Well, I've never been one to do things by half measures. I press the dagger deeper into the throat of the one I'm holding, nicking him with the wickedly sharp edge of my blade. A tiny drop of blood slides down his neck, but before I can even blink, his hand comes up, knocking my knife out of my grip.

He looks at me with a wide smile and feral eyes, but I'm not going down so easily. I kick my foot back, knocking the twin behind me in the dick. He grunts and drops his weapon, making the pressure at my back ease as I round on the blond one again. My fist almost connects with his face, but before I can move another inch, a second dark and seductive voice stop me in my tracks. One that *does* set my body on fire— even if I hate that it does.

"Stop, Sadie. Fucking *stop*," Elian growls, making my teeth grind together as he lowers his crotch knife from the second twin. This is the first time I've ever heard him call me Sadie and I find I like hearing the rasp he says it with. "Let's hear them out." He gives me a long look, trying to convey something with his eyes that I don't quite catch. All I can focus on is how I'm going to murder him later. *Maybe, I should fuck him first though. Get him out of my system.*

Wait, where the hell did that thought come from?

Bad libido.

His statement did the trick, however. Everyone is currently at a standstill. Dante, Kaos, and Reed lower their weapons, sensing the threat is over for the moment and move to stand beside me again. The ringleader's shoulders relax and I bend over to grab my blade, making sure to keep my eye on them while I do so.

"I apologize. I think we got off on the wrong foot," he says, stepping toward me to cross his fist over his heart. He slightly bows his head when I give him a *what the fuck* look. Our power brushes up against one another with him being so close and the reaction is not what I expect. I figure he'll feel slimy or oily, like tar, but if anything, he feels comforting, yet firm and unyielding.

"My name is Adam." He watches me from underneath long blond eyelashes that match his hair. The tinkling cadence of his voice washes over me like it's trying to burrow into my skin, but it's not purposeful. It's like he can't help but be seductive, and once again I wonder if it might be a part of his power. "These two are my Circle members. Nick and Niall. As I said, we've come to strike a deal with you. No tricks, no ploys, no dishonesty." His eyes sparkle with mischief, setting my senses on edge.

I open my center and caress him with my intuition, but he comes back clean again, making me even more suspicious.

Something has to be wrong, right? Why else would the Elders' sons need our help?

My gaze slides over to Kaos and I motion for him to take the lead. I don't trust myself to be diplomatic, and I trust Elian as far as I can throw him. Which isn't far at all. Dante is too much of a hothead like me. Reed would likely be diplomatic also, but Kaos knows how to navigate the Night Weaver world.

"A deal, you say. What does that mean, exactly?" Kaos asks, returning Adam's gesture with a slightly lower head nod. I'm assuming it's their sign of respect.

Adam sighs as both of them straighten back up. "As your Link has already gathered, we have her brown-haired friend—"

I attempt to jump forward again but a strong band of steel wraps around my middle before I can get very far. The scent of leather and amber hits my nostrils as the arms bring me into his chest.

Elian.

If heartbreak had a scent, he'd be the poster boy. I take a deep breath and count to five before continuing. When Elian is satisfied I won't go anywhere, he relaxes his hold and drops his arms, but his presence is still firmly at my back, and I have to bite back the tingling desire crawling up my spine. Now isn't the time.

"I swear if you have touched even one single hair on her head, I'll—"

Adam puts his hand out placatingly, stopping me before I

can threaten him. "I can assure you she's unharmed. We managed to get to her before our fathers could do any real damage."

"That's all fine and dandy, but you're dancing around the real shit. Why did they take her in the first place?"

Adam looks contemplative for a moment. "We're not certain why our fathers wanted her so badly. We're never sure what their end game on anything is. But it doesn't matter right now." He pauses to pull his sleeve up and check the time on his watch. "We have approximately six more minutes before our cloaking spell ends and we still haven't gotten to the bit about the deal."

Kaos interjects before I can. "What do you want from us?"

"It's simple really. Consider it an eye for an eye of sorts—"

I pinch the bridge of my nose. "Adam, I swear to the Night Goddess herself, you had better spit it out before you end up like a certain enemy of mine with a blade in your chest and six feet in the ground, okay? Tell us what you need for all of our sakes."

"Fine, but it's important. Probably the most important thing you've ever been tasked with—"

One of the twins, Nick, I believe from Adam's introduction, sighs, cutting off another one of his rambling episodes. "You'll get your human back if you agree to protect our mate." He wrings his hands, looking uncertain.

Mate?

They're mated?

Why do they need us to protect her?

Black mist starts to pour from his hands in a steady stream, curling and stringing through the air. My first reaction is to take a step back, but there's no time before a girl pops into existence. An awfully familiar girl.

A gasp escapes my lips, and it takes me a moment to realize that my eyes aren't betraying me. "Emma, is that you?

What are you doing here? Did these fuckheads steal you from the pet shop?"

Emma's wide eyes meet mine and she smiles, stepping toward me with her arms outstretched for a hug.

Elian snarls, keeping her from reaching me and she flinches. "Don't touch her. Who is this and how do you know her?" he directs his question to me.

I wince. "We met right before Tyler's attack. She actually works at the pet store in town. It's where I got Hemsworth's tag on his collar." I focus back on Emma. "Seriously, did they steal you from there?"

Can we take her back? Maybe erase her memories or something? I mentally ask my mates.

Dante cracks a smile. *I'm afraid that's not how it works, Angel.*

Emma's face pinches in confusion. "Of course they didn't steal me, silly. Why on earth would you think that?"

"Huh?" Here I am thinking they've stolen an innocent human to dangle in front of our faces but she doesn't seem to be a prisoner… "I don't—I thought—well, I don't know what I thought. You're a Weaver?"

Her usual smile falls. "Um, not exactly."

"Four minutes," the second twin, Niall, interrupts.

"Skip the back-and-forth for now," Adam says. Pot meet kettle, asshole. "Do you agree or not?"

"Yes," I say at the exact moment a chorus of *no's* echo around me. My eyes snap over to my four traitorous mates who at least have the decency to look a tiny bit sheepish.

Minus Elian. His lips curl as he says, "Fuck no."

"No? Care to enlighten me why?"

Elian's jaw grinds. "Have you forgotten who they are? They're the sons of the Elders. How can we trust that this isn't a trap? For Gods' sake, Sadie, you haven't even seen Ash yet. How do you know they're not lying?"

Damn it all. He's right. I don't know that at all. I was blinded by the prospect of finally getting my best friend back.

"What else are we supposed to *do?*" My voice cracks on the last syllable and I glance away, staring at the copse of trees around us. Cracking under Elian's scrutiny again is not something I'm comfortable with. Once was enough. Twice if you count the training room earlier.

"Decide. Now. We have 2 minutes."

I step forward, extending my hand for Adam to take. He looks down at it in confusion. "You have a deal, boys. Give me my best friend and we'll take Emma. Wait—" I pull my hand back before he can take it. Something tells me deals are very literal in the magic community, and I don't want to be held responsible for anything out of our control. "But we don't make any promises to keep her safe. We will shield her as best as we can, but there's no guarantee that she will be unharmed. Danger follows me and she's her own person."

Better safe than sorry.

Adam's nostrils flare. "You had better do everything in your power to make sure she's *not* harmed, or we will come to collect our revenge." I put my hand out once more and he gives it a firm squeeze. An invisible force seems to snap into both of us from where they're connected.

"I'd expect nothing less from the spawn of the Elders," I snarl, making him wince and drop my hand.

"I'm sorry that was a bit harsh. We only just found our dear Emma and we do not want to lose her so soon." His gaze travels to his mate and softens. The eyes say so much that our mouths do not. "If the Elders found out about her... well, they'd kill her. That is why we need you to keep her here. Forgive me for speaking rashly, but we'd do anything for her. Anything."

Honestly, how can you argue with that? I feel the same way for my Sworn and I know they'd do the same for me.

"We're on your side," Nick says, confirming Adam's words.

"That has yet to be determined," Kaos responds, coming over to rest a hand on my shoulder.

"Very well. We'll visit her two weeks from now after Niall has time to recharge his powers. That will be one week before your challenge." Adam nods. "Bring her in, Nick."

My heart stutters in my chest as Nick starts working his hands again, his black swirling magic wraps around all of us until Ash pops into existence. Her sad eyes snap to mine and for a moment, time seems to grind to a stop.

"We won't forget this. Like I said, you've found an ally in us." Adam gives me a small wink and casts a longing look over at Emma before they disappear as quickly as they came.

I rush toward Ash, as fast as my stupid feet can carry me, and practically tackle her. My arms go around her as I pull her into my embrace and inhale her comforting scent. She smells like *home.*

"Ash! Are you okay?" I ask, rubbing my hands up and down her arms. I back away a bit so I can get a good look at her. Other than a little bit of dirt on her cheek, she looks fairly good to have been missing a week. And judging by the slightly girly clothes she's wearing, I'd say she borrowed some of Emma's.

Ash tilts her head to the side. "Yeah, I'm good! Totally peachy. It'll take more than those dickwads to bring me down."

My mouth pops open in shock because her words confuse the shit out of me. Here I've been worried out of my mind about her... and she seems totally fine. "I was going to burn the world down for you," I admit with a careless shrug.

Her eyes widen into saucers. "Jesus, babe. I appreciate the sentiment, but I'm fine, really."

I think she's full of shit, because I know her better than that, but I don't call her out on it. "Did they hurt you?"

She shakes her head, but the pain behind her eyes tells a different story. "The Elders' stupid minions locked me in an underground room for a while. Only one of them would come and visit me. He was a vile fucker, Sadie. You need to be careful."

"What else happened?"

Her gaze goes faraway, looking haunted, before she refocuses on me. "He showed me—" She breaks off with a confused wince. "They had—" Her mouth opens again, but no words come out. Her face starts to turn redder and redder the longer the seconds tick by. What the hell?

Is she choking?

"Shh, it's okay, Ash. You don't have to relive everything right now." I figure it's likely the trauma of what she experienced choking her up. My best friend probably needs a minute before rehashing everything. She'll come to me when she's ready, she always does.

I clear my throat and wrap my arm through hers. "What do you say we go inside and binge on some homemade pizza?" I mentally flinch as that thought sends a pang of guilt through me. Vinson is the best at making pizza because he knows exactly how I like it. Not too much crust or sauce and a shit ton of cheese. What can I say? Cheese is my weakness.

Even though he's still living in the estate so Kaos can continue to try and heal him, he hasn't been working as much. Because the blackness is slowly taking over his veins. Because he protected me. Because of my stupidity. We have to figure out something for him, and soon.

"That sounds exactly like the distraction I need. Thanks, babe." We start to walk into the estate, but I don't hear anyone following so I glance back only to find everyone still standing around gaping at us.

Reed gives Ash a curious look. "What were you going to say, human?"

Ash glances toward the ground. "I don't want to talk about it right now."

"Don't want to, or can't?"

Her eyes widen and tears begin to pool in her eyes. I cut off her response. "Obviously, she's been through a lot, Red. Let's cut her some slack."

He doesn't look certain, but he respects my wishes and doesn't press the issue. I glance around us, taking in our bunch. A human, four Night Weavers, one Light Weaver, and a talking familiar. Then there's the matter of Emma. What are we going to do with another human to protect?

Hell, is she even human?

She doesn't seem surprised about any of this so I'm guessing no, but what is she then?

So many questions, so few answers.

Doing what I do best, I shove it all down into a little box and throw away the key. My bestie is back and I've missed the shit out of her. She may be a weakness of mine, but she's also a strength because she shows me the true meaning of friendship and it helps keep me grounded. Without her or the guys, I think I'd lose myself to the darkness sometimes.

I shake myself out of those thoughts. "Would someone mind getting Emma settled in for me?"

Kaos gives me a nod but is interrupted by Ash. "Actually, if you don't mind, Emma can come with us. We got to know each other a little bit while we were in the brothers' care. Plus, I think it'll do us all some good to have a girls' day."

"Sure, whatever you want, Ash." I lead them both inside, catching a flash of guilt across Ash's face before it's quickly replaced with a smile. There's no way I'm going to let anything else happen to my best friend.

Sadly, I know what I have to do to protect her, and that's having her nowhere near me and my crazy life until this world is safer. She's not going to like it either, but I decide to let it go for now and just enjoy her company.

12

SADIE

My fingers sink into Hemsworth's fur as I stroke his back, loving the calming effect he has on my nerves. Sitting on the floor is starting to become a little uncomfortable and I stretch out, making my back crackle and pop like popcorn. A sigh escapes me, and I readjust into a more comfortable position.

This week has been incredibly long and it's nice to finally feel a little relaxed. Oddly enough, there's still a storm brewing in my chest, but instead of letting the dread consume me, I refocus on the moment.

Turns out that Emma can put down as much, if not more, food than Ash and me. The three of us are now four pizzas deep and halfway into our third movie. For this one, Ash decided on some suspense flick with lots of fighting and very little talking. It starts to take on a bit of a darker note when the main character is kidnapped and locked into a tiny box inside her assailant's house. Ash flinches when the lid snaps closed, and the screen descends into darkness. She's up on her feet, flicking the movie off before any of us can even blink.

I spill my popcorn trying to get up, which Hemsworth doesn't mind as he scarfs it all down. "Shit, babe. Are you okay?"

Ash nods her head, waving me off when I go to put my arms around her. The rejection stings a little. "I'm fine. I just can't do the dark anymore. I didn't think it would affect me like that, but it brought me back to those moments down there. I'm sorry for ruining the—"

I cut her off before she can finish. "There's no need to apologize, babe. We totally understand. You've been through more than any one person should." The guilt of her being captured is weighing on me heavily.

Emma nods her head in agreement. "You didn't ruin anything."

Ash groans, placing her hands over her face. "Okay, but can we talk about someone else's problems now? Like you, Emma. We still haven't addressed what the hell is going on with you and those three hotties."

Emma's face turns into a bright shade of crimson and she ducks her head. "They really are dreamy, aren't they?"

"Yes, they are," Ash says, fanning herself for dramatic effect. "Now spill the fucking beans."

"It's complicated," she responds with a sigh, her gaze seemingly far away. "They're complicated. I'm starting to think the whole dang world is complicated."

The three of us sit and scoot in closer to one another, forming a circle in the middle of the room where Hemsworth snuggles between all of us, soaking up the attention. "So then start from the beginning," I tell her, sensing her confusion and frustration. "How did you meet?"

She shoots a sheepish look my way. "They came into the pet shop looking for information about you."

My heart sinks with her admission. Does that mean the

trio isn't actually friendly? Were they making everything up and they're really foes in waiting?

That doesn't make sense though. They returned Ash and they literally handed us their mate to protect. Either way, I was always taught to keep my friends close and my enemies closer. I intend to do just that, even if Emma and the trio's intentions are harmless.

My face must give away my thoughts because Emma puts her palms up placatingly. "They were only looking to warn you about the ambush, but it was too late by the time they got there. Something strange happened as they were leaving..." She trails off with a dreamy look in her eye.

"And?" Ash asks, nudging her arm lightly. "Rein it in, lover girl. Tell us the damn story."

Ah, how I've missed my person.

"Adam shook my hand as he was leaving, likely thinking I was a regular human—" I guess that confirms she's not human. Now I'm wishing the guys were here for this conversation, but they're all working out in the gym, trying to give us a moment to ourselves. Which is thoughtful of them. "—and that's when it happened. His palm stuck to mine and we were frozen in place. The twins were stunned, but they were also so excited. I still remember the look of awe on each of their faces."

That sure sounds familiar. It makes me wonder about the influx of true mates lately. What is the Goddess up to?

Emma smiles before continuing. "This is the best part. All of a sudden, my body became heavy and it felt like I was floating until my wolf appeared out of nowhere. Guys, it was the single most happy moment of my life. My wolf and I took off into the woods outside the shop and the guys followed me. The sights and smells were incredible..."

Shock ripples through me. She's a shifter, a fucking

shifter. "Wait, how did Vinson not pick up on your scent at the pet store?"

Her eyes dart to the ground. I've noticed that she can't seem to hold eye contact with me for long. "That's because I'm a weakling. I barely register on any shifters scale." Her words come out harsh and full of self-loathing.

"I'm sorry, Emma. Your power shouldn't define you. That's one of the things I'd change, if I could."

She shrugs like it's no big deal, but I see the spark of hope in her eyes. "Don't worry about it. I'm used to being snuffed by everyone."

Hemsworth gets up and finishes off the rest of the popcorn before laying between my legs, pushing his snout into me until I start petting him. "Well, I may not be able to change things, but no longer will you be ignored." She tilts her head, giving me a questioning look. "You're going to train with us and learn how to mold your body into a weapon. Like I have."

She perks up, excitement dancing in her eyes. "You mean it? You'd really take the time to help train some lowly nobody like me?"

"Of course, I would. You're not a lowly nobody, you hear me?" She nods, but still doesn't seem convinced. I continue on. "I'm curious about something you said though."

"Sure, ask me anything," she responds, bobbing her head eagerly.

She's so bubbly. Gods, what I wouldn't give to have that sort of innocence again. Actually, I take that back... there's always someone willing to take advantage of that and I'd rather know than be left in the dark, waiting for the other shoe to drop. "Earlier you said your wolf *suddenly appeared*. What did you mean by that? Can't shifters, you know, shift?"

That knocks the smile right off her face again as she goes solemn. "You don't know?"

"Uh, know what?"

"Shifters can't morph into their wolves until they meet their true mate. Our wolves live chained in our heads until that moment and then we can finally set them free." That revelation sends me spiraling.

Ever since the night of Tyler's attack, I've wondered why Vinson didn't shift and get the fuck out of there and now I guess that explains it. He couldn't. If I were a betting woman, and I am, I'd say he doesn't have a mate. And it's evidently possible for Weavers and shifters to mix. Adam, Nick, Niall, and Emma are proof of that.

A bud of hope blooms inside of me, but I crush the metaphorical blossom before it can take root. I already have four mates. Vinson's not mine. He probably has a hot shifter out there somewhere waiting for him to find her. That thought sends a rush of jealousy straight through me, and I barely catch the tail end of Emma's sentence. "—it's such a rare occurrence to meet your true mate these days, with the Elders keeping us apart from our packs."

"I guess that explains how they keep you under their thumb so easily. Kind of hard to fight back when you're basically human."

"That's so awful," Ash interjects. For a moment I'd completely forgotten she was there, but I guess that was the point. She didn't want the highlight of our night to be on her and her abduction.

Even though I know I shouldn't, I still feel responsible. If she had never come with me, the Elders wouldn't have found out about her. A part of me feels like I should've left her at the concert, but I snuff that down quickly. I'd rather have her in my life, but I also want her to be safe.

"One of these days they will pay for what they've done," I say, mentally ticking off all the Elders' offenses. A yawn breaks through my mouth, and I check my phone, eyes widening when I realize exactly how late it is. It's well after two am. "For now though, I'm going to go take a shower." I still faintly smell of Dante, and while it's nice, I'm starting to feel crusty. "Catch you guys tomorrow."

"Later gator," Ash says.

"Night!" Emma echoes.

Hemsworth raises his head and pops an eye open when he hears I'm about to leave. He rises from the ground and tags along after me. "Did you know about the shifters?" I ask, stroking his fur as we walk.

"I did," he admits.

"And you didn't think to tell me?"

"There hasn't exactly been time, but the guys are wanting to change that and have a more in depth discussion. They have plans for you to visit the compound and test your magic next week."

I stop in my tracks. "Wait, the compound that was attacked? If they're anything like the one we raided looking for Ash, I'm good. I'd rather not go back."

"From what I've gathered, this is more of a community center for Night Weavers. Nothing like the prison. Besides, it would do you some good to make an appearance, anyway."

I raise an eyebrow at him. "Why's that?"

Hemsworth gives a shrug, or as much of a shrug as a dog can manage. "Apparently, you caused quite the stir after you ended those miserable fuckers lives with Tyler. Plus, your escapade through the Elders' dungeon didn't go unnoticed. Rumors are already spreading about you and what you can do. You're powerful and people always gravitate toward power."

I huff, not able to hold it in. "I'm well aware of that fact." I reach up to finger Skylar's necklace for comfort. "How does this shit keep getting out?" I don't and have never wanted the spotlight on me. I know what happens to people who do end up in that light and it's rarely ever good.

"You weren't exactly inconspicuous at the festival from what I've heard. You bonded to Kaos right out in the open, killed a Weaver, and while Ben was low ranking, he was still in the Elders' good graces."

"Why does that not surprise me?" I should've known those two were in cahoots with the bad guys... but how does it all fit into place? I feel like there are still pieces of the puzzle missing, knocked under a couch somewhere, and completely forgotten. Until we find those pieces, I doubt anything will make sense.

I come to a stop at the corner before our rooms when a dark presence brushes along my spine. My intuition lights up at the same time my skin does. Why does Elian have such an effect on me?

Hemsworth continues on, none the wiser to my feelings or Elian. Either that or he knows Elian's waiting for me and doesn't care. "Not to mention all the shifters you saved. They talk, Sadie. They're ready for change to happen."

He's right, but how?

This conversation is heading for dangerous territory, so I drop it and I round the corner, locking eyes with Elian. He's leaning against my door, his posture casual, unbothered, though his eyes are anything but. He's sporting a tight-fitting long-sleeved shirt and a glorious pair of black sweatpants that highlight his package, which I ignore. Sort of. I'm only human after all.

Oh wow, I can't say that anymore. I'm a Weaver after all?

Nah, it doesn't hit the same.

When his gaze travels the length of me and back up my skin tingles and his nostrils flare. I can't help but picture the lust he showed this morning watching Dante and I in the training room. I sincerely hope that's not what he's going to talk about. That is one conversation I will be dipping out of. I close the distance between us until I'm standing in front of him. "Elian." My voice is breathier than I'd intended.

He inclines his head as if this is a normal occurrence for us. "Mercedes." I guess we're back to that now.

"Yeah, that's my cue to make myself scarce," Hemsworth says. Elian nudges my door open with his foot and Hemsworth slips inside, not even bothering to wait for my okay, leaving the two of us alone in the hallway.

"Why do you insist on calling me that? I know you know it bothers me."

He stares at me like he's trying to see through me and maybe he can, I'm still not sure what his powers are. "Mercedes suits you," he finally responds.

Moons, I think that's the nicest thing he's ever said to me even if I still hate the name because of who always called me that. I study him while he studies me. "Did you need something?"

"Not exactly." He doesn't elaborate but uncrosses his feet and repositions himself in front of my door, likely so I can't run through it and slam it in his gorgeous asshole face.

"Then why are you standing outside my door?"

There's a long, silent pause as he assess me before he sighs heavily. "I came to tell you that you will be training with me the rest of this week." Ah, no wonder he's blocking my only speedy exit. "We're going to work on your hand-to- hand and magic skills. Next week you will train with Kaos and he will teach you how to master your weapons."

Giddiness flutters through me and I speak before I think, "Can we skip this week and head straight into the weapons training? I'm pretty proficient at hand-to-hand, if you haven't noticed." Shit, that was rude. He probably thinks I don't want him to train me, but it's more the fact that weapons excite the hell out of me.

His lip curls, confirming my suspicion. "Absolutely not. You may be proficient, but you are not on the Elders' level. Or mine, for that matter."

He leans in until our foreheads are almost touching, but I don't look away from his hard emerald stare. Instead I narrow my eyes at his words, knowing I should probably set the record straight, but for some reason I don't. "All high and mighty, aren't you? Why are you such a dick?" The question comes out before I can stop it.

He ignores it and my jab like usual. "Get some sleep. I expect to see you bright-eyed and bushy-tailed in the morning." He shoots me a small lip quirk before he disappears into a cloud of shadows.

I groan, smacking my head against the wall, ignoring my racing heart and wet panties. "Bastard."

13

SADIE

The next morning gets here far too quickly for my liking. I slip downstairs before the sun rises to grab some breakfast from the kitchen before the cook arrives. He's an okay guy, but he's not Vinson. Uh, I mean, his abilities are not on the same level as Vinson.

Speak of the devil, I round the corner to find the man himself standing over the stove, making biscuits from the look of it, and I rush over to assist him. "Vin, what are you doing? You need to be careful!" He smacks my hand before I can put it in the dough, like a grandma scolding a child stealing a cookie. "Ouch, you fucker. Let me help you." He smacks my hand again, sending a white-hot jolt of lust through me.

He doesn't take his eyes off the dough. Man, he really takes cooking seriously. "If you're going to insist, then at least wash your hands first, please," he says. I swallow thickly and head over to the sink. As I'm drying my hands, he speaks once more. "Grab an apron from the rack. I don't want you to get flour on your outfit or accidentally burn your stomach."

I glance at my bare abdomen, tight sports bra, and running shorts.

Yeah, he's got a point.

"You didn't answer my question." I make small talk while tying the apron strings around my waist, trying my best to ignore the scrawling black lines that are visibly crawling up his neck.

He sighs. "I can't stay cooped up in that room forever. This gives me an opportunity to actually do *something* while being able to keep my mind off everything that's going on."

Grudgingly, I get that. I wouldn't want to be cooped up and feeling useless either. My eyes travel up and down the length of him, sizing up his condition as I note his usual work attire. Black tux, pants, and tie. That shit can't be comfortable. But he does seem well enough to do small things like this. "Fine. As long as you don't stay on your feet all day or else I'll sic Kaos on you." He gives me a small smile while kneading the dough in his hands. "What can I do to assist?"

"Have you ever made biscuits before?"

"Nope, but I'm a fast learner."

He chuckles and slaps the dough on the counter then gives it a few small smacks. The dough jiggles like an ass cheek, which shouldn't be erotic at all, but with him, somehow it is.

Get it together, Sadie.

Maybe I need to smack my own cheeks to snap me out of his trance. Wait, that would be weird, wouldn't it?

"I'll roll it out and then you can help me cut it into circles, if that's okay?" he asks, looking over at me. His cheeks turn a slight shade of pink.

"Sure, sounds good," I respond.

Vin grabs the roller and starts going to town on flattening the dough. The muscles in his arms expand and contract with each swipe and I advert my attention to the dough itself lest I start drooling. His gaze flicks over to me once more before returning to his work. "I heard you had a run in with the Elders' sons yesterday."

Wow, word does travel fast. "I did. They weren't as scary as me though." I shoot him a wink and he cracks a bright smile.

"I doubt anyone could be. I'm glad they returned your friend. I was worried about you for a while." He doesn't give me a chance to respond, but the sentiment is nice. "Now that we have the consistency and the flatness we'd like, we're going to cut it into circles." He tosses me the lid to a mason jar. "My mother was always old school, so we don't keep any shape cutters in here. We use whatever is available."

Huh, my kind of cooking. Between Ash and I, I'm the better cook. Not by much though, so we'd alternate between cooking meals. Most days we'd skimp on food for rent though.

I get to work cutting out the biscuits with Vin. He takes the left side and I take the right. It doesn't take long between the two of us and after placing them on a pan, into the oven they go to bake. Sweat beads appear across Vin's forehead, and I'm not sure if it's from the heat coming off the oven or if it's from overexertion.

Using my hands, I lift myself onto the counter to be able to reach him better and Vin makes a strange noise of objection from the back of his throat. "What are you doing? Now we'll have to clean that space again."

"Meh, so be it." I give him a small shrug. He moves toward me, and my legs shift of their own accord, allowing him entry between them. I place my hand against his forehead and hiss when I find he's burning up. "Shit, you need to go cool down."

Vin shakes his head, making his man bun bounce and a

stray strand of hair fall down into his face. I brush it away and he leans into my touch. "I'm fine. Shifters always run hotter than humans and Weavers. It's in our blood." He nuzzles his cheek against my hand and my heart flutters in my chest as he reaches up to wipe a bit of flour from my nose. I blush from the contact. What is it about him that makes me feel like such a giddy schoolgirl?

The timer dings, signaling that the biscuits are ready. "Dammit," Vin curses, pulling away to grab an oven mitt from the drawer to take them out. He sits them on the counter and starts rapidly yanking ingredients from the shelves and cabinets.

"What's wrong?"

"I got distracted and forgot to make the gravy."

Whoops. "I'm sorry. That's probably my bad."

"Don't worry about it. I can whip up homemade gravy faster than my Grams." And he does. That man is a machine when it comes to cooking. I've never seen someone so passionate in the kitchen as him. Everything is a labor of love and it really shows.

Once the gravy is done, Vinson makes me a plate, scooping a little extra gravy on it for me. "You better eat up. From what I've heard, you're training with Elian today. You're going to need your strength."

"I'll be fine. How bad could the asshole be?"

Apparently, pretty bad.

Elian moves with such grace and strength that he outdoes every single fighter I've ever seen before. I've never witnessed anyone move like him. He's almost exotic—wild and untamable... And there's an elbow coming for my face.

I barely duck in time to miss it and it sends me flying off

balance. I quickly shuffle on my feet to find my footing, but Elian is already coming for me once more. This time he goes for my legs, trying to sweep them out from under me, and I have to jump to avoid him. "You're good at this," I pant.

He doesn't respond.

We've been at it for a few hours now and he's fucking relentless. He acts like he's been training his whole life and maybe he has. I wouldn't know. Elian is worse than a closed book. As someone who is curious by nature, it's hard to not know much of anything about him.

Elian suddenly flashes in front of me, using his handy shadow-walking power. His fist snakes out for my cheek, but I catch it in my hand. "Hey now, asshole. Watch the face."

"You think your enemies are going to give a fuck about your pretty face?"

"Aww, you think my face is pretty?"

He quirks an eyebrow at me. It shouldn't be an angry gesture, but it is with him. "Answer my question."

"Well, no but—"

"Then shut up and keep fighting."

This motherfucker. Someone needs to put him in his place and it might as well be me. I double my efforts on trying to take him down. Unsurprisingly, the fucker meets me blow for blow, but I have a secret up my sleeve.

Taking a deep breath, I call upon my shadows, using the anger he stirs in me to do so. I pull them in slowly at first to not alert him of what I'm doing. When I have a sizable amount, I launch them at him. My beautiful little minions surround his wrists, pinning them against his side.

"What was that about 'keep fighting?'" I taunt. "Oh, you mean like this?" I land a blow to his torso and Elian smirks. The fucker smirks and disappears into *my* shadows.

It's not until it's too late that I realize he's behind me. The pressure of his forearm against my neck is my first indication, but the feel of his skin against mine is so much more. It buzzes and crackles, then I feel his ginormous, rock-hard cock brush against my ass. It takes everything in me not to make a sound.

"Never get cocky," he says, and then the pressure eases. Heh, I may be cocky but so is someone else. When I turn around to tease him of that fact, he's already halfway across the gym. "I think that's enough hand-to-hand for today. Let's move on to magic. Although, it looks like you've already started."

"Fine, let's get this over with."

How does he turn me away so easily?

Why does he hate me so much?

The world may never know.

Ha, yeah right. I fully intend to get to the center of this Tootsie Pop. Even if I have to lick until I fully expose his core. Wow, okay, that was definitely cringe worthy. Totally not weird at all, right?

A featherlight tap on my shoulder startles me out of my thoughts. How is he so gentle, yet so unyielding?

"The first thing we're going to do is work on centering ourselves. Without control and focus, you'll never harness your full potential." Elian slinks down to the floor and folds his legs in like a graceful house cat. He motions for me to mirror his pose, so I do. "Close your eyes, clear your mind, and focus on breathing."

"Is this some sort of meditation mojo type thing?"

"Hush and do as I say."

"Fine." I blow a stray piece of hair out of my eyes before closing them as I try to clear my mind, but my thoughts don't want to leave me. Sweat is pouring down my back from our workout and my skin is sticky. Plus, being so close to Elian makes me tingly. It's a strange combination of cold and fire. He's the ice in my veins, but also the raging bonfire.

"Do you ever stop thinking? I can practically hear your thoughts from here," he snaps.

"What was I thinking about then?" I taunt, hoping to call his bluff.

His breath feathers across my face. *When the hell did he get so close?*

"Something tells me you were thinking about me."

"That's actually true," I begrudgingly admit. "But did you know I was imagining all the ways I want to strangle you in your sleep?" This draws a dark chuckle from his lips, but I keep my eyes closed, not wanting to look into those hard emerald eyes and see the hatred there.

"What if I would like that?" he asks, voice deep and husky. I do my best to ignore the funny way it makes my insides feel.

I pop one eye open to find him leaning in closer to me. "Then I'll have to figure out another way to torture you, I guess."

"Your presence is enough," he responds before moving away, leaving me wondering what the hell he means by that?

"Close your eyes and focus on nothing more than your breathing," he barks. "Inhale. Exhale. Inhale. Exhale." He repeats this phrase over and over until everything in my mind dissolves. Until there's nothing more than *his* presence left. He invades my consciousness even when I'm not actively thinking about him. The fucker is imprinted on my soul.

"Now, I want you to picture your magic. Where does it reside?"

"In my chest."

"Good, and what does it look like?"

"Like a bright ball of silver, with threads that connect me to Kaos and Dante. Oh! They've changed a bit. Kaos' thread is now blue, while Dante's is a bright orange."

Somehow, I know he nods even though I can't see him.

"Your powers are settling and will evolve slowly. As will theirs."

Before the thought even processes, I blurt, "I wonder what color yours will be." It's official. I'm an idiot.

Instead of the snarky reply I'm expecting, Elian simply says, "Probably black. Just like my soul."

"Bit dark, aren't we? Are you really this much of a brooding asshole all the time? It has to be exhausting."

"Always," he responds. "Back to the lesson. I want you to focus on expanding that energy. Think about weaving it into the world, out of your soul and into existence. This is how our powers work, and how we unlock our potential. We weave a piece of ourselves into the universe. Everything is energy that can be wielded if you're strong enough."

My eyes open again. "Is that how you walk through the shadows? And is that only something you can do or do all Weavers have the ability?"

"Certain Weavers have the ability, yes, but it's quite rare to have shadow-walking powers nowadays. Nick's portal power is also rare." So that's what that was. Interesting.

"How do you do it then?"

"Walk through the shadows? It's all about weaving my magic to pull me through to another plane. It's quite basic once you learn how to do it properly."

Something tells me he's full of shit. This man is powerful. Probably the most powerful of my mates, if I'm being honest, and I don't even know what exactly he can do. Elian is dangerous, and yet, I don't think he'd hurt me. Unless I asked him to, anyway.

"If you say so. So are your shadow powers the only thing in your arsenal or what?" I figure what's the harm in asking directly? He sure as shit doesn't have a problem asking about my magic.

"I've always had an affinity for the shadow's but they are

not my main source of power. I'm gifted with several abilities."

I make a hum of approval. "What else can you do besides shadow-walk and cast wards?"

There's a long beat of silence before he eventually says, "I can read auras. Amongst other things."

"Was that so hard? I think that's the first time you've ever directly answered one of my questions. What other things?"

His eyes flash. "You don't want to know my true power. You'd fear me like all the rest."

For some reason his admission makes my heart twist, but I know better than to push him. "All right, what's next on the agenda for the day?"

"What, you're not going to poke and prod about my life some more?"

"Contrary to what you might believe, Elian, I'm not a total ditz. I know when to drop the subject and let things go. You're obviously untrusting of me and that's fine, even though I wish I knew why." I know if I poke at him too much, he'll close up tighter than a nun. I'll have to make do with getting tiny slivers of information from him at a time.

He clears his throat. "Since I'm the only one with experience with shadows, I'm going to teach you about wielding them. For today though, we're going to focus on you pulling in your power and then releasing it. Without using your anger." He motions with his hands. "Whenever you're ready, begin. We won't be leaving this room until you can control the shadows as easily as breathing."

I hold in my groan, knowing it won't do me an ounce of good. Never in my life have I ever wanted anything more than to simultaneously smack and fuck a man. Screw him and his damn control issues.

Elian wasn't joking either. Apparently, we skipped dinner. Although, Reed was kind enough to bring me down an apple and some toast. Dante and Kaos popped by too. Mainly to watch the spectacle.

I finally told Elian to fuck off with his whole meditation bullshit and got to my feet. For some reason, standing and using hand motions helps me channel my shadows better. I think the movement allows me to focus more intently because without rage fueling me they're a bit sluggish. My emotions seem to play into controlling them, something that Elian picked up on quickly.

The back-and-forth with him has become a game between us. Elian will do anything in his power to distract me until my focus slips and the shadows flutter away. Each time he does this, he makes me wait until I'm calm again before continuing. I get why he's doing it. It's going to make me stronger and more disciplined in the end but it's really starting to test my patience.

Frustration flits through me, making my next set of movements sloppy. Elian takes the opportunity to strike, wrapping his muscular arm around my torso. My back lands on the floor, but I don't bounce because his other arm comes up to cradle my head. What the fuck?

Is the brooding bad boy being considerate now?

"Weak, so weak," he murmurs and with the way he landed, his lips brush up against my skin as he speaks, sending a shiver straight down my spine. Then his words register in my brain, and I buck him off.

"Fuck you," I spit. "I'd like to see you do any better."

Without warning, the air shifts, a chill sneaks its way down my spine and into my bones. The room goes absolutely frigid as Elian pulls on the shadows without a thought, stalking toward me with a blast of magic in his hands. It's pitch black, exactly as he said. The color of his soul.

"Like this? You want me to show you how pathetic you're being?"

"I'm not weak and you know it," I snarl at him and get in his face. My heaving chest brushes up against him. I pretend like my nipples aren't hard, even though they definitely are.

"Then why haven't you put me on my ass yet, huh? I know you're dying to beat me, so fucking do *it.*"

My lip curls and I let the anger he's provoking enter my veins. I fill myself up with it, letting it enter my center. So many shadows slink into my hands that the room grows dimmer with each passing second, making his eyes widen, but there's not an opportunity to move before I sic them on him. One large strand wraps around his ankle and I yank with all my might.

His feet go out from under him and he ends up on the mat, breathing hard and glaring daggers at me, but he surprises me by cracking a bit of a smile of all things. It comes out as more of a cross between a grimace and a smirk, but it's a smile, nonetheless. Did hell suddenly freeze over outside?

"Finally!" he says before returning to his feet.

The shadows drop as my rage flees. "The fuck do you mean, *finally?*"

He stalks toward me, but I don't give him any ground. "I've been waiting for you to do that all afternoon. For someone who challenges me in every other aspect of life, you sure didn't give me much of a fight today." He comes to a stop directly in front of me, staring me down with those hard emerald eyes.

My eyebrow raises. "You were testing me?"

He nods. "And you failed... miserably."

"You were supposed to be teaching me!" With all the fire I can muster, I shove him away. He obviously doesn't expect it but he doesn't stumble. The dick. "You've been preaching patience and control all day, so how was I supposed to know you were actually trying to get me riled up to see me lash out?" My chest heaves with anger as a little bit of that heat returns to his eyes until it ignites into a flame. Then he seems to realize it and throws water on it, putting the fire out before it can spread to his brain. "Bastard!"

His eyes darken. "Unfortunately, I'm not a bastard, but I wish I was."

"What the fuck is that supposed to mean?"

"Nothing. You're dismissed for the day." I reach out to grab him, but my hands pass through empty air as he shadows away. A frustrated scream tears free from my throat. That infuriating man!

And I have to go through a whole week of this?

Fine, then I'm going to make him regret taunting me.

Fuck this hot and cold shit. I want his heat all the time and I'm going to push him until I get every ounce of it.

14

SADIE

Sometimes things eat at me. Well, more than sometimes but I usually don't let them show. One thing that's been eating at me, now that Ash is back home, are the shifters we stole from the prison compound. I know Kaos and Dante managed to get them settled into the pack house, but I can't ignore this feeling in my gut any longer, tugging me to them. I find myself wanting to know more about them. To learn their stories and know about their culture.

I guess that's why my feet are carrying me in their direction. Hemsworth trails along behind me, my somewhat silent guardian. Which is unusual for him. "Penny for your thoughts, Hems?"

"That saying has never made sense to me," he chuffs. "My thoughts are worth way more than a penny."

I chuckle, ruffling the fur on top of his head. "What's on your mind then?"

"What are you going to give me if I tell you?" he counters.

"Hmm... can you be convinced with a steak?"

He licks his lips with a dreamy look in his eye. "Deal, but I want two. I was thinking about you, actually. About how much I've seen you blossom in the short time you've been with your mates. Happy is a good look on you, Sadie."

I've never been one that's good with compliments, so I simply say, "Thanks, Hems. I'm so glad we found you. Although, your entrance could've been a hell of a lot better."

"Ah, yeah that was Bedi's idea. I was safe the whole time, you know. If she can control a boulder from a hundred miles away, why not a car?"

A chilling thought to think about. Definitely want to keep that woman on my good side. "She's a powerful ally."

"And an even more powerful enemy," he warns. "Now, do you want to tell me why we're out here?"

"I need to know they're okay and that they're starting to fit in around here, I guess. I don't know, to be honest."

Hemsworth cocks his head, staring at me like he's seeing me in a different light. "Maybe it's a blessing you weren't raised around Weavers so you don't hold the same prejudices as they do."

"Maybe it was," I agree. "But sometimes I do feel pretty lost trying to navigate this world."

"You'll get there. Rome wasn't built in a day."

I snort. "Yep, definitely sounds like something you would say."

As we crest the hill, a sprawling house pops into view, nestled into the trees. If I had to guess, I'd say it's every bit as big as my Sworns' estate which makes me extremely happy. At least they're not cramped into a tiny house with absolutely no space to move around.

Before we can make it to the pack house, we're intercepted by an enormous wolf. My hand automatically goes to my switchblade in my pocket, but Hemsworth knocks my hand out of the way before I can pull it out and subtly shakes his head.

I give him a nasty look which he pointedly ignores while the wolf stares at us. He's massive. His body is gray while his paws and snout are white. He bares his teeth at me when I move to step around him. Shifter or real wolf?

My question is answered a millisecond later when there's a flash of light, and where a furry body once stood is now a buff and totally naked shifter.

"Moons above." I'm totally *not* checking out his package. Nope. Not at all. But if I were, I'd say Godsdamn, shifters are *packing.*

You're mated, Sadie.

Oh, yeah. Whoops.

A second later, another male comes running up to us and at least he's clothed. He tosses the wolf a shirt and I shield my eyes until he covers his junk with it. When his dick is out of sight, I return my gaze to them and study them both. The naked one has dark hair and gorgeous blue eyes while the clothed one is blond and has that hard-working vibe going on. They both do. Must be a shifter thing.

"What business do you have at the pack house?" Dark hair asks, locking gazes with me. Bad idea, bud. I'm good at winning these things. Eventually, the weight of my stare becomes too great and he's forced to look away. "Who are you?" His eyes stay slightly above where my actual line of sight is.

"The name's Sadie Sinclair. Who the fuck are you?"

The blond one chuckles and his companion smacks him with his free arm. "My name is Darren and I'm this estate's Alpha. Nice to meet you, Miss Sinclair. We've heard great things about you from one of our own."

This makes my eyebrow rise. "Oh, you have?"

"We have," the blond guy confirms, speaking up for the first time. "Vinson will not shut up about you. Ever."

Darren smacks him again. "Ignore Carter. He's my Beta, or second in command."

"It's nice to meet you both." I give them a slight head nod. "Actually, Hems and I were hoping to meet some of the shifters from the prisons."

Darren's jaw clenches and he looks away from me for a moment. "They're not adjusting well. Most of them have been in captivity and tortured for years. We're very protective of them."

"I'd never hurt them, but I do want to make sure they're okay." I don't take offense at what he's implying. I'm a part of the society keeping them oppressed, after all. *Not forever though,* I remind myself. I don't know how or when, but I'll set them free one day.

Darren and Carter's eyes glaze over and I assume they're having a mental conversation. They finally come back to the present and Darren inclines his head. "Right this way."

The pack house is quite spacious on the inside. They really managed to do the most with the area they were given. Nearly all of it is housing from the looks of it by the cots littered throughout. Darren leads us up a flight of stairs and down a hallway, stopping at the door at the end. "They wanted to stick together and I couldn't deny them that. They've been through so much."

"I understand. Thanks, Darren." I pause, taking a deep breath to center myself and clear any negative thoughts away. "We won't be long. I just needed to see them."

He nods like he understands, but still doesn't seem certain about allowing us inside. "We'll be right outside if you need anything."

Ripping the proverbial band-aid off and not giving myself any more time to think about it, I slowly turn the doorknob and step into the room with the shifters that I helped rescue. They're all huddled in the corner of the room, not talking, just staring at me with wide eyes. Hemsworth whines at the state of them and I have to agree. Shivering, covered in dirt, likely the same grime from their prison.

"Hello," I murmur awkwardly. "My name is Sadie, and this is my familiar, Hemsworth." I keep my voice soft and low, hoping not to spook anyone. Hems lowers his head and we both make sure not to make eye contact with any of them for too long. "I wanted to come check on you all and see how you were doing now. I, um, helped them rescue you."

A girl in the front stands up, seeming to be the bravest of them all. "I know we aren't who you were wanting to find but thank you for getting us out of there nonetheless," she says.

"No need to thank me. Um, is there anything I can do to help you all? Would you like a bath?" One of the males in the back cries out and I recoil. "Shit, I'm sorry. Was it something I said?"

The same girl speaks up again. "His punishments were always water based," she hisses, and for once I feel totally out of my element. Usually, I'm good at adapting but I have no idea what I'm doing here. Being soft isn't my thing. I stand there with my mouth opening and closing for a bit before I close it and start to turn around. Maybe this was a mistake. I might only make things worse.

Suddenly, the door opens behind me and Kaos steps in. "You followed me?" I ask.

"I figured you could use some help."

Please, I gratefully say into his mind.

A few of the shifters perk up when Kaos turns his attention to them. Out of fear or respect, I'm not sure. "Does anyone have any injuries that need healing? I don't even need to touch you to do it," he adds when a few of them cast wary glances at him.

The brave girl assesses us for a long moment before standing and making her way over to us on unsteady feet.

"Look me in the eye and tell me why two Weavers would help a bunch of outcast shifters. Do I need to remind you it was your Elders who put us in this state?" No, she doesn't honestly. I've thought of nothing else since we found them in this condition.

"Kaos is one of the most compassionate men I've ever met, and I wasn't raised around their kind so I don't hold any ill will against you. The reason we want to help you is because we owe it to you to correct *their* wrongs."

Another long pause of silence, then she finally inclines her head. "A few of us are injured. Most internally. Let's see what your magic can do." She signals for the shifters to rise and form two lines. Critically injured and stable. The majority slide to the former side. I'm surprised by their willingness to listen to a female when the societies around them seem to be led by males.

Kaos' hands glow black as he starts on them. After he heals two, he motions for me to come forward. Thinking he's going to ask for a recharge, I place my palm against his arm, but he shakes his head. "This is the perfect time to test out if you have gained any of my abilities."

"You want me to try and heal them?"

"Yes. I think it's about time we work on it, don't you?"

"Sure. I'll give it a shot." I should be nervous but with Kaos at my side, everything feels possible.

"Okay, I want you to place your hands above her stomach and imagine your magic flowing to you and then through her. Weave in your intentions as well. Focus on healing and mending any wounds."

I close my eyes and center my magic, trying to push it out of my body and into hers. Nothing happens for a while, but eventually I feel a small spark. Kaos nods at me encouragingly and I coax that spark into a small flame but instead of turning it into actual fire, I channel its energy into mending rather than destroying. It works, slowly at first until I feel the girl's internal wound start stitching itself together. I ignore the slight discomfort healing her causes, even though it itches like a motherfucker.

"Very nice, Little Flame. Keep at it and you'll be a healer in no time," Kaos praises.

It takes a while but gradually, we heal the shifters. One by one we bond with them as we go and listen to their stories. My rage against the Elders vastly grows as each of them tells us what they went through.

Most of them were sold as payment and happened to intrigue the Elders or piss them off. Some of them had been there as long as five years and others as short as six months. But all of them are thankful to us for rescuing them.

Several of the braver ones even come over to pet Hemsworth, smiling slightly when he nudges them or licks them.

Eventually, we leave their room with an open invitation from Darren and Carter to come back, and I feel lighter than I have in days.

15

SADIE

The next few days pass fairly quickly. My mornings start with Vinson in the kitchen and end with Elian smoking me in the training room. The latter wasn't lying about liking to see me riled up. He finds any and every opportunity to do just that.

When I make it to the bottom of the steps, I'm surprised to find the training room completely empty. There's not even a trace of Elian's usual signature. He always manages to beat me in the mornings, no matter how early I am. If I didn't hear him wearing a hole in the floor of his room every night, I'd think he slept down here.

Instead of being deterred, I slip my phone out of my pocket and connect it to the stereo. As soon as my music starts playing, I let out a sigh of relief. It's been difficult to train without it, but Elian denies me that pleasure saying it distracts him. Seems pretty on par with him though.

Working my muscles through each stretch really helps me work out the kinks. Elian doesn't pull any punches, and I have a few bruises to show for it. But so does he.

Speaking of, his aura brushes along my spine a second

before there's a featherlight touch against my shoulder blade as he corrects my posture. His touch is as frigid as he is.

"Why are you always so cold?" I ask.

"The shadow realm is freezing."

"Why are you late?"

He sighs. "I've been dealing with the Elders this morning."

I turn around to face him with that admission, quirking a brow. "Spilling all of our secrets to them, eh? I figured you were the rat."

"If I were the rat, you'd be dead by now," he deadpans, then clears his throat. "They were laying down the ground rules for our visit in two weeks."

When he doesn't elaborate, I push him. "Oh, and what are they?"

"All Weavers are required to wear formal attire. Something more suitable will be given to you to change into upon commencement of the challenge and we're not allowed to give you any information on what to expect from your opponent."

I groan. "You mean I have to wear heels?"

"I'm afraid so."

"That's fucking great. Perfect. What if I wear a long dress? Can I still wear my Converse?"

He makes a weird choking sound. "No, you cannot wear your Converse. I swear, it's like you want to get us killed."

"Why the fuck should my choice of footwear matter?"

"It shouldn't," he spits back. "But I don't make the rules."

"Whatever," I grumble, reaching down to retie my shoe. "Any more *good* news you need to tell me?"

He gives me a look, his icy eyes heating as he watches me while I'm down on one knee. "The *good news* is, Savannah will be going in as blind as you. You'll have the element of surprise on your hand."

"But so will she."

All he gives me is a small shrug. I can't tell if I should read into his words more and believe that he thinks Savannah is weaker than me or if it's just Elian being Elian. Something has to give between us, so I decide to try and play on his ego. "How about you and I play a little game?"

Knowing he's too stubborn to refuse, I smirk when he asks, "What kind of game?"

"Each day, we're allowed to ask each other one question and we have to answer truthfully. No matter what."

His jaw ticks. "By all means, ask your question."

Instead of wasting it on something like why he hates me so much, I decide to ask him about something that's been bugging me since the fight with Tyler. "Why wouldn't your ward let the others out the night Tyler attacked?"

His eyes flash. Is that guilt I'm seeing? "I didn't realize you were outside it. I'd only just gotten the distress signal from the vehicle the shifter taking Ash was driving and decided to lock it down tight. Unfortunately, it worked against me as well." He clears his throat and everything on his face vanishes as the mask slips back into place. "Why did you freeze up that night at the concert?"

My muscles tense. Maybe this was a bad idea after all. "Because Tyler was drunk and smelled like whiskey. It holds bad memories for me."

I expect him to comment on it but he doesn't, just studies me with those steely emerald eyes of his. "There's been a change of plans today."

"You're not going to ask me to elaborate further?"

"No. You said a question for a question and that would be more than one."

"Fair enough." At least he knows how to listen to rules, I guess. "What are we doing then?"

Dante bounds down the steps into the gym with Kaos following. "We're taking the day off!" he announces. My gaze strays to them and I have to do a double take because they look absolutely divine in their gym shorts and cut-off shirts. Their freshly showered hair is still wet, and I can imagine myself being trapped between them, one washing my hair and the other worshipping my body.

RIP my vagina. That bitch wants to jump everyone in this room right now.

Me, on the other hand, is curious. "Are we going somewhere?"

"We sure are. So get that pretty ass upstairs and change into something you don't mind getting dirty," Dante says, giving said ass a slap.

Kaos reaches over and rubs the spot like a good mate. "Good morning, Little Flame."

"Good morning, Steel." I reach over and palm his dick through his shorts. What do you know? Every part of his body is hard. His nickname does not let me down. "Seems like someone is happy to see me."

He groans, shooting me a panty-dropping look. Ha. They should know by now two can play this game and I always win. "He's never not happy to see you."

Elian's voice snaps me out of our back-and-forth banter. "For the love of the Goddess, can we get this shitshow on the road? Go get changed, Mercedes."

"Cock-blocking motherfucker," I grumble heading upstairs with the sound of laughter following me the whole way. I hear Kaos scolding Elian for using my full name on the way out and it makes me smile.

Hemsworth meets me outside my door with a tail wag and a bright doggy smile. "Hey, bud," I greet, giving his head a little pat. "Feels like I haven't seen you in a few days."

"You've been too busy training with your hot brooding asshole."

"Ugh, tell me about it." I run a hand through my ponytail.

"I've been meaning to ask, how are things going? Have you and Kaos made any breakthroughs on Vin's condition?"

His usual smile drops as his mouth closes. "Sadly, no. I'm sorry, Sadie."

I sigh. "That's okay. We'll figure it out." I refuse to believe otherwise.

"I'll hit the books again today while you're out."

"Thanks, Hems. You're the best." Apparently his mysterious familiar magic allows him to read like a human. He can even flip the pages with his mind. Have I mentioned that familiar magic is sort of freaky?

Once I'm in my room, I find the rattiest shirt in my arsenal that I promptly turn into a crop top by knotting the bottom since they told me it needs to be something I don't care about, which isn't hard considering all of my clothes are worn. Then, I tug on a pair of tight jean shorts that highlight the curve of my ass. If the guys think they won because we were interrupted earlier, they're sorely mistaken—I can make this old top and jeans into tools of seduction.

And judging by the thorough eye-fucking I'm getting going down the stairs, I made the right choice. Dante whistles appreciatively, Kaos' gaze follows my every movement, Reed looks like he wants to swallow me whole, and Elian's eyes are banked with desire. Their attention when it's fully on me like this is a charge to my self-confidence.

"Hot damn, Angel. You certainly called our bluff, didn't you?"

"Haven't you learned by now, Dante?" I give him a shy smile that couldn't be misconstrued as anything other than evil.

He looks a little wary as he asks, "Learned what, exactly?"

"I always win."

He chuckles, but it's Kaos who responds. "That you do, Little Flame. That you do."

"Whatever these two fucks did, I'm glad they did it. You look stunning, Love," Reed comments, giving me a once-over. I do the same, taking in his athletic shorts and t-shirt. This is the most dressed down I've ever seen him and the look suits him.

"You look pretty good yourself." I shoot him a wink and he ducks his head. Since it's more than likely not polite to drag them all to my bedroom and have my way with them, I decide to change the direction of conversation. Although I'm tempted, consequences be damned, when they clearly have something planned for me. "So, where are we going? Don't get me wrong, I'm excited to have a day off, but what's the plan?"

"You'll see," Kaos says cryptically, placing a hand on my lower back to lead me down the front porch steps. The shifters have done a lovely job of repairing where Reed dropped through it. If it weren't for the clear differences in the new wood and the old wood, I doubt anyone would ever know. Kaos informs me that staining them to match is next on their agenda.

I've tried to get close to a few of the shifters that are always milling about but every time one of them spots me heading their way they usually turn and walk in the other direction. I try not to take it personally, but I really do want to understand more about them and build a good relationship with them.

When we near the garage, my steps falter and my jaw drops as I spot three pristine four-wheelers sitting in front of the bay doors. Each of them are different colors, one black, one blue, and one green, and they're all equipped with a snorkel. Each has a backpack attached to the rack on the back.

I don't even question it. This seems exactly like the type of adrenaline rush I've been needing. I used to seek it out in other ways. Like training with Ben, but that's hard to do when he's currently six feet under somewhere. Good riddance.

With an excited breath, I stride over to the black four-wheeler, but a carefully placed hand around my wrist stops me before I can slide on. My eyes lift to the culprit, connecting with Elian's harsh emerald ones, then back to his hand around my wrist. My teeth grind together. Of course he didn't grab my hand. Wouldn't want the mating bond accidentally slipping into place.

"This one is mine. Go ride with one of your other mates."

Yet, my wrist stays firmly in his grip. "You'd have to let me go first." I relish in the way he drops my hand like it's burning him. His eyes narrow on mine and that's as much of a challenge as anything. I give a loose shrug, cackling as I wrap my legs around his four-wheeler and take my seat on the back.

Elian scrubs a hand down his face before sliding in front of me to grip the handles. "You asked for it."

My other mates gape at me, glancing between us like they can't quite figure out our dynamic. That'd make... four of us? Five of us?

Dante and Kaos give each other a look, their gazes sliding to Reed and the remaining two four-wheelers. A small smile graces my lips as I realize what that means.

Dante and Kaos break out into a game of rock, paper, scissors, and I absolutely lose it. Each heave of my chest brings me slightly closer to Elian and my breasts scrape his back, making him stiffen. I pretend to not notice his reaction.

Kaos' lips twitch as he wins the first battle and Dante shouts, "Best two out of three!"

Eventually, I have to declare Kaos the victor so we can get going. My skin is buzzing being this close to Elian, even if we're both doing our best to ignore it. I'm really starting to rethink my decision to hop on with him, but there's no way I'm backing down now.

Dante and Reed end up on the green one with Kaos going solo on the blue one. As soon as everyone is seated, Elian takes off. The loud roar of the engine thankfully covers up the surprised squeal that bursts from my lips. I didn't think I'd have to hold on, but Elian gives me no choice. The rumble of his chest against my hands is the only indication that he's amused. Yep, he definitely heard my squeal.

I wrap my arms around his torso, feeling every inch of us that touches while he zips through the trees. I have to dig my fingers into his skin, lest I fall off. Mercifully, I'm able to get my bearings fairly quickly, and once I do it's truly a thrill. The scenery is absolutely beautiful.

They must do this quite often because there's a worn trail that's just big enough for the machines beneath us to pass safely through the trees. Every now and then there are small paths that branch off in one direction or another, but Elian stays on the main one.

My fingers flex as I rest them against his taut abs. I count at least six before I realize what I'm doing and stop. He's still an asshole and I'm better than that.

Blocking all of that out of my mind, I let loose. With the sun bearing down on us and the wind whipping through our hair, I feel free. I feel alive. I feel more than I've felt in weeks.

Elian eventually makes it to a small creek. He turns and starts following it upstream, making the loose pebbles crunch under our tires. The rain from a few days ago is still evident in the mighty flow of the clear water.

I check behind me to make sure the others are still following and they are. Dante and Reed are behind us with Kaos bringing up the rear. Elian guns the throttle as we slam into a deeper part of the creek and water goes splashing across my heated, sweat slicked skin, jolting me to turn around, only to get splashed directly in the face with another spray of water. My hair is going to be an absolute wreck later.

I'm barely able to get my bearings again before Elian takes a sharp turn to the left and the momentum threatens to send me flying off. I have to grab onto his abs once more, which, if I'm being honest, isn't the worst thing in the world. And judging by the motions his shoulders are making, he knows exactly what he did.

"Smooth sailing back there?" he asks, taunting me. Is he actually *joking* with me?

How are pigs not flying?

I'm too stunned by the interaction to say anything for a moment. "Totally," I call back, raising my voice to be heard over the roar of the engine. "Where are we going?"

"You'll see," he responds, kicking the four-wheeler into a higher gear. We race through the creek, disrupting the crystal clear water. The terrain starts to change a bit from shallow water and pebbles, to deeper and murky. At one point, the water is so high that the machine is basically swimming through the water. Guess I know what the machine's snorkels are for now. When we make it to a shallow part again, Elian navigates onto a bank and out of the creek.

The path starts to take an upward climb, leaving me curious. "Is this still your property?"

"Yeah, we own quite a bit of land!" he hollers back. One thing about riding like this, it's not good for conversation. Which is likely a Godsend with me and Elian. His sharp tongue is like a whip, but then again, so is mine.

We come to a clearing a few minutes later and then an abrupt stop which makes me crash into Elian's back. "Ouch, give a girl a warning next time," I say as he shuts off the engine. It takes a few moments for my ears to adjust to normal.

"You're riding back with someone else." He stalks off before I can respond but I'm pretty certain I catch him adjusting himself. I ignore the thought that conjures and turn to my other mates instead.

"What did you think, Little Flame?" Kaos asks, looking me up and down, his eyes lingering on my legs.

Yeah, these shorts were worth it.

"It was actually quite nice. The fucker couldn't insult me over the roar of the engine."

Dante snorts. "You love to test him."

"And he likes to test me. I think that makes us even. Anyway, what did we come out here for?"

Reed gives me a slight shrug. "They didn't tell me either. Just told me to get ready for some bonding time. Not that I mind though."

The other two give me a salacious grin as they start stripping their shirts as a unit. My mouth waters as I run my gaze over each defined ab and muscle. Thank you Goddess for I have been blessed. "Come on, Angel. Let's show you around our favorite watering hole," Dante says.

Reed shifts on his feet, looking slightly out of place as he looks between us, so I make sure to walk beside him as we trail after Elian. "Did you enjoy the ride?" I ask him, my lips turning up at the corners as I try to hide my smile. Him and Dante riding together was a fun sight.

"Actually, it went quite well. I managed to... er, keep my junk off his ass as much as possible."

A laugh bursts free from my lips as I move a stray strand of hair from my eyes. "I'm glad you two are getting along better."

Hopefully, we'll be able to get to the bottom of this Light Weaver versus Night Weaver mate issue soon. My body reacts to him as much as the others, but even though I don't need it, I want the others' approval. Reed has to earn his place with them.

Reed gives me a meaningful look. "I hope I'm able to do that."

"Shit, was I talking out loud again—"

"Hurry up, Angel!" Dante interrupts. "You're taking forever!"

I don't have time to respond to anyone because the next thing I know, I'm hoisted in the air and planted on Dante's shoulder with my head hanging near his ass. Honestly, I could shake myself out of his hold if I wanted to, but I don't. His skin is scalding against mine, but it's comforting. I love how we fit together. How I fit with all of my mates really.

After a short walk uphill, he deposits me back on the ground and my jaw drops. We're standing atop a waterfall. Not a huge one like I've always seen in movies and magazines like Niagara Falls, but a small one with a large basin of water at the bottom. The water isn't as crystal clear as the creeks, considering I can't see the bottom because it's so deep, and the color is different, but it's lovely all the same.

I take in the whole scene with wide eyes. "What is this place?" We're surrounded by trees, but this little spot is carved out and eroded by the world, untouched by the horrors of mankind. It feels sacred, otherworldly almost. As if the Gods once occupied this spot themselves. Claimed the pulse of power here. Or, perhaps, it truly came from the Gods. "Do you all *feel* that?"

Kaos is the one who answers. "The power here is something else. It's why we come here every once in a while to recharge. Elian discovered it when we were kids, after our Circle bond clicked into place and we were still fighting for dominance. One evening here and we came back with clear minds and clear hearts. We've been unbreakable since."

Until I came along, a dark voice whispers in the recesses of my mind.

My thoughts must be clear on my face because Kaos' eyes narrow in on me. "We've always had petty squabbles, Little Flame," he says.

"And is that what I am? A petty squabble?" I caused a rift between them. This Circle that used to be tighter than brothers. Then again, Elian has definitely been hiding shit from them. Maybe I'm not fully to blame.

Before my thoughts can go any further, Kaos is upon me. Lifting my chin with a slight caress, as if he's asking me to look at him, not telling me. My gaze rises to his. "You are the furthest thing from a petty squabble," he says, blue eyes so soft. Like the sky on a clear, beautiful day. So full of love and life. I give him a nod because it's all I can manage. He takes my hand into his and leads me over to the ledge.

Dante gives me a wide grin which instantly puts me on alert. "Let's have some fun, shall we?" Before anyone can say anything, he takes a running leap over the cliff. A startled gasp escapes me as I watch him plummet into the water below with whoop and holler. Elian follows suit without so much as a backward glance. I swear everything around him leans in closer as he jumps, but when I blink everything is back to normal.

Reed gives me a surprised look, which I return. I give him a small smile before I back up slightly and take my own running leap over the edge. I'm a do or don't kind of girl, as they say. A scream leaves my lips as the wind whips through my hair and my stomach rises to my throat. I'm completely weightless for a moment but I make sure to close my mouth before I reach the cool water and slip through it with a splash. My toes hit the cool pebbles at the bottom and I push off those to rise to the surface.

Dante's face is the first sight to greet me when I emerge

from the water's hold and take a breath. He looks divine as he runs a hand through his dirty blond hair and swims closer to me. There's a splash next to me as Kaos jumps in, leaving Reed at the top, staring warily down at the four of us.

"Come on down, Red! The water is fine," I call out, splashing Dante for emphasis.

Reed still looks uncertain, but he takes a step back and then another until he's far enough away to get a running start. He holds my gaze as he takes the plunge, dropping like a heavy weight into the spot directly in front of me. When he rises to the top, a wide grin graces his lips making my heart soar with joy for him. Water drips from his glasses, which I'm surprised stayed on, and he pulls them off, trying to wipe them with his hands to no avail.

"Guess I should've left these up there. Oh well," he says, sticking them back on his face. He's so devastatingly handsome in that quiet, nerdy, way of his. Slowly, the darkness is fading from his eyes. Same with the haunted look that follows him around like a shadow.

Out of nowhere, a dark tendril drags its way down my spine as if to remind me it's still there, that it can get past my defenses, that it's always watching, always lurking. A strangled gasp tumbles from my lips from the sheer force of the invasion. Taunting me. Four sets of eyes and heads whip in my direction at the sound.

"What is it?" Elian demands.

I ignore him, focusing inside myself to hopefully find the intrusion, but it's as if there's an invisible hand clutching my heart, my spine, my mind. My intuition lights up as the presence caresses my senses once more, sending a tremor through my body, and then it vanishes like it was never there to begin with. But I see it for what it is.

A warning.

From whom, I'm not entirely sure, but one nonetheless.

16

SADIE

"What the hell was that?" Elian asks once more, suddenly in my face.

"You need to strengthen your wards," I manage to choke out.

He curses and disappears into the shadows without second-guessing me. I'm not sure what to make of that so I won't dwell on it. I scan the area, weaving my shadows through the air around us, but there's nothing.

"Whatever it was is gone now." I dart a glance to my other mates and they look wary.

It's Dante who finally breaks the silence. He ducks under the water, tapping on my legs to spread them, then he rises with me on his shoulders. "How about a game of chicken to lighten the mood?"

"You're not worried?"

"No, I am, but Elian's wards will keep them physically out. He must be slacking a bit if they managed to get through to you mentally."

Or he's exhausted, I think silently, remembering the past

few nights of him fitfully tossing in his sleep then waking at dawn to train me.

Reed and Kaos look at each other before Reed sighs. "Fine." He lifts Kaos out of the water and all thoughts of the ward and Elian are shoved from my mind as we battle it out atop our trusty steeds. Or rather, my trusty steeds.

They do a well and thorough job of keeping me distracted. Elian returns some time later, but he said he was content to watch us from the bank. There were several moments when I wanted to ask him to join us, but since we'd have to battle with our hands to try and topple each other, he refused. Because of the bond untapped between us. I didn't push it any further.

"Are you ready for some food, Angel?" Dante asks after I toss Kaos off into the water for the fifth time. Don't get me wrong, he managed to beat me a few times, but I totally won. Or he let me win. Either way I'm totally taking the victory as my own. "I don't know about you, but I am famished." He places a hand on his taut stomach, his abs in full view and pouts.

Pretty sure I'm already getting a feast... for the eyes. But I don't voice that thought aloud. Although I swear I see Reed's lips twitch. In a blink his face is normal as he and Kaos carry on a conversation.

"Take me away, you dramatic baby," I respond to Dante, teasing him with a wide grin. I can't remember the last time I enjoyed life this much. Or smiled this much, hell, *lived* this much.

"You got it." He takes my hand and leads me over to a grassy meadow where we lay out the beach towels from one of the backpacks.

Kaos retrieves the food, made by Vinson I realize, when he pulls out five of his special BLT's. A pang of longing hits me square in the chest, but I shove it down, shove the memories of us in the kitchen, of him wiping the corner of my mouth, out of my mind. Reed gives me a curious look, which I don't return.

"Was there a reason for this trip?" I ask around a mouthful of the tasty sandwich. It's as good—if not better—than I remember.

"We figured you needed a break," Kaos responds. "Especially since we're going to the compound tomorrow."

I snort to cover up the jolt of nervousness. "Two days off from training with the broody bastard? Sign me right up."

Said broody bastard rolls his eyes. "Just for that, I'm tacking on two more days to your regime with me. Besides, we're far from over. You're going to train until your fingers ache and it's second nature to use all your powers."

I groan and Dante chuckles. The others join him until we're all laughing. "Should've kept your mouth shut, huh?"

"Apparently—" I start to say but I'm interrupted by a dark flash as a shadowy figure emerges from the trees, stalking toward us. Whatever it is has a dainty gait and moves as though the world should take note of their presence.

Everyone is up on their feet in an instant, food forgotten. Kaos goes to reach for the weapons in his pack, but a tinkling laugh stops him short. "There's no need for that, child," she says in that familiar breathy voice.

My eyes widen as they fully take in the beautiful woman now mere feet from our picnic spot. Long flowing black hair that curls around a tiny waist. Her hair flows alongside her sheer skirt that is scarcely thick enough to cover the most important bits. Her round ample breasts cupped with that same fabric shake with silent laughter as I peruse her. Otherworldly. Unreal. *Ethereal.* Those are the first thoughts that pop into my head about her.

"Well met, Sadie Sinclair," she says, giving me a slight head nod. I note that she calls me Sadie, not Mercedes like most would. I manage a glance at my mates to find them on their knees with their heads bowed. You've got to be shitting me.

Is this the Goddess?

Completely unsure of what to do, I start to sink to my knees, but she holds a hand out to stop me. The Goddess herself is in this meadow—our meadow—and she stops me from bowing to her.

"You needn't bow for me, child. None of you should. Rise, my loves."

Each of the guys do with awe clear on their faces. They turn to me, staring at me with the same amount of reverence. Even Elian.

"What the hell is happening?" I breathe.

"I have come to give you some guidance, but I cannot stay for long." At my curious look she says, "This world was not built for me and it is far too draining on my powers, but I wanted to give you a little shove in the right direction."

"You're nothing like what I expected," I blurt.

"What did you expect, dear?"

"Cold beauty and grace," I answer honestly.

"Moons, no," she says with a laugh, extending a hand for me to take. Her skin is soft, warm, and welcoming as it brushes against mine. "I have always chosen to lead with integrity, kindness, and honor rather than with a firm hand."

"Then why are people like the Elders in power?" Once again my mouth moves before my brain does. It must be something about being in her presence that makes me spill the truth.

Her eyes darken and she looks away for a moment before her clear blue eyes snap back to mine. "The whispers are true. They were once blessed by me, but the three of them had seeds of evil in their hearts. Sometimes that is unavoidable with giving your people free will." She sighs. "Those seeds grew as their lust for absolute power grew. They were smart and resourceful, climbing the ranks by whatever means necessary. Then they started dabbling with the order of things, perverting everything sacred."

"What do you mean by that?"

"Long ago, after I created each and every one of you, I decreed that I would never take away your choices. That I would never interfere with your lives lest taking away your right of free will. I've been bound by those words and that decree for many millennia. So, I cannot intervene, but I can even the playing field a bit."

"That's where all of us fit into this?" I ask, reading between the lines.

"You would be correct. I saw the path those fools chose and decided to fight back, but I was not expecting their love of power to run so deep and now they have perverted the mating bonds too." Her body flickers in and out of focus in her silent rage. She gives me a grim smile before continuing, "I spoke a prophecy into existence twenty-three years ago. There would be a girl to come along that would shake this very world to the core. She will be darkness and light personified, dishing justice throughout the mortal realm. She will be mercy and grace rolled into one package and she will unite this world, no matter the cost. Our worlds have been divided for far too long." She flickers in and out of existence again. "Sadly, I can't stay much longer. It's taking way more power than I thought possible to remain here, child."

"Who is the girl in your prophecy?" I ask. Surely, she can't mean me, right? That would be absurd.

"You will have to figure that out for yourself. Listen to my next words very carefully because this is all I can give you without breaking my pact. Love is light, it is dark, and it is wholly yours. The path in front of you and your mates will be dark, but it can be light if you let it."

I sigh. Bloody fucking riddles.

"And what about Reed?" I ask, noting him watching the whole exchange with wide eyes under those black water-splattered glasses. "Is he a part of my Circle? What about the Light Weavers?"

"All living things on this earth are my creation. There was never supposed to be a divide," she says with sorrow as she looks to my red-haired mate. "I'm sorry for your loss but know that they are running free in a meadow quite like this one."

A lone tear slips down Reed's cheek. "Thank you."

The Night Goddess turns to me once more. "Your pairing was no mistake, my child. No bond blessed by me ever is." She studies my face and I'm sure there's more meaning under her words, but I'm not catching it. My mind is swirling with all of the new information.

There's a bright flash of white light and a man appears beside the Goddess, watching her with such love and warmth in his gaze that it takes my breath away as he grabs her arm. Two more appear beside them, one in a cloud of russet purples and oranges and another in the pre-dawn light on a spring morning.

The first one is the one who says, "Come now, mate. Your powers are draining quickly. The Weavers can handle it."

She gives him a small nod. "Stay close to your loved ones, Sadie. They will guide you through the dark."

"Thank you for calling me Sadie," I whisper. She must know the reason I hate my full name, must know that is all my uncle ever called me and that it haunts me in my sleep.

Her ancient eyes once again fill with sadness. "Of course. It is truly time for me to go but know that I'm always watching you. You're going to go far in this world, girl. I know it."

"Thank you."

The four of them give us one last look and then vanish like they were never here at all. Silence descends upon us as we mull over what we experienced.

Finally, Elian says, "What the hell just happened?" But I don't really have an answer.

17

SADIE

We wake the next morning to a loud bang on the front door and open it to find a raven, twisted at all the wrong angles lying on the doorstep.

Apprehension unfurls in my stomach as I stare at its broken body and the Goddess' words from yesterday filter into my mind. *Trouble is coming, girl. You need to be prepared.*

The same icy talons from the day before rake down my spine before disappearing entirely. All happening in the span of a heartbeat. Refusing to be cowed, I hold my head high as I once again tell Elian he needs to strengthen his wards. This time I even offer to go with him, aid him in whatever way I can with my own magic. He doesn't object so I take that as my opportunity to follow him.

The grass sways with the wind as Elian leads me to what he calls the epicenter of his ward. I can't see anything, but I feel the buzzing of his magic under my skin. The closer we get, the more intense it gets. Like a loose livewire readying to snap.

"How is this dark presence getting through?" I ask, watching him out of the corner of my eye. His hands are in his pants pocket and there's not a wrinkle in sight on his crisp button-up. He's the epitome of perfection, as always.

He runs a hand through those dark blond locks of his, his emerald eyes snagging on mine. I swear I see regret in them, but it's gone in a blink, leaving me to believe I imagined it. "It seems as if they're tricking it into thinking they're friendly."

"How is that possible?"

"I don't know," he admits. "Put your hand against the barrier and I'll show you what I mean." I take a step closer, examining the pulse of magic. The hair on the back of my neck stands.

"Is it going to shock me?"

His lips quirk. "Only if I tell it to."

"Will you?"

"No."

For some reason, I believe him. Closing the small distance, I place my hand fully against his ward. It's cold to the touch and feels so utterly like him that it takes my breath away for a moment. The magic tries to rush into my body to greet me and I have to focus on pushing it out. It doesn't hurt though. If anything, it's like a lover's caress, desperately reaching out. Too bad its master is a bastard.

"Imagine finding the loose ends and patching them," he tells me. I glance over to find him with his hand against the barrier also, eyes closed in concentration.

I close my own eyes. I'm not sure if it really helps but I've learned with Weaver magic it's about intention and I can concentrate better this way. As soon as my palm connects to the ward, the hundreds of threads making it up appear behind my eyelids. They're intricately interwoven into patterns that make absolutely no sense.

One could get lost looking at them but instead of focusing on the madness of the loops and swirls, I zero in on one strand in particular that seems a little dull compared to the rest. I send my magic thrumming through it until it stops abruptly. Each strand in that area is frayed, swaying along an invisible breeze.

Without Elian even uttering a word, I know what needs to be done to fix it. I reach inside that swell of magic in my center and caress it lightly before coaxing it into the frayed bits. It feels a bit sluggish at first, but once it powers through the sludge it snaps into place almost instantly—as strong as an impenetrable fortress.

I continue my search, checking along the wall and finding small areas that occasionally need patching.

When I deem the ward to be properly fixed, I open my eyes to find Elian staring at me, assessing me. "Do you even realize what you've managed to do?" he asks casually. Almost too casually, but I sense the steel underneath, the cold impenetrable walls of his own fortress around him, his heart and his mind. One's that I want to tear down and then rebuild when I'm inside. Then maybe I'd be able to understand his mind. "Not even some of the most advanced Weavers can strengthen someone else's ward like that. Yet you did it with half a thought. Your magic is so unlike any I've ever seen."

"Still think I'm weak?" I quip.

His lips tilt upward into that cruel smile he wears so well but all he says is, "No." Then he shadows away, leaving me to walk back to the estate on my own. At least I can breathe a little better knowing my power did something to fix the wards.

My power mixing with Elian's. What a potent combination indeed.

18

SADIE

We leave for the compound to test out my magic after lunch. Reed has to stay, not only to watch over the estate, but to avoid the other Night Weavers who would likely try to kill him. A strong fierceness enters my body at that thought. They could try, but I sure as hell wouldn't let them. No one hurts my mates.

Nonetheless, someone needs to stay and it might as well be him. Which leaves Hemsworth at my side, riding in the back of Elian's brand new Jeep and Dante on my other. Kaos and Elian are up front, with the latter driving. It doesn't take long before we're turning off the main road, pulling up short when the path ends abruptly.

Kaos senses my confusion. "See through the Illusion."

I take a deep breath and physically feel for the magic around me. The Illusion is strong and fights me at first since it doesn't recognize me, but I'm stronger and it finally lets me in. When I open my eyes, I find a sprawling wrought iron fence with two Weavers dressed head to toe in black. They leave their position at the gate and stalk toward us with grim faces. Their magic signature brushes up against mine as they prepare to face us. No one other than me seems alarmed. *Uh, guys?*

Elian rolls down the driver window, waiting for the men to see who it is, and a bright smile crosses the shorter man's face when he sees it's Elian. "Well met, brother. We sure are glad to see you all alive." He clasps Elian's hand through the window and then his gaze snags on me in the back. "With your mate in tow no less. Who would've thought the day would come? And that the Goddess would bless *you* of all people."

I expect Elian to scowl, maybe even deny me as his mate but he chuckles at the man's words, surprising the hell out of me. "Well met, Malachi. I see you haven't lost your sense of humor."

"You know me," Malachi says with a dismissive shrug. Kaos butts in before Elian and Malachi can keep going.

"How is everyone? Any news about the attack?"

Confusion bleeds into Malachi's expression. "What attack?"

My mates share a look. "The one a few weeks ago? Fedrick called to inform us not to show up to test Sadie's magic that day because there had been an attack," Kaos responds carefully.

Malachi rubs his jaw in thought, throwing a look over his shoulder to his companion. "There wasn't an attack. Actually, the last one was a few months ago."

Elian's jaw is tight with tension. "A ploy to keep us from coming here by you know who, I'm sure."

"To what end?" I ask from the back.

The others ignore my question and Malachi whistles, throwing up two fingers in the air as he signals the guard to open the gates. "Come on, let's discuss this further inside."

Elian doesn't need any more encouragement as the large wrought iron gates swing open and he pulls through them.

After a half mile or so a large sprawling compound starts to take form and it's nothing like I expected. Buildings of all shapes and sizes litter the grounds, all serving various purposes if I had to guess. The largest building in the middle is the one that catches my eye though. It's massive, built to shelter large numbers of people. This place is nothing like the small outpost we rescued the shifters from. Here... there is a pulse of *life*. A chord of liveliness the dank prison didn't have.

Dozens of Weavers mill around, heading to and from the different buildings. There are so many of them, more than I'd thought there'd be with their dwindling numbers. Some of them glance at us as Elian parks in the grass and we file out of the Jeep. Others outright stare at us and whispers start up amongst them.

"Do the Elders live here?" I ask, and Malachi gives me a funny look.

"As if they could be bothered with this lowly crowd."

"I'll take that as a no, then?"

"No," Elian says. "They have their own mansion. They only come here when necessary to keep everyone in line. Technically, no one has to live here but some choose to. Let's go get this over with, shall we? I don't want to be here any longer than needed on the off chance they do decide to show up unannounced."

As we walk, Hemsworth sticks to me like glue, and I thread my fingers in his fur, needing him to help keep me grounded with all the sights, the smells, and the magic pulsing around me. There are so many people here, more than I ever thought possible.

Kaos senses my discomfort and takes my other hand in his, sending me a thread of his calming peace. I hate being stared at but none of my anxiety shows on my face as I hold my shoulders and head high, following Malachi through the crowd. Dante brings up the rear, protecting my back and I give him a small nod of thanks which he returns with a lazy smile.

Malachi leans in toward Elian. "I managed to clear out the testing room today. It'll just be your Circle allowed inside for the duration. The monitors will be wiped as soon as you receive the results, as promised."

"Thank you for your discretion," Elian murmurs with dark undercurrents and a promise of pain riding his tone.

Malachi swallows thickly and merely nods before he opens the door to the largest building for us to pass through. "Right this way."

My Converse squeaks on the tiled floor as he takes a left and follows the hallway all the way to the double doors at the end. "Good luck," is all Malachi says, then he strides away, leaving me to glance curiously at my mates.

"What do we do now?"

"We figure out what you are and what we're working with," Elian says tightly. I think he's spoken more to me this past week than ever before.

I'm not complaining.

I break every test machine. Every single one of them. Not one of them withstands my power long enough to give us any answers as to what my magic truly is and what it might derive from. A sign from the Goddess if I've ever seen one.

At least we're not walking out completely empty-handed though. During the internal test that allowed me to see inside of my ball of power, I found a section of it missing and a part of me shackled and caged, begging to be let out. I'm not sure if I want to fully unleash myself on this world. Not yet, anyway. I'm certain the day will come. Why else would I have this locked power?

My mates are cranky as fuck. Not because I damaged irreparable machines, but because we're no closer to finding out my true potential.

"Does it really matter at this point? We all heard *her* yesterday," I say as they lead me toward the gym. They want to check in on everyone and it's a win-win because I'll get to see how the other Weavers train.

Kaos squeezes my hand. "I guess not. We wanted to know if there's anything else hidden in your arsenal we could use though. We want you to have every advantage, Little Flame."

I give him a squeeze back. "I appreciate everyone's concerns, but I've got this. I can handle myself."

He gives me a smirk. "I know. Goddess help the poor souls who ever stand in your way."

Hemsworth gives my leg a small nudge in agreement, and I smile down at him. He's been extremely careful not to reveal who, or what he is by choosing not to speak. Kaos claims it would spook everyone here to know I am powerful enough to have a familiar and we don't want to cause a panic. I'm cool with that. They're already ogling me enough for my liking.

The sound of flesh hitting flesh drags me from my thoughts as we round the corner to their gym and training room. The sight before me makes my blood start to sizzle in my veins, awakening that primal instinct in me that loves the thrill of the fight.

"We should've come here first." I slip into the fray with a chuckling Dante right behind me.

The fighters are a blur as they circle each other in their respective areas. They almost seem to move as one, drawing me into their fights. I carefully consider each team and watch their movements to learn their patterns. The heat sizzling in my veins turns to ice as I spot a massive oily looking man relentlessly beating a male that can't be much older than me and half the size. The poor thing is practically a scrawny shrimp.

The massive one lands another hit that he isn't able to dodge and blood sprays from his mouth. I wince. Shrimp's lip is already split and his left eye is swollen shut. A few of the Weaver's are watching from the sidelines, roaring their approval when the bastard sticks another punch to his gut. I take in their faces and memorize them.

I don't know what possesses me to do so but my feet are carrying me across the training room before I even make the conscious thought. I duck and weave through the crowd, using my elbows a few times when some of them won't move. I cross over the black tape indicating their fight circle and raise my chin. Dante curses and tries to yank me back but it's too late. The massive fuck has already spotted me.

"How about you pick on someone your own size, motherfucker?"

With his fight temporarily forgotten, he levels those muddy eyes on me. "Who the fuck do you think you are?"

My voice is not entirely my own as I say, "I'm the shadow men like you should fear." And just like that, this man's history is splayed out for me to pick through, much like the men from the prison compound. I instantly know his history and that he's a bully, firmly on team Elders. Imagine that. This level up on my intuition is coming in handy. He hasn't done anything worthy of death... yet. But I'd say now is as good of a time as any to teach him a lesson in humility.

He laughs, fucking laughs as he takes another step toward me. One of my mates snarls at him, making him glance behind me. His gaze returns to mine and he smirks. "You're the newest Link. What makes you so fucking special, huh?

You look like a normal bitch to me. Maybe your pussy is magic."

"Watch your mouth, Hunter, or I will watch it for you," Dante says, reaching for me.

"Ah, ah, not so fast, Dante. You know the rules. She stepped inside the circle which means she will have to fight in order to leave it."

I stare him down, assessing him. "That's not a problem."

"Dammit, Sadie—"

"Let her fight," Elian cuts in before he can finish. "We need to see how she does, anyway." Dante relents but he doesn't look happy about it, more worried than anything else. I appreciate his concern, but Elian is right. For once. Never thought that day would come.

Hemsworth gives me a sly grin, watching the scene unfold. *So overprotective,* he says into my mind.

Tell me about it.

It's not a bad thing, he responds.

Nah, it means they care but they're going to have to get used to me throwing myself into danger headfirst.

Shrimp clears his throat, bringing me back to the matter at hand. "You didn't have to step in on my behalf." His words come out garbled and barely understandable. He must have a will of steel to still be standing in his condition.

I don't want to look at him with pity but it's hard not to. I school my features, figuring I shouldn't deflate what little confidence he has left. "I'll always defend those who can't defend themselves," I tell him as he takes me in with his non-swollen eye. "How about you head over to my mate, the tall one with the black hair, and he'll take care of your injuries, okay?"

Now his non-swollen eye widens, and he glances over my shoulder then back to me. "You mean... *Kaos?*"

"Uh, yes?" It comes out more like a question, and I clear my throat. "He'll heal you while I take care of this asshole."

Please heal him, I project to Kaos. *That last blow to his ribs probably broke them. I don't know how he's still standing.*

Kaos winces. *Yeah, it was an unfair match.*

So you'll heal him? I ask again.

I'd do anything for you, my Little Flame, he responds. *Knock that bastard down a peg or two for me.*

You got it, Steel.

Once Shrimp is out of the circle, I level my gaze on my opponent, sizing him up. "You stepped into the wrong fight, bitch," he says. "I'm going to crush you between my fists and then dance over your corpse."

Yeah, this asshole definitely has it coming. He doesn't know that I know he's never killed anyone before.

I pointedly ignore his jeering and turn to face my mates. "What are the rules?"

Elian rubs his jaw. "When you step into a fight and interrupt, there are no rules. Hunter has free rein to tear you apart."

"That's totally reassuring," I respond with an eye roll and slowly shift back to face Hunter. Oh man, if I thought he was simmering before he's about to boil over now. Turning my back on him like he's not a threat really makes the veins in his neck stand out with rage. "Magic or hands only?"

Hunter pops his knuckles. "You can use your magic, sweet cheeks. You're going to need every ounce of it to defeat me."

"Wonderful. Let's get this over with. I have other important things to do today." My statement makes his lip curl into a snarl, and he charges me. I deftly step out of the way and he barely manages not to bowl into the crowd. This only serves to enrage him further. The crowd watches me warily, some of them exchange money, betting on my opponent. Idiots.

I decide not to use my shadows, instead, I call Dante's

flames to my hands. It comes to me slowly at first but when the whoosh of heat finally takes over my body, I sigh. I love that rush. It warms me like a bonfire on a cold winter night. I toss a ball of it at my opponent and he doesn't even move. *Wow, maybe this is going to be easier than I thought.* The flame bounces right off his skin, not harming him a bit.

Shit, spoke too soon.

"How'd ya like that? My skin is tougher than rock and harder than diamonds."

"Looks like I'll have to be more precise in my attacks then."

While he's circling me, I take a moment to sort through what I know about him. Since his entire body is a weapon, I definitely need to avoid getting in close contact with him and avoid his fists. They're huge and would likely drop me like a ton of bricks. Jeez, how *was* that guy still standing?

"Why attack the scrawny guy?" I ask, trying to buy myself some time to think through my life decisions. Of course, I'd pick a fight with a fucking rock man.

Hunter steps toward me and I notice he's favoring his left leg. *Old injury, maybe?* He does it again and I know that's my ticket to bring him down. The question is, do I make him suffer first or end it quickly?

The image of his fists hitting the scrawny kid flash through my mind, and I have my answer.

"Everyone has to earn their place here," he says, and while I do agree that everyone needs to be trained properly, doing it this way is not the way to go about it. I'm sure there's someone closer to Shrimp's size and skill level than this beefy asshole.

Hunter spits to the side and then charges me. His nostrils are flared like an angry bull charging at one of those idiots waving a flag. Yeah, I don't understand that sport.

I'm so much lighter on my feet that I'm able to avoid him

again and while he's regaining his footing, I center myself before reaching into that basin where my power lies. I latch onto it and unleash myself throughout the room. The lights dim as the shadows from everyone's forms slink toward me. The crowd starts shifting on their feet as they watch the spectacle. More money exchanges hands as a few start betting on me, Elian included. The fucking prick is actually betting on me? Huh.

My momentary lapse in concentration costs me. For someone so big, Hunter's pretty quiet and I barely duck under his arm to miss his hit. I swivel, blocking his fist from hitting me while I'm crouched and the force of it reverberates up my arm. There's absolutely no give to his skin whatsoever. I need to steer clear of his hands at all costs.

My shadows rear up behind him, taking him by surprise as they sweep his feet out from under him, but I don't stop there. Curling my fists, I lift him feet first into the air, stringing them up from the ceiling. It strains me to use that much power because the dude is heavy as fuck, but I manage. He snarls and growls at me, watching me while being upside down.

"Hunter, you are a bully and a bastard. Next time you come into this room, you will remember this, remember me, and you will only pick fights with someone your size and skill level or my shadows will know. Do you have anything to say for yourself?"

"Fuck you," he snaps, veins popping out in his neck from the exertion of trying to break free. Sweat beads on my forehead from expending so much of my power, but I don't let it show.

"Fine, have it your way," I say, then snap my fingers. Immediately, my shadows dissipate and Hunter falls, smacking his head on the floor with enough force to knock him out. "Goddess, I hate fucking assholes like him."

A few boo's reach my ears under the roar of the cheering and four men step into the circle with me, looking me up and down. I yawn, playing it off like I'm unbothered. "I guess you'd like me to make an example of you all next?"

The crowd cheers, some of them even saying, *"Go, Shadow Girl, go!"* Their chants help fuel the fire inside of me and I wave my hand toward the four men, beckoning them forward.

They charge at me at once, one throwing a ball of water which I block with my black shield from Kaos. Another one's arm extends from his body, snaking toward me like that mom from the Disney movie *The Incredibles*, which I also block with my shield. The third one levitates from the floor and starts zooming toward me through the air.

"Don't you dare intervene, Dante," Elian snarls from somewhere behind me. *"She can handle this on her own. Watch."* And maybe that's the boost of confidence I needed.

Fire flares to life in my palms as I drop my shield and I start firing on my opponents. One of the balls lands on the bendy one's arm and he cries out in pain. I should probably feel bad since I also sense that he's not worthy of death but teaching these asshole's a lesson is the only thing on my mind. That's what healers are for.

The fourth one stays behind his other companions to observe the show. Something tells me he's the one I'll need to watch the most, but there's another ball of water aiming for my face so I don't have time to contemplate it too much. I throw up my shield, blocking the water blast just as the levitating one reaches me. My shadows lift from the ground, chasing after him which he expertly evades.

The other two advance on me and I decide to take the Water Weaver down first, heading straight for him. He manages to dodge my first hit but not the second and goes down like a sack of potatoes from the blow to his head, and the water in his hands soak my Converse. Ugh, I hate soggy shoes.

I shake it off and round on bendy man, making his eyes widen at whatever he sees in my expression. I smirk and rush toward him with my extra strength. He sends both arms flying at me and he manages to latch onto my ankle. *Shit.* He yanks and I go down with a thud and an oomph as the breath whooshes out of me.

Somehow, I manage to regain my footing before he can use his other arm to pin me down. I snatch his bendy arms out of the air, lay my molten hands on both of them. I don't let go even as he yelps and tries to yank them away from me. Using my hold on him to my advantage, I use his outstretched arms to catapult me to him in two large pulls and then knock him out with one punch to the temple.

Meanwhile, my shadows are slowly catching up to the levitating fuck and when they finally find him, they latch on, knocking him out of the air. He lands on the training mat in a heap and doesn't rise again. Too easy. The shadows return to me, whipping around me as they sense my agitation, and my palms are full of blue-orange flames as I face my last opponent.

My rage is definitely the key to unlocking my magic fully. I've still been struggling with calling my other powers to me at will in training with Elian. This is the most I've managed to do and I know it's because my emotions are fueling me.

I tilt my head to the side as I take in my last opponent. "What else do you have in store for me?" I ask him, and he's still watching me from his spot across the mat.

"I don't even have to touch you to kill you," he responds, eyes gleaming with hatred. My spine prickles with awareness, but it's too late to put up my shield.

Agony spreads throughout my head, bringing me to my

knees with a blinding headache as pain starts to become unbearable. Distantly, I hear my mates snarling for me to get up, but I can't focus on anything other than this debilitating ache. It's like he's boiling my brain from the inside out. I let my victory over the other three distract me and put my guard down.

A dark voice breaks through the fog, *Push him out, dammit. You have all the power here. Fucking remember that.* Leave it to Elian to be the only one calm enough to be the voice of reason that gets through to me.

Push him out how?

Out of your mind, he says just as another spike of pain sears through me, and I almost lose myself to it.

Straining with all my might, I wrap my shadows around me like a protective blanket, then I work on finding that invading presence. My magic is sporadic inside me, shooting around like lightning as if it's trying to protect me but it doesn't know how. I sort through everything until I find a thick, slimy tendril leading from me to him. There.

Using my mental switchblade, I cut the tie between us, causing him to hiss in pain and his magic explodes out of me. The agony holding me in its embrace starts to recede until I can finally see again. I find Elian holding both Dante and Kaos back while Hemsworth paces the line of the circle. He couldn't intervene without giving away he's my familiar and more than a simple dog, which is fine. The rest of the crowd is watching every single movement we make with bated breath.

"Cool trick," I say, stalking toward him. Severing the tie must've knocked him on his ass because he's currently on the ground looking up at me with wide eyes.

"How?" he demands, looking livid as he tries—and fails—to invade my mind again. He huffs in frustration.

"How what?" I ask, and his mouth twists into a line.

"How did you break my mental hold? No one has ever been able to do that before." He genuinely seems confused.

"Like I said, I'm the shadow men like you should fear. I'm the light in the darkness for the ones who can't help themselves." I swivel, kicking him in the temple with the side of my Converse and he winks out like the light of a candle being snuffed out.

Everything is silent for a moment, minus the beat of my heart in my ears, and my heavy breathing. It lasts maybe a second before everything erupts. The Weavers standing around close in around me, giving me pats on the back and several "good jobs." Shrimp is the last one to greet me and he gives me a hug, his tears soaking into my t-shirt.

"They've been a menace to us for so long. None of us could stand up to them with their powers and you did it without a second thought. Thank you so much." He starts to head back into the crowd again, but I stop him.

"Wait, what's your name?" Shrimp isn't the best nickname.

"Oliver!" he hollers and then disappears.

"All right! Back it up!" Dante hollers, pushing everyone back until my mates are the ones surrounding me. My mind is still a little sluggish from the hold that guy had over it, so I'm grateful for them getting everyone off of me. It seems most of the Weavers are staring at me with some level of respect and more than a few give me grateful head nods as they watch me with my Sworn.

"You all aren't mad that I interrupted your training and kicked five of your own asses?" I ask.

Malachi steps from the crowd with a cocky smirk. "Gods, no. Those bastards have had it coming for a long time. You did us a favor, Shadow Girl." Ah, it must've been him who started the chant.

"Wait, I did?"

"You did," he confirms, sticking his hand out for me to shake. I do so without a second thought... until I hear the hissing of my mates as our skin connects. *Oh, shit.* I forgot about Weavers and their whole touch thing. Thankfully, nothing happens when his palm connects with mine. Neither of us freeze and there's no jolt of magic. Malachi looks a little upset when he realizes the same thing.

"I could kick your ass for that," Dante interjects and yanks me away from Malachi. Apparently, there's only so much Dante can tolerate and an unsolicited touch is his limit. I'm grateful to Elian for not letting them intervene though. I know their protective instincts want to keep me safe, but I can handle myself and I more than proved that. To everyone. Which will hopefully work out in my favor later down the line.

"Sorry, man, but we're all a little desperate to find our mates now that you've found your bond," Malachi says and there's not an ounce of remorse in his tone. I kind of feel bad for them in a way but it's still disrespectful of him to be so outright. Something tells me that mate bonds will be making a comeback... but maybe not in the way everyone is thinking. Who knows how that will blow over.

The guys don't look back at Malachi as they lead me out of the room with whispers and votes of respect trailing me the whole way out.

19

KAOS

Sadie keeps her head held high as we make our way through the crowd and pride shines through me at her fierceness. My Little Flame is not cowed easily, but her shoulders are still tense, her posture rigid like she thinks she'll have to pounce on someone again. Like she's waiting for someone to pop out of nowhere. Not if I can help it.

My eyes scan the room, watching the crowd as I help watch her back and find mostly everyone staring at her in wonder. Before her, no one would dare mess with the Marsh Circle. They're some of the toughest pricks here, favored by the Elders for their ruthless pursuit of climbing the ranks. Doing anything they can to stay on top. It's disgusting.

Truthfully, I'm not certain if Sadie knows the extent of the favor she gained for sticking up for Oliver. His whole Circle, none of which could defeat the Marsh Circle on their own, would probably follow her to the ends of the earth for the simple kindness alone. The others and I used to watch out for this sort of thing and step in when we could, but life has been a tad hectic since we found Sadie.

Looks like my mate also managed to make quite a few enemies. I mark each one, those with a scowl on their face or murder hidden in their eyes, remembering their names for later. Too many have fallen for the Elders' charms and lies or are too afraid to dare stand up against them.

Fear breeds cowardice and a coward is a dangerous tool.

And while Sadie is a force to be reckoned with in her own right, she's not invincible and I'll do everything in my power to keep her as safe as possible—without stifling her natural glow—as I know the others would as well. We'd go to the ends of the earth for Sadie. Especially Dante who is absolutely smitten with her and yeah, even Elian, who still hasn't admitted it to himself yet for some reason. I'm not an aura reader like him, but I can tell she brightens a room as soon as she steps inside one, even if she doesn't notice it herself. She's like a beacon in the darkness, a siren singing her sweet song, and we're the sailors trapped in her lure. I wouldn't want it any other way either.

Thankfully, she doesn't seem to be hurt but I have a feeling she would turn down me healing her in front of everyone anyway. She's smart and knows when to play her cards right, and right now that means acting as if she is unaffected from the fight.

Sometimes my protective instincts take over and I want to scoop her up and hide her from the danger, to fight her battles for her like Dante. I know it's from the mate bond pushing me to protect her, but Elian is right. She deserves to stand on her own two feet. I'll have to tamp down on the urge more the next time she's in danger. Which, let's face it, likely won't be long before something else happens. Trouble seems to follow her no matter where she goes.

"There's one more place I'd like to show you before we leave," I say, veering left at the next break in the hall and heading toward the unmarked door. The Elders will be pissed that we're not only killing their soldiers, but stealing from them as well, but what's one more infraction at this point?

"Lead the way," Sadie says, turning her head slightly to watch her back only to find Dante and Hemsworth have it covered already. Without thought, we've started to assume protective positions around her, something I'm sure she has noticed every time we've left the house.

The Elders are probably going to kill us after Savannah's challenge anyway or force us to do something far worse than death, but I don't let myself dwell on that thought. I swing the door open to reveal the racks on racks of weapons hidden inside. Sadie stares at the various weaponry with wonder in her bright green eyes.

"What is this place?" she asks.

"It's our special armory. When Weavers come of age at eighteen, we're brought here and given a weapon of choice. Are there any that speak to you?" Her gaze lingers on the knives the most, and I marvel at the glint in her eye. "This is where I received my karambits," I tell her as I lead her around the room, letting her peruse each shelf and weapon, in case the knives really aren't what will choose her, but with the way she normally favors the blade, I suspect it will. I guess we'll find out.

She turns to Dante with an inquisitive look on her face. "What did you choose, Blondie? I don't think I've ever seen you with anything but your crotch knife."

Dante bursts out laughing and I can't help but join him. Even Elian cracks a smirk that he tries to hide behind his hands. "Oh, Angel. Crotch knives? That's what you call them?" He steps closer to her like he's trying to figure out if she's fucking with him or not.

"Well, you always seem to be pulling them out of your

dicks, so what am I supposed to call them? Where *do* they come from? Is there a hidden crotch pocket somewhere?"

"*A hidden crotch pocket?*" he wheezes and slaps a hand over his stomach. "This is golden. You're never going to live this down."

Sadie crosses her arms and Hemsworth starts chuffing at her too, making her throw her hands up in exasperation. "Oh, fuck off, you guys. Just tell me where they come from!"

"Nope. They're officially crotch knives now," I say and watch her roll her eyes at our behavior, but there's a small smile gracing her lips.

"Fine, whatever. Keep your secrets," she says, then levels her gaze on Dante. "You didn't answer my question. What did you pick?"

When he finally manages to stop laughing, he says, "You don't pick the weapon, the weapon picks you, Angel. My *crotch knife,* as you call it, was the weapon that was given to me as the blade can be imbued with my fire to make it stronger."

"The weapons usually enhance our powers in some way," I add, then realize she's not listening anymore. It's as if an unseen hand is guiding her steps as she makes her way over to the rack of knives once more.

I knew it.

Sadie

A PHANTOM HAND REACHES FOR ME, TUGGING ME IN THE direction of the knife display. Some are cushioned by velvet pillows while others are lying in display cases. A pulse of magic trickles down my spine, sparking my intuition. My gaze lands upon a beautiful dagger with an ebony blade. It's smaller than all of the others, more like the size of my switchblade—as if it were tailored just for me.

"What is this?" I ask, fingering the dagger.

Kaos glances at it and his eyes widen. "That is a blade forged from shadestone, the rarest form of weapon here. Some say the rock originated in the Goddesses realm and that it only allows those who are worthy to wield it. Others say the stone itself has magical properties, even healing properties, but that's likely hearsay. It's considered a very sacred item if one is gifted to you."

"Wait, that name sounds familiar." I dig around in my pocket and pull out a similar stone to the one the dagger is made from. "Bedi gave this to me after my ritual at her treehouse."

Kaos raises an eyebrow. "Really?"

I nod. "She said to always keep it on me because it was charged during my ceremony and might help me one day."

"Interesting," Elian says from across the room. He's not even near us anymore and yet he still knows exactly what's happening.

"Bedi wouldn't give you that without a reason," Hemsworth cuts in. "In other words, she thinks you're worthy, Sadie. Which is a huge deal."

I shrug because I'm not good with things like that. I may be able to charge into a fight with a rock man, but dealing with compliments? Hell no. "I kept it on me this whole time. Never hurts to be too careful, right?"

Kaos murmurs his agreement as my hand lands on the ornate silver handle adorned with a crescent moon on each side. A shock reverberates up my arm as my fingers clasp around it and I test the weight in my grip, giving the air a few quick jabs and swipes.

"Do you think this is the work of the Goddess?"

"It's highly likely," Kaos responds, standing beside me with his hands in his pocket and a look of awe on his face.

"Uh, I don't think that's all the Goddess left for you either," Dante says, pointing to a table to the side of the bows where a set of armor now rests that definitely wasn't there before.

"Whoa, where did that come from?"

The armor is far too small for me, but... I glance down at Hemsworth as I finger the plated dog vest and send a silent praise of *thanks* up to the Goddess, hoping she can hear my gratitude in that single word.

Ever since the night where Hems, Vin, and I were attacked, I've been terrified for my familiar, and this will allow me to breathe a little easier. My hands make quick work of the straps and Hemsworth preens when the last buckle clicks into place. "Thank you, Goddess. I feel like a fucking badass," he says, turning in a circle for us to admire the Goddesses' handiwork. It fits him like a glove.

"That's because you are, pup," I respond, feeling lighter than when we first came here.

I should've known that feeling wouldn't last though.

20

SADIE

Elian stays true to his word. He trains me the rest of his remaining days with me, plus the two more he promised. Each day my powers become a little easier to control.

By the end of our training together, I'm not sure if I'm ready for it to end or if I want more of the back-and-forth banter between us. We're dancing on an extremely fine, tenuous line. One that could snap at any moment. Sometimes I wish it would.

Vinson looks a little paler than usual today, but he's still on his feet and cooking when I head down for breakfast, which I'm glad for. I'm terrified I'll wake up one morning and he won't be in his usual spot. No one can quite figure out what to do with him since none of our healing methods have worked, and Kaos has tried everything he knows. Even I tried the other day, but it was no use. Our magic bounces off of him like there's a repellant bubble around him.

I refuse to give up on him though and so does Kaos. I know he visits him nightly to try different things and I'm grateful for it.

There has to be something that we're missing and it's infuriating to be absolutely no closer to an answer. I have a feeling we'll have to put a call out for help soon. Hell, I'm not above trying to steal information from the Elders, if that's what it takes. They have to know something about it. Especially since that orb was aimed for me and not Vin.

Unless it reacts differently because he's a shifter…

I push all of that out of my mind for the moment as I focus on what I can control. It's finally Kaos' turn to show me what he can do with weapons, and I have to say I'm dying to find out what he has in store for me. Dante calls him the weapons master, which is a title, he says, that isn't given out to just anyone.

The man in question is waiting for me in the basement, giving me a beaming smile when he sees me coming down the steps. He's sporting a cut-off tee and tight-fitting gym shorts which highlight the toned muscles of his legs. I give him a mock bow and say, "What have you got for me today, weapons master?"

He snorts, returning my bow with one of the signature Weaver poses. A hand fisted over his heart and a slight dip. "Actually, I'm going to teach you a bit more about daggers and how to properly wield yours." My eyes light up in excitement, which he doesn't miss. This man is always watching, always assessing, and always trying to figure out what makes everyone tick. I find it comforting that he cares so much about those around him.

"Well then, teach me, *master*." I punctuate the last word and definitely don't miss the downright salacious look he shoots me either.

"I'm going to make you say that right before you come one of these days."

My toes curl with his demanding tone, and I catch the

rapidly hardening outline tenting his shorts. Yep, he means that too. "Bring it on."

The next thing I know, a dagger is being thrown my way. Time seems to slow as I watch the hilt spin, waiting until the blade is down and the handle is up before snatching it out of the air.

"Hey, what gives, Kaos?" I watch as he draws another dagger from his belt.

He shrugs a shoulder. "I wanted to see if you could handle it and you did, exceptionally well, like most things that are thrown at you."

My eyes narrow. "Did you expect anything less?"

From under his thick lashes, he says, "From you, no."

"Then give me your best."

He throws his own dagger up in the air, watching as it spins before catching the hilt—much like I did. He jerks it up then down in rapid slashing motions then repeats the action several more times before lunging at me.

"You're in a mood today," I observe, stepping back to watch as his jaw clenches.

"You let Malachi connect *palms* with you," he says with a quiet flash of his teeth. Ah, so that's what's wrong with him.

"I didn't think, Kaos. You have to remember I'm not from this world."

He runs a hand through his hair. "I know, but I'm still angry. What if he had something malicious planned? There are those like Tyler that would and say damn the consequences."

"They wouldn't like my wrath if they did," I respond and the shadows flare to life to punctuate my point.

Kaos grabs my arm and pulls me into him, wrapping his hands into my hair. I savor his embrace and wrap my arms around him, enjoying the way I fit into him like a puzzle piece. His taut abs are a plus too. "They wouldn't like mine either, Little Flame."

Dante appears at the bottom of the steps seconds later. "Think you can take both of us on at the same time, Angel? I believe we have a little lesson to teach you." My stomach tightens with the unspoken meaning of his words and hell, I wish he *did* mean that, but we need to train. There's only two weeks left until my showdown with Savannah and dinner with the Elders.

"Bring it on, boys." I back away from them with a broad smile. "It'll be fun to test my abilities on you both." I let that innuendo hang between us and they both groan.

Kaos is the one who breaks first. "Training only," he states, then grumbles, "this time."

"I'm anticipating the next." I strike with the dagger he gave me and he raises his to block me in time.

Dante chuckles. "Easy, Angel. You don't want to ruin these perfect faces, do you?"

"So cocky." I smile, then sweep his feet out from under him.

He jumps up and rubs his tailbone. "What the hell? I'm supposed to be your favorite!"

"I take my training seriously, what can I say?"

And I do.

Kaos teaches me how to properly wield a dagger until my arms are exhausted from the exertion. By now he's had to heal several cuts and scrapes from both sides, but I really feel like I got a challenge today taking them both on. I guess my training with Elian is coming in handy after all.

Just when I think we're finally finished, Reed appears at

the bottom of the steps. He's dressed in a tight-fitting tank top and a pair of running shorts. "Hey, Red. What's up?"

"I was wondering if you would be willing to train me?" He gives my body a once-over, sees all the sweat pouring off of me, and grimaces. "But we can do it another day if you're too tired."

I want nothing more than to shower and sleep but how can I deny him this opportunity?

Besides, it's another chance to get to know him better and I'm curious to see where our connection leads us.

Dante steps in between us before I can respond. "If you're going to train him then you both need to wrap your hands."

Valid point.

"That's not a problem," Reed responds to Dante and reaches over to grab the tape that's sitting on the shelf by the weight benches. "I know the Night Goddess said she doesn't make mistakes, but you all were an established Circle and I'm an outsider. I get that and I'll do whatever it takes to earn my place." He pushes his glasses further up his nose before starting to tape his hands.

Kaos grips Dante on the shoulder. "We also need to respect Sadie's wishes, brother. All of it isn't up to us. If he proves his worth, then the rest is our mate's decision."

They turn to me, and I sigh. "I won't deny that there's a pull between Reed and I because I would be lying if I did, but I would like to take my time and get to know him. Considering my last two bonds were pretty *rushed*." I shoot them a wink so they know I'm joking. "Should we get this party started? I'm exhausted and quickly running out of energy. How much do you know about fighting, Red?"

"Not much of anything really. My father was grooming me to become the next leader, not a warrior."

"Hold up. The next leader?"

His eyes widen at my question. "Don't you know? I am

the heir to the Light Weaver throne." He winces and shakes his head. "Which, I guess, technically I'm the ruler now." *The heir to the Light Weaver throne...* So, since I'm his mate, what the hell does that make me?

Nope, I haven't had enough coffee or sex for that conversation.

I wrap my hands in tape while contemplating everything he's telling me, attempting to mull it over in my brain. Yeah, still not enough. "How many of you are there?"

"Several thousand or so, I'd say. My father had jurisdiction over the mid-western faction of Light Weavers. Our faction is more spread out but there were a lot of us back home. The Soleil family actually lived at our community compound."

"Wait, there are more factions of Light Weavers? I was thinking you were wiped out entirely." His eyes flash with guilt and it makes my heart squeeze. "That was insensitive to say, I'm sorry, Red."

"It's okay." He takes a deep breath. "No, we were not all wiped out. The United States is broken into three factions. Western, mid-western, and eastern factions."

"Wow, okay. Interesting. Thank you for entrusting us with that information." I turn to Dante and Kaos. "How much do the Elders have control over?"

They wince. "The entire United States, unfortunately," Kaos tells me.

Fuck, that's a lot of Night Weavers to have control over. I guess it's good that Reed's father wasn't aiming for total world domination like the Elders though.

"When will you go back?" I ask Reed.

"Soon. Probably after your challenge but I—I," he takes a deep breath. "I'm not ready to yet."

"That's fine, Red. There's no rush." I may be dying to know more about his people, but there's no way I'm going to press him about it if he's not ready. He suffered enough that day. "Let's start with the basic fighting stance."

From the front, I move his arms up and help him keep them in position to protect his face. Occasionally, I'll correct his stance or posture as I give him directions, but he seems to pick up on things really quickly. His ability to adapt likely stems from his social position.

I'm the mate to the Light Weaver throne. Somebody fucking pinch me, I've awoken in Oz.

SADIE

Adam, Nick, and Niall show up at our doorstep exactly like they said they would at the end of the week. Adam stares me down as he walks up the driveway while the twins scope out the trees around them.

I keep my posture lax, leaning against the porch frame with my arms crossed, but in reality, I'm ready to spring at a moment's notice. The others in my crew mirror my calm posture, but I can tell they're as tense as I am.

My thoughts start to wander while I study the dangerous men traipsing closer to us. Their magic brushes against mine, showing me just how powerful they are. I don't want to question the Goddess' judgment here, but surely she's leading a lamb to slaughter entrusting Emma into their care?

But I'm not fate's guiding hand, nor do I want to be, so I keep my thoughts to myself as they come to a stop at the bottom of the porch. Our elevated ground gives us a slight advantage over them if anything were to go awry. Though, the trio doesn't seem intimidated at all.

"I trust you managed to keep our mate safe and out of

trouble the past week?" Adam asks, sweeping his knowing gaze over me.

"Your mate is her own person, but yes, not a hair on her head was damaged this week. Unless she burned it while straightening it," I respond, thinking back to the girls' night we had with Ash last night. Who knew straightening your hair at midnight because you're nervous to see your mates would be a bad thing?

He lets out an audible breath. "Thank the Goddess. Now, where is she? We'd like to spend our time with her."

I give him a long once-over before finally stepping to the side to allow them to pass. "Through this door, down the hall, and to the right. She's in our game room. Help yourself to anything in there."

A soft tap on my shoulder causes me to turn slightly. Emma clears her throat. "Actually, if you all don't mind, I'd like for everyone to join us." Her eyes nervously dart to her newfound mates and I can't say I blame the girl. They're quite the intimidating Circle.

"Of course." There's no way I'm leaving this poor girl to fend for herself if she wants me to be around. Besties before testes, right?

I hardly know her, yet I feel a sense of comradery with her. The same sense that makes up mine and Ash's bond.

When we're all settled in the game room, things continue to grow awkward. Everyone alternates between staring at each other and the ground and shifting in their seats. Elian and Niall are standing against the far wall facing everyone, while Adam and Nick are sitting on the loveseat, with Emma in the gaming chair and Reed, Dante, Kaos, and I on the other couch across from them.

What the hell do you say to the men who are the direct offspring of the villains in so many of your friends' stories?

It's hard to get over that fact, though if we're going to form this alliance, I guess I'll have to. We'll all have to.

Adam clears his throat and warily looks over to Reed, who is sitting beside me, as if he's trying to see through him like the Light Weaver going to pounce at any moment. I'm starting to think the Light Weavers are extremely misunderstood and not the monsters that the Night Weavers believe them to be. "You so easily allow one of their kind into your home and into your ranks?" Adam directs his question to me.

My eyes narrow and I almost say according to the Goddess she makes no mistakes, but I bite my tongue, not revealing our hand so easily, even though it's my first reaction to prove him wrong and defend Reed. Who's to say how they would react if they knew we had an actual conversation with the Goddess herself?

Something tells me that's not an everyday occurrence.

Instead, I simply say, "As you so easily accepted a shifter as your mate?"

Nick and Niall give me an assessing look while a broad smile overtakes Adam's face. "Touché, Shadowbringer. Tell me, how is your training coming along?" He doesn't give me the opportunity to reply. "A certain ruthless girl is gunning for your head. We can't let her succeed in killing you."

My lips curl at the mention of Savannah. I know he's talking about her without him even having to say her name. "She'll get what's coming to her, don't you worry." I pause, thinking about something that's been bugging me. "I have to ask though. The fight with her is seriously to the death? We can't just… I don't know… beat the shit out of one another until she concedes?" I hate the bitch for trying to steal my men, but is that really worthy of death?

That shit is kind of permanent.

Adam gives me a solemn nod. "Unfortunately, it's the law

of challenges. One of you will walk out alive while the other will take their last breath in the arena."

Emma lets out a surprised gasp and her already milky skin pales further as she looks between me, my Sworn, and her own mates.

Nick makes a noise of objection. "This isn't the type of conversation we should continue in front of Emma. We've upset her."

I turn to Emma with a confused frown. "Surely you've dealt with worse being with the shifters?" I ask, thinking about the things I've already been through. She's been a shifter for far longer than I've known I'm a Night Weaver. The poor girl needs to grow some thicker skin and fast if she wants to make it in this world.

Emma shakes her head. "The other girls were awful bitches to me, but beyond that though, we were an extremely tight-knit pack. All of the horrors I've endured in my lifetime have been at the Weavers' hands."

The trio's eyes flash before they look away from their mate, jaws clenched with guilt from her admission. The Goddess sure does have a twisted sense of humor pairing them together. I still haven't been able to figure out her motive surrounding it but then again, it's not my relationship or my place to judge.

Hemsworth strolls through the door, taking in the scene with a knowing glint in his eye. That pup doesn't miss much. "Moons, who died?" he asks, making each of us crack a bit of a smile. It helps alleviate some of the thick tension permeating the room. If our companions are surprised by his ability to speak, they hide it extremely well, telling me they likely already knew. So, my hunch is correct, someone is still leaking information to the trio and the Elders somehow...

I reach for one of the untouched glasses of water on the

coffee table, taking a small sip. "I take it you knew I have a familiar?"

I figure Adam will take the lead like he always does, but I'm surprised when it's Niall's voice as he speaks up for the first time today. "We know many things about you, Sadie. Our fathers see all, know all, hear all. They have more spies than the amount of flies buzzing around outside." His tone is filled with self-loathing and bitterness.

His admission doesn't surprise me, but what does make me curious is how they're here without their fathers knowing if they're apparently so powerful. So I voice that thought aloud, "Then how are you here without them knowing?"

A muscle in his jaw feathers. "My specialty is concealment. I can hold a cover spell over this estate long enough for us to have a thirty-minute conversation without prying eyes, but it's too taxing to hold it any longer without being mated." He looks over to Emma longingly but she's busy picking at her nails and doesn't seem to notice, or purposefully avoiding his gaze. It's going to be fun watching them have to win her over.

"What about my wards?" Elian asks. There's a dark undercurrent to his question even if his posture is casual with his hands in his pockets and his foot dropped against the wall. "Does it hold their eyes out?"

"For the most part, but even the shadows have ears."

His words send a chill down my spine. Does he know about how sentient my shadows feel? Surely not, so I dismiss the thought, chuckling to myself. There's no way he could know.

Adam glances at his watch. "We only have ten minutes left. Emma, would you mind if we had a word alone?"

Jeez, it's been twenty minutes already? Thank the Goddess.

Emma glances at me and gives me a small nod. I get to my feet, going around to her side so I can give her shoulder a squeeze as I walk past. "We'll be in the kitchen if you need us."

She lets out a grateful breath that the others don't miss. "Thank you."

My mates and I exit the room, filing out in a line to give them their moment. A small snort escapes me as I catch the tail end of Emma standing her ground about waiting to mate before the rest of their conversation grows too soft for me to hear. They've got their work cut out for them, that's for certain.

"What do you all think about them?" I ask as we walk into the kitchen, hopping up on the granite island as I grab a box of Ritz crackers out of the cabinet where Vin keeps them just for me. My lips curve up into a smile. He told me that he doesn't allow anyone else access to his kitchen like this. I must be pretty damn special if he keeps an entire cabinet of stuff for me.

Dante wrinkles his nose at my choice of food, opting to find a bag of cheese cubes in the fridge. I snatch a couple from him, inwardly pouting that I didn't think of those first. "I don't know what to think about them," he responds to my question, and holds the bag out for me to grab more. He's a better sharer than me. "They've always been an untouchable force, held onto a pedestal in front of the rest of us. We've seen and even experienced their cruelty firsthand. Now we're supposed to accept that's not who they really are?" He scoffs.

"Maybe they had to adapt? Like all of the rest of us," I say quietly, not looking at the rest of them.

"If she really is their mate, they wouldn't harm her, you know," Kaos says, and his gaze softens as I glance up at him.

"It's true. The mating bond eventually overrides every

emotion, every need, everything," Dante adds.

"Hey, Weaver, you're supposed to feed me, you know," Hemsworth interrupts with an impatient huff. "Would you mind passing me the jerky sticks before you delve into this conversation? Vinson said he had the grocery store order some especially for me. I'd do it myself but you're sitting in front of the door."

"Oops, sorry, Hems. Here you go." I laugh and reach into the cabinet to grab them. I toss him a couple and he lays down to chew on them, using his paws to keep them stable. Ugh, why is he so fucking cute?

"Thanks, you may continue," he says between chewing.

"Wow, we see what Hems uses us for. A free pass for food." I shoot him a wink and he chuffs. I hop down from the island and Kaos immediately comes over to start rubbing the tension out of my shoulders. My brain wants to go blank, but I know I can't leave this conversation untouched. "Okay, back to the part about the mating bond bit. You said it eventually overrides everything. Do we not get a choice in the matter at all?"

"Of course you get a choice. The Goddess would never force two souls together if they didn't truly want to be together, but from what I've read, severing the bond is painful and some say that the souls never recover," Kaos responds, and my thoughts drift to Elian unbidden. He's supposed to be my mate, but he's been nothing but an asshole to me. Could I ever really forgive him for the way he's acted?

Maybe if he got on his knees and groveled or maybe if he stuck that head of hair between my thighs and begged for forgiveness, worshipping me like his own Goddess. Another groan escapes my lips, one I totally blame on Kaos' fingers and not the thought of Elian's filthy ways of apologizing.

That sure would be a sight though, wouldn't it?

Reed's cheeks heat as he looks over at me with wide eyes when my gaze meets his. I see the heat, the pent-up desire, the restraint within them. So to keep myself from doing something stupid, like climbing him in the kitchen, I extend a Ritz cracker toward him. His eyes widen as he takes it, staring at it curiously.

"Please tell me you don't have the same reservations about junk food that the rest of my mates do, Red."

He pushes those black-framed glasses up his nose. "I'll try anything once," he says and shoves the crunchy cracker in his mouth. His face scrunches up while he chews, looking slightly uncomfortable when he swallows. "Not bad."

"Fuck's sake. Who doesn't like Ritz crackers?" I huff. "I swear you four are all the same. Oh well, more for me and Ash." I pop another one into my mouth, ignoring the stares of my Sworn. They shouldn't be surprised by my antics at this point.

"And me," Hemsworth chimes in, finished with his jerky. He gives me the sad *puppy-dog* eyes until I toss him a cracker.

"So pitiful. All you have to do is ask, Hems."

A commotion from the game room startles all of us into action. We burst through the door at the exact moment Emma cracks Adam across the cheek with an audible thwack. I'd wince in sympathy if I weren't in kick-his-ass-mode.

"What happened?" I demand, reaching for my switchblade in my pocket while the rest of my mates reach for their crotch knives. Fucking crotch knives.

"They're such bastards," she seethes. "They want to complete the rest of the mating bond now because they said it'll make me safer but I'm not ready yet. I'm not—" she takes a deep breath and turns pleading eyes onto me. "I'm not ready. They're still *their* sons."

"Please, Emma," Adam begs with eyes as pleading as hers.

"You don't understand. We're not our fathers. We—"

"Don't, Adam," Niall says, cutting off whatever he was about to admit. "Our time here is up. Nick, portal us out of here before they track where we are."

Emma starts to sob as they dissipate in a cloud of smoke. The sound of it breaks my heart for her. "Come here, Em. It'll be all right." I place my switchblade into my pocket and pull her into my arms.

"Will it though? How could the Goddess pair me with them?" Her tone is full of despair.

"I don't know, hun. I don't know what her end game is, with you or with me."

Emma wipes the tears off her cheeks. "I love my wolf. I love her beyond anything, and I know I'd have never met her without meeting them, but I'm not ready."

I shush her softly. "There's nothing wrong with that. They'll either respect your boundaries or I'll make them respect them. You're safe here. You're safe with us. Who knows, maybe one of these days the Goddess' vision for us will be clear."

Suddenly, she looks frail. Far too frail for my liking. "I think for now I'd like to go lay down if that's okay?" I do as she requests and carefully get her upstairs to the guest room and then settle her into bed. As I'm turning to leave her soft voice stops me in my tracks. "It hurts, you know."

My body tenses and I turn back around, keeping a pleasant smile on my face. "What does?"

"Being away from them." I wasn't expecting her to say that. "The bond is tugging us to be together, to be close, but they can't. Because of *them*. Because of this damned world. I think the Goddess made a mistake," she admits the last part so softly, I barely catch it. She glances over at me expectantly and I realize she's waiting for me to give her my opinion.

"I can't tell you what to do, Em. You're the only one who

can make that decision. You're in charge of your own life. Don't ever let anyone put you under their thumb."

"That's all I've ever known."

"And that's not an excuse. My childhood was awful and I learned to become stronger for it. To wield my hatred and my anger into a weapon I can use. You can do the same if you want."

She takes a moment to mull over my words then gives me a nod. "I think I'd like that."

"For now though, get some rest." I shut the door to her room quietly and then make my way downstairs, my feet traveling almost of their own accord.

I'm surprised to find Elian standing at the door to the basement with his legs crossed, head against the wooden frame, waiting for me. He flicks his pocket watch closed and uncrosses his feet. "Need an outlet for all that anger?" he asks with a glint of fire in that icy gaze of his.

This moment feels heavier than it should be. Almost like a crossroad. I can either ignore the olive branch he's extending, or I can accept it and the torrential downpour I'll likely bring down on my head with it. I decide I no longer want to look for cover. Besides, I know how to dance in the rain. Actually, I'm starting to crave that sensation.

Swallowing past the lump in my throat I say, "Please."

This earns me a small lip quirk. Not quite a smile, but I'll take it. "Come on. I'll let you work out your aggression until you're an exhausted puddle at my feet."

I start to rethink my decision, already feeling the drops of rain speckle my skin from the storm that is Elian King.

Still... I could use the release.

Despite my better judgment, I follow him down the steps to our training room where he delivers on his promise, and I relish in the moment between us, feeling some more of his ice begin to melt.

22

SADIE

After my unexpected training session with Elian is over, I head back to my bedroom to take a shower and wash our sweat off me.

Surprisingly, working out with him was quite enjoyable this time. He even let me blast one A Day to Remember song and didn't insult me other than barking orders about my "horrible" fighting moves. What to do with the broody bad boy. What to do.

Ah, well. Compromises, right?

Something moves in the shadows next to the desk in the corner of my room and I whip toward it, blood still racing with the need to fight. I throw my hands up, calling the shadows to me to reveal my assailant. A growl slips past my lips when I realize it's only Ash—who also looks mighty sheepish at the look on my face and let my hands drop. "Jeez. You almost gave me a heart attack. What the hell are you doing hiding in my room, anyway?"

"I'm going to take a wild guess and say you were pretty lost in thought considering I waved and called your name twice, babe."

I wince. "Sorry, there's been a lot on my mind lately." Namely, Elian.

"Mhm, and I'm sure it has nothing to do with a certain asshole?" She doesn't give me a chance to respond before ordering me to get dressed.

"Uh, why?"

A smile forms on the corner of her lips instantly making me skeptical as I notice the nice attire she's wearing. She only gets that look in her eye when she's up to no good. "A couple of the shifters invited me out tonight and by extension, you."

"So, what you're saying, is that you're trying to get me to crash a party?"

"Yep. Now, are you going to get ready or not?"

If it'll make that spark stay in her eyes?

Definitely.

Every time I catch her wandering around the mansion there's a haunted look about her and I don't like it. It's why I haven't pushed her any further about what she experienced at the hands of the Elders. Everyone deserves time to work through their trauma and she'll come to me when she's ready.

"Fine. Give me a second to get changed and we'll go."

She squeals as I make my way to my closet and slide a fitted black tank top over my sports bra then shimmy into a tight pair of skinny jeans, sans a shower since there's no time. My mate mark from Dante and Kaos stands out strikingly against my skin and I have to admire it for a moment, running my fingers across the moons to make them turn silver. Absolutely gorgeous.

"Who invited you, anyway? I never can get any of the shifters that work in the house to talk to me."

She gives me a small shrug. "That's because you're a Weaver and they're not *supposed* to talk to you."

My nose wrinkles. "I don't care about the stupid societal rules. Seriously though, who was it?"

Her gaze darts away from me as she says, "Carter."

"Oh, snap, Ash. He's the beta." My eyebrow hits my hairline when her cheeks start to turn pink. "Wait, do you actually *like* him?"

"No!" she blurts quickly—almost too quickly—then scrubs a hand down her face. "Really, I don't. How could I? I know nothing about him."

"Mhm." I'm not buying it. "The girl notoriously known as *hook-up only Ash,* in high school actually has a crush on a shifter, huh?"

"I don't know what you're talking about. He's cute, that's all. Actually, he's one of Vinson's friends. Haven't you been paying attention?"

To any shifters other than Vin? Not really.

"Nice diversion, bitch."

She smirks. "Gotcha."

Suddenly, Emma opens the door interrupting our conversation. "Hey! Are we ready?" she asks, bounding into the room with a bright smile on her face.

"Moons above, was everyone invited to this party but me?" I demand, looking between my oldest friend and my newest one.

Ash, at least, has the decency to cringe. "Like I said, you're a Weaver, Sadie. You're on a completely different level than them."

"Maybe in title, but not in life experiences."

Emma gives me a placating look. "Come on, I'm sure it's started by now." Thankfully, she looks much better than she did earlier today and it's nice to see her in better spirits. "I can't wait to meet the other shifters!"

"Speaking of which, where is your family? And how were you allowed to work at the pet shop?"

Her cheeks burn with embarrassment and she looks between the two of us carefully. "My family were some of the lowest ranking shifters in our original pack. We ran away a few years ago and they presumed us dead because most wolves need a pack to survive. We found our small group of shifters shortly thereafter and the Elders weren't aware of our little band of misfits because most of us are fairly low in ranking. We weren't enough to even register on their scale. They're only concerned with the ones they can trap into servitude or torture."

My heart twists. "Gods, that's awful."

"It is, but no sad stuff tonight! We're supposed to go have fun!" she says, bouncing on her toes. It's amazing to me how quickly she bounces back, such resilience.

Emma and Ash carry on a conversation while we walk but I can't seem to focus on it. *They're only concerned with the ones they can trap into servitude or torture...* The weight of her words follow me all the way to the pack house.

It doesn't take us long to reach the building where the shifters live and my steps falter when a thought strikes me. I didn't tell my Sworn where I'm going and I'm *definitely* not making that mistake again.

Ash and I are at the pack house. The shifters are having a party tonight and we were invited, I project to them.

Thanks for letting us know, Little Flame, Kaos responds immediately, the relief flowing through our bond. There's a pause before he continues, *Hemsworth is on his way to meet you.*

Have fun, Angel, Dante tells me.

Their combined affection reaches me all the way down the bond as they both stroke our connection. It gives me the little push I need to let go and stop worrying. We're behind Elian's wards and I haven't felt any weird weaknesses or disturbances lately.

For the most part, the shifters seem to be milling around outside the house, chatting amongst themselves. The other half congregate around a large bonfire. The majority of them are shirtless and it highlights their muscular bodies. One thing is for certain, there's a lot of testosterone in the air and just as many muscles on display.

The flames flicker, reaching toward the sky as little embers float off in every direction when someone throws another log on. When the light of the fire finally reaches Ash, Emma, and I, bathing us in its fiery glow, all heads snap in our direction. Their focus immediately narrows in on me and every single one of them freezes. After a beat, they seem to take a collective breath and that's when the whispers start.

A Weaver?

What's she doing here?

Who is with her?

One girl nudges her friend and says, *oh no, pay attention.*

Mercifully, Vinson rounds the corner of the house and spots us before anything else can be said. The grin that lights up his face could juice up the sun. "Hey, Sadie! Over here!" he calls out.

I return his smile as his gaze slowly travels up and down the length of me before returning to my face. He douses the yearning behind his eyes but not before I catch a glimpse of it, making guilt smack me right upside the head. I'm certain that same yearning is likely reflected in mine, and I shake myself out of it.

Pull yourself together, Sadie.

When he reaches me, his arms band around me in a quick hug and his woodsy scent envelops me, tickling and teasing my nostrils as I inhale. "Hey, Vin. What are you doing here? I figured you'd be resting."

I hear several gasps behind me as we break apart and find several of the shifters around us staring with their mouths wide open. I'm guessing he's not supposed to hug me. Ah, well.

"And miss the opportunity to see you?" He grins. "Never."

I return his smile with one of my own. "How'd you know I'd be here? Ash only told me about it ten minutes or so ago."

He gives me a look. "Carter and I made the mistake of talking about a party in front of her. She hounded us about coming until we finally relented, and I knew you wouldn't let her come alone."

Huh. Well, he's not wrong. Maybe I'm not as much of a puzzle as I think I am. "Parties and Ash go together like water and fish."

"So I noticed."

"Quit talking shit, Sades! You know you love me."

A laugh tumbles from my lips. I've missed her snark.

Vin glances at Emma and Ash behind me like he's seeing them for the first time. "Oh, how rude of me not to say hello." He inclines his head and looks at all three of us. "Ladies, would you all like to come inside for a drink? Food will be passed around in a bit so we should probably grab that and then a seat."

"Sure, lead the way," I respond.

Ash, Emma, and I follow Vin inside, both of them with goofy looks on their faces as they look between the shifter and I. They quickly drop their smirks when they see me looking.

When we enter the living room, I spot several of the shifters from the prison milling around, some on the couches and others keeping to themselves, but still within a short distance of the others.

Thankfully, most of them seem much better. Looks like they've all put on a little bit of weight, changed clothes, and showered. There's still a little bit of sadness permeating around them, but it's way less than the last time I saw them. I hope they're able to move forward with their lives. The brave girl from before spots me, giving me a small wave, and approaches us slowly. She's still far too pale and skinny, but leagues above where she was a few weeks ago.

I give her a smile to let her know it's all right. "Hey! It's good to see you all out and about. How's everyone doing?"

"Better now that we're here." Her gaze darts around us and she lowers her voice before continuing. "We really lucked out with this property. Your mates are the kindest masters we've ever known."

I frown. "They are not your masters. No one is."

She gives me a look that seems a lot like pity. "Girl, in this world, someone is always on top and everyone else must file in line underneath them. You need to decide if you're going to be the one on top or if you're going to submit like the rest of us."

She shoos me away before I can say anything else, telling me to enjoy my night and not to worry about them, but I can't help but to mull over her words as Vinson pours us all a drink. She's absolutely right and I don't plan on bowing for anyone but my Sworn. Maybe not even all of them. *Cough, Elian.*

On the flip side, if we're going to come out on top then we have to remain fair and just. I refuse to let any of us become like the Elders. Power hungry monsters?

No, thanks. I'll pass.

A soft, ancient breeze feathers across my face and I smile. The Goddess must be listening in on my thoughts. You'd think I'd be afraid or even intimidated but she has a way of settling any doubts. "Thank you, Goddess," I whisper.

"Huh?" Ash asks with a confused frown, and I realize they were waiting for my response about something. I totally zoned out.

"Uh, nothing. I'm sorry, what did you say?" I motion with my hands for her to repeat herself.

"Vinson asked if you wanted water or shifter beer," Emma chimes in.

My eyebrows crinkle. "Shifter beer?"

"Yeah, we metabolize normal beer faster than humans so it doesn't really do anything for us. We brew our own special blend here."

"Oh, interesting. I'll take some water, please. I don't drink."

Vin nods and reaches into the cooler on the ground, tossing me a bottle of water. The outside of it is wet from being in ice but I'm not complaining. It's still hot outside and the bonfire makes it even hotter. Fortunately, the nights are starting to get cooler.

As we're walking out the door to grab a seat outside, Darren, the Alpha is heading in. "Why, what a pleasant surprise," he says when he spots us. "It's nice to see you again, Sadie." His gaze snags on Emma and his nostrils flare as he scents her. His stance goes rigid. "And who are your friends?" I'm guessing his Alpha powers are stronger than Vin's if he scents her that fast.

"This is Ashley." I gesture to my left and then right. "And this is Emma. She's under, uh, under our *protection*," I tell him cryptically. The Alpha is smart enough to catch my meaning and even though I can tell he's extremely curious, he doesn't prod the situation further.

"Interesting." He looks her up and down and she shifts on her feet. "Well, if a shifter is going to be on the premises, she will need to come down one day and do a meeting with the pack. I'll let it slide for tonight though since I'm needed elsewhere."

"Yes, Alpha. I will come back tomorrow if that's okay?" Emma asks.

"Sounds like a plan." Something crashes behind us and someone cheers. Darren sighs. "The job of an Alpha is never complete. Make yourselves at home. You're welcome any time." He gives me a pat on the back, squeezing my shoulder as he leans in close to my ear. "Thank you for what you did with the prison shifters. They're leaps and bounds better than before. I'll forever be in your debt."

"There's no need to thank me, Darren. It was the least I could do. Honestly, I wish there were more I could do for you all."

He tilts his head, assessing me. "You're a good person, Sadie. Never let anyone tell you otherwise." With one last glance back at us, he delves further into the house, calling out for someone to stop roughhousing.

One thing I'm beginning to notice is that these shifters are more like one big family than anything else and I was just given an open invitation to come back.

Score.

As we reach the fire, I notice there are already pillows and blankets strewn alongside for anyone to take and quite a few shifters already planted around them. A few try to offer us their spots but I refuse and politely tell them to stay where they are. Eventually, Vinson manages to find us two empty blankets next to each other. Well, empty minus Carter.

Ash casually sits on the spot beside him and he gives her a peck on the cheek as a way of greeting. Yep, they're definitely fucking or if they haven't already, they will before the night is over. Emma, Vin, and I take the other blanket and they stick me in the middle, which I don't mind. I crack the cap on the water bottle and take a sip. Vin watches as my throat bobs, but quickly glances away as my eyes find his.

I glance at the crowd, enjoying the easy peace they have amongst each other. "I didn't realize there were so many of you here," I say conversationally.

"The Kings watch over the most shifters in this area minus the Elders. Their Circle is one of the most prominent Night Weaver families because of their grape vineyard. Most of us work there."

"Right. I keep forgetting my mates own a fucking vineyard," I mutter. "I need to bug them to take me to it sometime. I bet it's gorgeous."

"It is," Vin agrees.

"What about the rest of the shifters?"

"The rest have jobs that are more up close and personal, like Carter and I. We do anything your mates need us to, from cooking to valeting to mechanics."

"Both of you are men of many talents, for sure." I glance over and notice Emma, Ash, and Carter are chatting amongst themselves, giving Vin and I a moment to ourselves. I watch the little line of sweat travel down the side of his neck. The black vines aren't as noticeable with his shirt on, but I know they're still there. I'm sure the other shifters have noticed it too and it makes me wonder what they think. "How are you feeling, Vin? *Really feeling?*" I add when he gives me a look.

"Look, Sadie, I appreciate all of your efforts to heal me but I'm managing. And I'm planning on making the most of the time I have left so don't worry about me, okay? I'm going to be fine."

Easier said than done, I want to say but I take his words for what they are and drop the conversation. He obviously doesn't want to talk about it and I can't blame him for that. I clear my throat and change the subject. "I've been meaning to ask, have you had any time to look at my car to see if it can be fixed?"

He winces. "It's not looking good, I'm afraid. The magic managed to damage the engine and the whole brake system. Not to mention all the body damage..."

I run my hand through my ponytail. "I figured as much. It's a shame it was so messed up. I spent many hours, blood, sweat, and tears on that car fixing her up."

"I'll do my best to repair it for you."

I wave him off. "Don't overwork yourself. It's probably time to let it go anyway. She was kind of a piece of shit."

Vin chuckles. "Yes, she was."

I shoot him a mock outraged grin and take another sip of my water. "But she was my piece of shit. So, do you all have these gatherings often?"

"Every month. The mated shifters go for a run in their wolf form while the rest of us stay behind and sit by the fire."

"How many of you are mated?"

"Six extremely lucky couples. The Elders don't allow us to socialize outside our assigned houses much, so most of us have never found our mates."

"That's awful."

"It is, but it's our reality. If the Goddess wills it this way, then we will endure it." Sounds like a bunch of shit to me but I don't say that. The Goddess wouldn't want them to suffer, but she also can't intervene. Quite the combination.

"Are shifters like Weavers, with more than one mate?" I blurt before thinking it through. What is it with me and blurting shit out without giving it proper thought?

Vin cracks a small smile while taking a sip out of his own water. "No, shifters only have one mate. We do mate for life like Weavers though. Well, like the true mate bonds you and your Circle have."

"Really?"

"Yes."

"And are you mated?"

We're already heading for this line of questioning, may as well be direct and not beat around the bush. His usual smile dims and he glances away from me. Shit, I struck a nerve.

"No. I have not yet found the one whom I will share my soul with."

I swallow the lump in my throat. "You'll find her, I'm sure."

He takes a deep breath. "Sometimes, I wonder if—"

"There you are! Jeez, I thought dogs smelled but wolves are so much worse," Hemsworth says, plopping down between my legs, interrupting our moment. I can't decide if I'm relieved or upset that I'll never know what Vin was going to say.

"They don't smell so bad," I respond.

"Once again, the strongest nose in the entire world right here." I raise an eyebrow at him and he gives me a look. "I can still smell Elian's sweat on you."

"Okay! I believe you, you little shit."

Something in the corner of my eye catches my attention and the smell of charred burgers reaches my nostrils, making my mouth start to water. I glance over and watch as a group of male shifters pass a plate of grilled burgers to the females.

The males work as a team to get all the women around us fed until it's my turn. Vin's eyes find mine as he hands me a burger. Our fingers brush against one another and his eyes glisten. They flash to a pure animalistic glow as his wolf seems to peak through the surface. I start to point it out but the moment between us breaks as he turns to hand the plate to Emma, and I'm left wondering if I imagined it.

I shake it off and decide not to comment because I don't want to strain him anymore than I already have. Maybe I'm going crazy because Vin's staring directly at me and his eyes are no longer glowing. "What is happening? Why are we being fed first?" I ask.

Hemsworth chuffs at my bewilderment.

Vin is unperturbed by my confusion. "We make sure our women eat before the men do. It's tradition. After this, the wolves will run."

Ash giggles, like full on giggles, at Carter as he passes her the plate of food and it distracts me because I haven't seen her look so smitten. Ever. Not even with rock star Brandon Luck, though it comes close. I wonder how he's doing nowadays and if he's still obsessed with Ash or if it was all for show.

"Hey, Vin. Is Carter mated?"

He follows my line of sight. "No, our Beta is not mated." He ponders for a moment. "They'd make a cute couple, you know."

I snort. "Good luck getting Ash to commit to it though."

"Good point."

AFTER EVERYONE FINISHES EATING, THERE'S A SHIFT IN THE AIR. The chatter starts to die down and everyone turns to watch as six couples, including Alpha Darren, walk toward the tree line. They immediately start stripping their clothes and my eyes widen. I turn away to give them their privacy, but Vin says, "Watch."

I turn back around in time to see a bright flash, and the sound of bones cracking and reforming reach my ears. The next thing I know, where humans once stood are now twelve beautiful wolves. Most of them are gray and white mixed but they all have distinguishing features whether on their backs, paws, or snouts.

Each of them tip their heads back in unison and howl.

Their combined song sends shivers down my spine, and then they take off, yipping at each other's heels and chasing one another through the trees. A pang of longing shoots through me watching them run so freely like that.

A small whine grabs my attention and I turn to find Emma also staring after them. "Are you okay, Em?"

Her eyes don't leave the wolves. "Yeah, I'm just taking everything in. Do you think they would mind if I joined them?"

Carter gives her an assessing look and I'm fairly sure there's some jealousy behind it also, since unmated shifters can't shift. "I don't think they would mind at all."

"Are you sure?" she asks quietly.

"We're a pretty accepting pack. Besides, Darren is out there with his mate. He'll keep everyone in line."

"Is that okay with you, Sadie?"

"Absolutely. Go," I wave her on when she still looks uncertain. "Go catch up to them. It'll be good for your wolf to run with some of your kind."

Emma smiles and with one last glance back at us, she takes off, shedding her clothes. Like with the others, there's a bright flash and the sound of bones realigning before a small all gray wolf appears. She darts into the trees, striving to catch up with the others.

The sense of camaraderie in the air lingers long after their forms dissipate. Ash and Carter stand up a moment later. "We're going to head in for the night, Sades. Will you be all right with Vinson?"

"Of course. Have fun." I wiggle my eyebrows. She knocks her fist into my arm playfully before she takes Carter's hand. Right before they disappear from sight she turns around and gives me a thumbs up while he's not looking. A laugh bursts from my lips. That's typical Ash for you. Hopefully, I won't have to go looking for her later only to find her spread eagle under Carter.

Still scarred from that.

Vin lays a gentle hand on mine pulling me back to the present as he entwines our pinkies together. Even the barest brush of our skin is enough to electrify my senses, bringing them to life. Warmth travels from our connected touch up and down my entire body but I'm also exhausted from training with Elian and it's not long before a yawn racks my body.

The combined feeling of the crackling fire and Vin's soothing presence makes my muscles relax and all I want to do is sleep. I'm not the only one either. Even Hemsworth is snoring softly at my feet.

"I'm tired, Vin," I finally admit.

He laughs softly. "Come on, my Moon. Let's get you home." His strong arms lift me from the ground, then cradle me to his warm chest. Almost as warm as the fire. He walks us slowly to the mansion and I savor every step that I'm this close to him.

"Maybe my nightmares will stay away tonight," I murmur, half asleep.

Vin's forehead crinkles when he frowns. "I'll keep them away from you, my Moon. Don't you worry."

The last thing I notice before I fall down the rabbit hole of sleep is the sound of Vin's heart beating in time to mine.

"Sadie," a husky masculine voice calls out in the dark recesses of my mind. The hypnotizing sound wraps around me in an affectionate embrace, like lovers calling out to one another. There's something extremely familiar about it, but I can't seem to put my finger on who exactly it is.

Suddenly, glowing golden eyes appear in the darkness as they sprint toward me. The presence slams into me and I gasp, expecting it to hurt, but if anything it's amazing. A pair of arms wrap around me as we both go sprawling backwards into an endless abyss of black. What the actual fuck?

"Sadie, I'm here," the voice says again, louder this time. The owner of the voice seems to change the direction of our descent and we go flying sideways. My head spins.

"Fucking hell, these nightmares are getting out of hand."

What other explanation is there? I've always had vivid dreams but this is some next level shit and I don't plan on sticking around for whatever fresh hell is heading my way.

"Wait, stay with me," the same voice begs. "We're almost there."

Seconds later we land on something soft and the spinning in my head finally stops. I open my eyes and look around. Immediately, my mouth pops open in shock. The sky around us is a gorgeous shade of orange with purple tones mixed in and there are thousands upon thousands of white puffy marshmallows floating by us. If I'm not mistaken, the puffy white surface underneath me is also a cloud.

If this isn't a nightmare, then what the hell is happening? Am I still dreaming?

My eyes snap to the man next to me and I have to do a double take.

Vin.

He's only wearing a flowy pair of white trousers and his gorgeous tanned abs are on full display as he leans back. Instead of checking out the scenery, he's staring at me. My heart skips another beat. He looks like a God with the sun beaming down on his skin, casting a glow in his golden eyes. He pulls me into his arms and helps cradle my head. My eyelids start to droop once more.

"Sleep softly, my Moon."

I feel the tug of sleep coming to claim me but I'm not ready to leave this serene space, to leave this dream version of Vin's arms. "Wait! Will I remember this when I wake up?" I ask.

He shakes his head. "Don't worry, Luna. I'll watch over you."

And then sleep takes me fully and I go under its embrace.

23

SADIE

An arm shifts around me and I'm snuggled further into a warm, smooth chest, at peace with my waking thoughts for once. I arch my back into them, feeling their hard length press into my ass. A chuckle and a groan reaches my ears as consciousness returns to me.

Thoughts from last night drift into my mind. Emma running with the wolves, Ash disappearing with Carter, Vin's golden eyes, and his promise to keep my nightmares at bay. For once, I'm not waking up covered in a cold sweat from a bad dream, so maybe his words do have some merit.

Wait, Vin!

I shove the blanket and arms cocooning me off my body. My heart is racing as I sit straight up, searching for him but the watchful eyes staring back at me do not belong to Vin. No, these intense blues are all Kaos. The corner of my mouth tilts up into a smirk when my gaze moves to find Dante pressed into Kaos' back, arm around his middle, fast asleep.

"Having a cuddle party without me, Dante? I'm heartbroken."

His eyes pop open and I see it in his eyes the moment he

realizes what he's doing. He jolts away from Kaos like his ass is on fire and he can't put it out. "Shit, sorry, bro. I thought you were Sadie."

Mirth shines in Kaos' eyes. "To be fair, you did cuddle her first, but it was relatively easy to slide in between the two of you."

The sheet puddles around Dante's middle and his delicious abs are on full display. Kaos' too. I groan, looking them up and down. "Please tell me you don't sleep nude." *Or do, but I definitely won't be getting anything done today.*

I'm only so strong and their nakedness would completely do me in.

Dante grimaces. "I don't but Kaos normally does. He's a hot sleeper. Always bitching about how he wakes up sweating."

I laugh. "And you're not? You're both fucking infernos."

"Relax, bro. I'm wearing boxers," Kaos says and shows us his plaid boxers. Huh, I took him for more of a briefs guy.

Dante lets out a breath and then he turns those twinkling eyes on me. "You know this is like every girl's wet dream, right? Two of her boyfriend's already half-naked and both hard as steel?"

I groan again and smack the pillow over my face, noticing I'm still in the same clothes from last night. "As much as I'd like to take you two up on your offer, today marks six days until the challenge and I have plans with Hemsworth in the library."

Kaos raises an eyebrow. "What sort of plans are you and the familiar concocting without us?"

"Nothing." I sigh. "Well, it's not nothing, per se, but I don't want to say anything until she agrees to it."

"She?"

"Bedi. Hems knows how to get a hold of her so we're

going to ask her to come here to watch over everyone while we're dealing with the Elders."

Kaos rubs his chin. "I still don't know if I trust her. I read up on seers and they used to be notoriously neutral, which might not seem like a bad thing, but they usually stay out of things or keep on the winning side's good graces. Whichever side it might be."

"I'm assuming since she's the last of them that it hasn't worked out so well?"

"No. The Elders wiped them out because they were too powerful and then outlawed their practices. She has to be holding one hell of a grudge… and she does seem to have a soft spot for you."

"I trust her, Kaos."

He still doesn't look certain but he doesn't fight me on it anymore. "Does Ash know about your plan to send her with Bedi afterward?"

I jolt. "How did you know that?"

He shrugs. "I know you, Sadie. I saw the gears turning in your head the moment the trio returned her and each time you noticed Ash flinching at a sound or saw her with that haunted look in her eye. I guessed you'd want to protect her from anything like that ever happening again. Bedi seems like the logical choice."

Sometimes he seems to know me better than I know myself. I think it's those watchful eyes of his. "No, she doesn't know and we're going to keep it that way. I'll tell her before we leave, not any sooner. I don't feel like spending my last week fighting her tooth and nail about going to stay with her."

Kaos inclines his head. "As you wish, Little Flame. Let's get dressed. I want to check over the archives once more and see if there's anything I missed about Vin's condition."

Dante glances over at me. "Speaking of Vin—" My heart

skips a beat. Oh no, this is it. Dante's going to scold me for last night. "I need to thank the shifter for getting you home safely."

"Nothing happen—" I stop and replay his words in my mind. "Wait, you want to thank him?"

"Yeah, apparently you fell asleep at the party and he found me straight away. I want to thank him for watching over you."

Kaos nods his agreement. "He's a good man. I wish I could do more for him."

"Me too," I admit. More than anything.

BEGRUDGINGLY, I LEAVE THE COMFORT OF MY MATES TO GET showered and dressed. Hemsworth is already waiting for me in the library, sitting at the desk when I walk in. He tells me in order to contact Bedi, I need to write her name down on a piece of paper with my message and then set it on fire. Supposedly, that will reach her anywhere in the world, but I'm still slightly skeptical.

"Are you sure this will work?" I voice my concern aloud, hand hovering over a scrap of paper. Hemsworth spins in his chair to face me and I almost laugh. So studious. I swear all he needs is a pair of reading glasses and he'd be a mini librarian. It's hard to take anything he says seriously when he looks like this.

"All Fire Weavers can send messages with their abilities. You have Dante's fire ability. Bedi has a fire ability. Bam, connection."

"Okay, Mr. Snarky Pants, I'll take your fucking word for it." After scribbling down my message, making sure to tell her exactly when to be here, I inhale deeply and call the fire to me. "Here goes nothing." A blast of heat flares to life inside of my belly, searing me on the inside, but it's not painful. If anything, the fire caresses me lovingly. Exactly like Dante would.

I concentrate on moving the fire to my fingers, smiling when a bright blue and orange orb appears in my palm. I fold the note in half and catch the tip of it on fire. It doesn't take long to burn the whole note, reducing it to ash that safely dissipates at my feet.

Kaos walks through the doorway a second later with a raised eyebrow. "Hey, Little Flame. All done with your fire message to Bedi?"

"Fire messages are actually a real thing?"

"You just sent one, didn't you?"

"Well, yeah! I didn't think it was real though. I just sent it because Hems said it would work."

He chuckles while Hems gives me the stink-eye. "Are you up for a bit of research? I figured we could scour the few books we have on healing. A fresh pair of eyes might do me some good."

"Absolutely. Point me in the direction of where to start."

He leads me over to one of their floor to ceiling bookcases and pulls out a few ancient tomes. Each of them are bound in leather and weathered. There's no writing on the outside of them besides a small Roman numeral and crescent moon on the spine. He tosses me the one labeled number five, and I take a seat at the desk to get started.

As soon as I crack the book open, dust particles fly out of it and I sneeze. "Moons, how old are these things?"

"Old," Kaos responds, sitting across from me. "They're handwritten."

"I can see that." The perfect, looping script of the writer is absolutely gorgeous but insanely hard to read. "This is going to take ages."

"Look for anything related to healing and skip the rest."

Flipping through the pages, I do as he says and scour for any information on healing or black vines crawling underneath the skin or anything about shifters. But sadly, there's not a single mention of anything in all nine hundred pages. Just a vague description of what healing consists of—which we already know. I sigh as Kaos tosses me another book. I do the same with it and the next ones that Kaos gets up to grab until the pile of books next to us are completely and thoroughly searched.

We're no closer to figuring anything out, and now I have a massive headache. "What are we going to do, Kaos?" I ask, rubbing my temples.

"I don't know," he admits.

"I can't let him die," I tell him, tone somber.

"I know. We'll figure it out." He rises from his seat and extends a hand to help me out of mine. "Since we're done researching for the day, would you like to check out the rest of the books?"

"Hell yeah. What kind of question is that?" I bounce up with renewed energy at getting the chance to look around the library and all that it holds. I've been dying to do it since I saw it on the tour with Dante.

He chuckles as he leads me over to the other side of their library. There's a wide variety of books on the shelves. Some are old, maybe as old as the magic tomes, while the others look completely new. Some have classic titles and some are more obscure. My gaze snags on the bottom of the shelf and I catch one of the titles, making my eyebrow raise. Are those raunchy romance novels I spy?

I turn my attention to my observant mate, trying and failing to hold back my grin as I point to one facing us with a shirtless dude on the cover. "Who's reading smut?"

Kaos boops my nose and I playfully nip his finger as he

pulls it away which makes heat flare in his eyes. "Men are allowed to read romance novels too," he defends.

"I never said they weren't, did I? I'm asking because your girl is a romance novel freak and all of mine were destroyed. It's about damn time I start collecting again, don't you think?"

"I'd give you the moon if I could, Little Flame. Find some you're interested in and let me know, I'll purchase them for the library."

"It doesn't bother you that anyone could find them here?" I ask, scanning the various titles.

"Uh, no?" He responds and it comes out as more of a question. "I'm perfectly fine with my masculinity and I don't particularly care what anyone else thinks about my taste in reading. Minus you, of course."

I groan. "Have I told you how sexy you are lately?"

His lips quirk. "Probably, but I like hearing it anyway."

I smack his abs. Little good that does, the man is made of steel. Heh. Steel. "Cheeky fucker."

"I'll show you a cheeky fucker," he says, eyes ablaze with desire. His arms wrap around me as a voice interrupts our banter.

"There you are, Sadie! I've been looking everywhere for you." Reed stops in his tracks when he sees Kaos and I together in a somewhat intimate position. "Oh, sorry, I didn't realize you had company." He clears his throat before running a hand through his reddish locks.

"Hey, Red, what's up?"

"Nothing. I wanted to see if you needed any help." His gaze flicks over to Kaos. "But it looks like I'm intruding on a moment."

Kaos shakes his head. "No worries, bro. You can join us." Reed looks shocked and so hopeful that it makes my heart swell. Gods, I really lucked out in the mate department.

"We're going to have to get used to having you around it seems," Kaos says with a wink.

"Valid point," Reed agrees with a smile. "Because I don't plan on going anywhere."

I glance between them curiously. I'm totally picking up budding bromance vibes.

"I respect that," Kaos responds. "Anyway, Sadie and I were about to read a romance novel, if that's all right with you?" Kaos plucks the one with the super sexy model on the cover I pointed at earlier, and leans in conspiratorially. "Our little mate seems to need a distraction."

Reed's cheeks turn a twinge of pink as he looks down at the cover of the book in Kaos' hand. "Actually, I've read this one before."

"I fucking knew it!" I exclaim with a little fist pump.

Kaos looks between the two of us curiously. "What am I missing?"

"When Reed came into my workplace, he had a book with him, but wouldn't let me see the cover or title. I had a hunch it was lady porn, but I couldn't call him out on it because of customer service and all that shit."

"It's true." Reed chuckles. "You caught me red handed."

"Which book was it?" Kaos asks eagerly, beating me to the punch.

No wonder he knows how to play my body like a fucking fiddle. Can all men start reading romance novels with us?

Maybe then they'd know where to find the fucking clitoris.

My two mates take a moment to discuss their favorite books while I bask in their closeness, not really paying attention to what they're saying, but merely enjoying the way their bonding.

Besides, my focus shifts to the giant windowsill that's suddenly calling my name. It's filled with blankets and pillows like someone had the same idea as me to use it as a nook. It's the perfect space for us to cuddle up and read a really good book together. "Shall we move somewhere a bit more comfortable, boys?" I interject.

"You like that, do you?" Kaos asks when he sees me pointing toward the windowsill. "Fine, I guess I can share my book-nook with you. What's mine is yours after all." He grins at me before sliding into the blankets first, motioning for me to crawl in next, and Reed files in behind me. Kaos wraps his arm around my shoulder, giving me a place to rest my head. The pillows were fine but I'll take his arm any day.

"Who wants to read first?" I ask, trying to distract myself, lest I jump their bones right here, right now. I'd really like to hear them read me a dirty book first.

Kaos lifts the book he chose and gives a small shrug. "I will." He flips it open to the first page and starts reading. Immediately, I find myself entranced by the cadence of his voice. Moons above, he needs to be an audiobook narrator. Women everywhere need to hear the rough quality of his tone. A fierce jealousy threatens to rear her head inside me. Yeah, scratch that. That shit is all mine.

"Skip to the good stuff," I tell him breathily. I'm dying to know what he sounds like while reading a sex scene.

"If you say so, my Little Flame."

Surprisingly, I don't recognize the book in his hands, but the cover leads me to believe it's a bit of a dark romance.

"Page fifty-three is a good one," Reed pipes up with a sheepish grin.

Kaos nods and when he finds the correct page, he clears his throat and his eyebrow raises. "The paddle descends onto her pussy, striking her clit, and drawing little mewls from her lips with each hit…"

Oh, Gods. I'm an idiot. What was I thinking when I told him to read a spicy scene? But he does it without even stumbling over a single word. Suddenly, our little fort starts to seem a lot hotter than before. Or is it me and my skyrocketing libido? Shit, I'm going to spontaneously combust.

"Yeah, that's my cue to leave," Hemsworth says with a snort as he jumps down from his chair. "Let me know when you hear back from Bedi."

Crap, I'd totally forgotten he was still there! Poor guy really is going to be scarred for life one of these days.

Kaos continues, not caring that Hems left us all alone, and the words grow dirtier and nastier by the second. Heat pools in my core and my legs shift, seeking that friction I'm craving. Gods, *I wish nothing more than for Reed to touch me while Kaos reads in that sultry voice of his.*

Almost as if Reed hears my thought, he slowly moves his hand up my thigh under the blanket. He starts off slow, rubbing small circles on the side of my knee.

Higher, I need him to go higher. A soft groan escapes my lips when his touch travels up toward my core but he keeps his movements unhurried like he doesn't care if Kaos sees us or not. *Gods, I want Kaos to see what he's doing to me though.* A thrill shoots through me. Is that wrong of me? To want one of my mates seeing another while they play my body into a hot mess?

This whole time I've wanted nothing more than to please them, to not upset them. It's why I've only ever had one on one time with them in the bedroom. But it's my life and according to the Goddess, Reed really is my mate—

Reed's fingers go even higher, cutting off my thought process. It takes everything in me not to react. My skin tingles, my breath quickens. I love the rush that he's creating. I want them. Fucking hell, I want both of them, right here, right now. Reed leans in close to my ear and whispers, "Do you want me to keep going, Love?"

I suck in a sharp breath, causing Kaos to pause in his

reading. His smirk is all-knowing. "Is something the matter over there, Little Flame?"

Is he fucking with me?

Because I refuse to hold back any longer.

"I need to know if everyone is okay with things moving forward with Reed."

"We were all there the day the Goddess said she doesn't make mistakes. I do think there's a lot more we need to uncover about him and his culture before you bond. But I'm not in the business of denying my mate pleasure so if you want him to finger fuck you, I don't see why he shouldn't."

That sends a jolt of pure lust straight to my clit and my chest begins to heave as the weight of their combined stares bear down on me, making me dizzy and light-headed with need. "Keep reading, Kaos. I need both of you. Please."

"Pleasure her," Kaos demands, leveling those intrusive eyes on my lighter counterpart. A moan escapes my lips as Reed does as he's ordered and inches his fingers toward my aching center.

"I'll take good care of you, Love. Don't you worry," he whispers, repositioning himself over me. He captures my lips with his and our kiss is softer than what I've had with the others, as if he's testing out the waters. When I open my mouth to allow him entry his tongue darts in, swirling around mine. He tastes like the sunshine coming out on a rainy day. His touch is pure light, soft and explorative as he runs his fingers down the side of my body.

Kaos reads another sentence that has my desire spiraling even higher. "My mouth descends on her glistening pussy, licking up her slit to her sensitive nub. She tries to buck and writhe but I pin her down with a hand on her hip, pushing her further into the mattress—"

Reed pulls my focus back to him by inching my shorts and panties down. "I want to see you. All of you, Love." No arguments here. I lift my ass and help him get them the rest of the way off. My shirt and bra follow soon after and I wonder why I even got dressed this morning.

"Because it's fun undressing you. It's like unwrapping a present."

I glance between them both and cross my arms over my chest. "Nope, I'm not going to be the only one starkers. Clothes had better start coming off."

Kaos shrugs and undresses quickly and after a moment, Reed does the same.

"Better?" Kaos asks.

"Much," I respond, uncrossing my arms as I eye their delicious muscles. I half expect to find a crotch knife holster still attached but sadly, there's nothing of the sort.

Oh well, mysteries for another day.

Reed taps my knee, motioning for me to spread them. I oblige and he starts a sensuous trek down to my heat which is already soaked for him. He swipes a finger through my wetness and smirks at what he finds. Then he pops that digit in his mouth, sucking off my juices, and I gasp because the sight sends a zing straight to my clit.

I reach down to start playing with myself and Kaos tuts, pausing his narration once more. "I said for Reed to pleasure you, Little Flame, and if he doesn't get a move on, I'm going to take his place."

"I don't see why you both can't get something out of this as well," I respond, shooting Kaos a salacious grin.

"Oh? What did you have in mind?"

I bite my lip in thought. "I want you to touch yourself while Reed touches me, but I also want you to keep reading. Can you do that?"

"I can for you, mate." His eyes blaze as his hand travels down to his hardened length. He hisses as his rough hand wraps around it. I watch, enraptured, while he gives it a few strokes, spreading the bead of liquid at the top for lube. He suddenly pauses and swipes his hand through my wetness, combing it with his own. "Much better," he says, swirling his cock with his hand before repositioning the book in his other hand.

My skin flushes with desire and shock. Holy hell, that's hot as fuck. Reed chooses this exact moment to stop teasing me and sticks a digit straight in my molten core. He curls his finger at the perfect angle to brush against my g-spot with every move he makes.

As Kaos continues to read and work himself into a frenzy, the lust in the room grows. Reed plays my body like a fucking fiddle and another moan escapes my lips. "That's right. Give my mate what she wants."

Reed's eyes flash. "Our mate."

Fuck me. Why is it so sexy when he's assertive?

I wish they would both dominate me. It's so tiring being in control all the time.

Reed's eyes snap to mine. "I think our little mate wants us to take control, Kaos."

My mouth pops open in shock, but Reed claims it again before I can utter a word. Our lips graze and our tongues clash in our fervor. When we finally have to break for air, I level a look at him. "How did you know I want that? I know didn't say it out loud this time."

He winces, looking sheepish. "You didn't have to say it. I read—"

The thought hits me before he can even finish his sentence. "My mind!" All those times I thought I accidentally said something out loud filter into my thoughts. "I wasn't going crazy and talking to myself after all. You're just a mind reader!"

His face flushes, but he doesn't stop curling his finger. Shit, he's a good multitasker. "I'm sorry I didn't tell you sooner, Love," he rasps. "I didn't want you to be mad and think I was intruding on your thoughts and—"

"I'm not mad, Red. You really should have told me sooner though. That shit is going to come in handy." His palm brushes my clit, pulling a gasp from my lips.

"We'll discuss this later," Kaos interjects. "For now, this is about our mate and her desires." He motions for Reed to back up and hooks a leg around mine, flipping me onto my stomach. My head lands in Kaos' lap with his hardened length in my face. "Is this okay?"

My mouth waters at the sight of him. "It's more than okay," I say before licking his tip. The taste of me and him combined swirls on my tongue as he threads his fingers through my hair, the raunchy book forgotten, but thankfully, unharmed and out of our way.

Reed places his hand on my ass, letting me know he's behind me. It's strange not being able to see what's being done to me but it's also thrilling to let go. I trust these men with my life. Why not my body?

My lips wrap around Kaos' head and I run my tongue down his length to help coat him. Meanwhile Reed is circling my clit with his tongue. I jolt from the sensation causing Kaos to groan. "Fuck, her mouth feels incredible."

I hum in approval. Up and down, bobbing my head all the while allowing Reed to bring my body to the brink with his mouth. It doesn't take long between his skilled fingers, his expert tongue, and knowing from my thoughts exactly what makes me tick for me to reach the peak. My core tightens and I come with a scream around Kaos' dick.

He follows suit moments later and hot ropes spurt down the back of my throat. I swallow down every last drop, not wanting any to go to waste.

Completely and utterly spent, I collapse into the blanket fort. "We should do that again sometime."

Both guys laugh.

"As you wish, Love," Reed says, and I reach for him, but he waves me off. "Not today. This was about you."

"If you say so."

We spend the rest of the afternoon cuddling naked, relishing in the feel of our bodies pressed together and it becomes apparent to me how badly I need to win this challenge. I never want to give these men up. Much less to a shark like Savannah. Or die. Not dying is a plus too.

Less than a week to go.

24

SADIE

The sound of a tortured scream wakes me in the middle of the night, and for once it's not my own. Startled, I jump from the bed with Kaos, Dante, and Hemsworth on my heels. It seems as though the scream is coming from Elian's room, so we hastily make it to the hallway and I wrap my hand around his doorknob, only to find it locked up tight with an extra ward around it for protection.

Kaos bangs on the door until a bleary-eyed Elian finally opens it. "What the fuck do you all want?" he demands.

"Uh, you were screaming?" I say slowly.

"I'm fucking fine. Go back to sleep." He slams the door in our faces, leaving all of us slightly stunned.

"Goddess, I just want to knock him upside the head sometimes."

"He's always had night terrors, Angel. Most of the time he only sleeps for a few hours and doesn't like to be bothered," Dante responds placatingly.

"Whatever. I'm going back to sleep." If he's going to be an

ass then he can deal with his shit on his own. I'm not his keeper.

"Can you try not to snore so badly this time, Dante? You're ruining my beauty sleep," Hemsworth grumbles. Leave it to him to be the comedic relief we all need.

Kaos

I find myself outside of Elian's door the next morning. He might've brushed his night terrors off, but I know him better. He's struggling and I intend to find out what's going on with him. Thankfully, he opens it on my second knock, looking exhausted with dark circles under his eyes. His clothes are in disarray, which is quite concerning. He's normally more put together than this.

We move into the room and Elian sits at his desk, popping open the top to his crystal whiskey decanter, and pours himself a drink. I take the seat across from him and my nose wrinkles. "A little early to be drinking, don't you think?"

He glances at his pocket watch before snapping it shut and putting it into his sweats pocket. He never goes anywhere without the thing. I think it was his mothers. "It's five o'clock somewhere." He takes a sip and makes a face.

"You know Sadie hates that shit, right?"

"Yeah, and I had a rough night, so I don't really give a shit."

"What's going on with you, bro? You're so fucking cold to her some days and warm with her the next. I don't get it and frankly, I'm tired of it."

That's an understatement really. I've never seen him act

like this. He's always been a bit of a surly bastard but it's as if Sadie gets under his skin like no other. We usually let it go because we know he has been through a lot in his life. More so than normal people. If only he and Sadie could connect on that level, I think they'd find they're more alike than either would like to admit.

"I thought she was going to tear us apart and having her here ruins my plans with Elron. All that work, straight down the drain."

I sincerely didn't expect an honest answer from him because of how evasive he's been about her so far. "Why is that?" I ask, but then it hits me. "Because you care for her?" Elron, his father, would use any advantage over him he could get and Sadie would be a massive target. Although, she's already got a bullseye on her.

He shrugs. "Savannah was expendable."

"You fucking bastard. You know she's already yours, right?"

"I know."

"Then why do you keep fighting it?"

He takes another sip. "Fuck, I don't know anymore. I guess I thought I could spare her the trouble of taking on a broken fucker like me."

His words piss me off and I rise from my chair, leveling a stern look on him. "Here's a bit of advice, brother. You need to figure your shit out and fast. She doesn't deserve the way you've treated her and I'm tired of making excuses for you. Dante and I both are."

This time he swallows the remaining whiskey in his glass and stares at the ceiling. "She'll never forgive me for the way I've acted."

"I think you might be surprised."

I walk out of the room, leaving Elian to sort through his

thoughts, hoping he makes the right choice because I love him... and I think I'm starting to love Sadie too.

Shit.

I think it's time to go for a run and expend some energy.

Maybe I need to sort through my own thoughts.

25

SADIE

Another scream wakes me a few nights later, the night before my final showdown with Savannah. This time Kaos and Dante are nowhere to be found when I wake. I do my best to ignore it since it's Elian and I don't want to bother him after his night terrors again.

Eventually the sound fades away, but my brain is now wired. With a sigh, I realize there's absolutely no way I'll be getting any more sleep tonight. My eyes are wide open and my mind is spinning a mile a minute. *I guess I could go for a walk.*

I slip out from the rumpled covers and put on a pair of ripped shorts. I opted to sleep in one of Kaos' band tees so I'm already good to go there. The shirt is so large it almost swallows me whole—exactly the way I like, but I tie the end of it into a knot so it doesn't cover my shorts.

Hemsworth raises his head from the edge of the bed and gives me a look when he notices I'm getting dressed. "What are you doing?"

"Going for a moonlight stroll," I respond, fixing my bed hair with my fingers.

"Would you like some company?" he asks groggily, barely able to keep his head up.

"No, but thanks for the offer. Go back to sleep, pup. I know how you are when you're sleep deprived."

Once my Converse are laced up, I head out of my bedroom, down the stairs, and out the back door into the night. The moon is extremely bright, and the nocturnal life is out in full force. A lone bat flies over my head, the crickets chirp, and an owl hoots in the distance.

It's the rustling of some branches up ahead that capture my attention though. Confused, and wondering if I'm about to run into an actual bear or something, I turn in time to see Elian slip into the trees. What the hell is he doing sneaking into the woods when he was just in his room screaming?

Elian disappears from sight and my feet are moving before my brain even makes the conscious decision to follow him. As quietly as possible, I trace his steps over to where he entered the woods and catch a glimpse of his body as he makes another turn. I pick up the pace, doing my best not to crunch on the twigs and leaves under my feet. One snaps, making a loud crack. I hold my breath for a moment, waiting to see if he noticed. Luckily, he continues on without stopping.

Elian takes many twists and turns until he finally disappears into a clearing. I stop at the edge of the trees, trying to stay hidden, watching as Elian makes his way up the large hill that leads to the edge of a cliff.

Once he reaches the top, he tilts his head up to the sky. With his chest heaving, he lets his mouth pop open, and he screams. Never in my life have I seen someone look so broken down and defeated. It startles the shit out of me.

Moons, if the asshole would just talk to someone about his problems, maybe we could get somewhere, but instead of letting my anger rise to the surface, I shove it down, and watch the tortured soul in front of me.

When he runs out of air, he takes a few deep breaths, and then he starts screaming again. His shout cuts off as he drops his head into his hands. In that moment, I feel a tug in my soul for this broken man and my chest aches.

"What the fuck, Goddess? Why tie a broken man like me to a woman like her?"

My feet are carrying me closer to him, but I pause, using my enhanced hearing to catch exactly what he's saying.

Her.

As in me?

"Dammit, Goddess. She's fiery and she doesn't take my shit. But I'm all twisted and volatile inside. My father broke something inside of me that I don't know can be fixed. I don't understand why you'd pair us together." While I'm busy contemplating his words, he sighs and suddenly takes off running, launching himself off the side of the cliff.

My stomach drops all the way to my toes, and I scream his name as I race after him but I know I'm not going to make it in time, and I haven't mastered walking through the shadows yet. Elian is already sailing toward the ground like a high-powered missile and then I can no longer see him. *Oh, Gods. Why?*

A twig crunches behind me and I whirl around, feeling utterly hopeless, only to find Elian's emerald eyes on mine. The faint glow from the moon shining down on him highlights the lighter tones in his hair. In the day, it almost looks muddied, but out here under the light of the night, it seems luminous. Like I've said before, the dark is where Elian thrives. The silence stretches between us for a moment as he stands there, staring at me. What was I thinking following him out here?

I feel like such an intruder, a voyeur trying to peer into his life, an outsider.

"What the fuck are you doing?" he asks, breaking the silence.

"How—how are you alive?" I ask instead, wiping the tears from my face.

"I used the shadows before I hit the ground." I didn't even think of that. Of course, Elian wouldn't actually try to kill himself. Seek a thrill though? He'd definitely do that. Motherfucker. I'm an idiot. "What's the real reason you're out here?"

"I couldn't go back to sleep after you woke me up, so I came outside for some fresh air only to find you disappearing into the woods…" I trail off because he can make his own connections from there.

With his eyes still locked on mine, he storms toward me. For the first time, I realize he's completely shirtless and only wearing a pair of low-slung black sweatpants that highlights the delicious V of his abs, and damn, is the dude fucking tatted. Every inch of his torso is covered in ink. I seem to lose myself in the patterns for a moment, and when I look back up, I find his face no less than an inch from mine.

Instead of backing up like he probably expects, I stand my ground and don't move. I inhale deeply, drawing in Elian's leathery scent as I ready myself, for what, I'm not entirely sure. I never know with him.

His eyes flash as he drinks me in. "Why are you so infuriating?"

"Me? I'm infuriating? You're the one who jumped off a fucking cliff! Why are you such an asshole?" I throw back, giving him a taste of what he dishes out.

Instead of looking pissed, he smirks. "Would you like to try it?"

"What? No! I don't have a death wish, fuck you very

much."

He raises an eyebrow in challenge. "Are you afraid?"

I scoff. "Of course not."

"Then jump with me."

Damn him. If I don't do it, I'll look weak and he knows it. "Fine, but you better not let me hit the ground. I know quite a few of your fellow Circle members that will kill you if you do. And I'd haunt you from the afterlife."

His lip twitches. "I promise I won't let anything happen to you," he says, his tone the most soft and sincere that I've ever heard it. Is he sleep deprived or am is he finally letting me in? Before I can contemplate it further, he takes off running.

I follow suit, feeling like a complete idiot for giving in to his demands. The edge of the cliff comes up fast and I use my momentum to push myself off the ledge behind Elian. My stomach drops as gravity takes hold and I fall down, down toward the hard unforgiving ground. Unlike in the meadow, there's no lake beneath us. Elian is in front of me and somehow slows his descent to wrap his arms around me and I cling onto him for dear life. He's quite literally holding my life in his hands. Ah, hell I'm probably fucked.

A blast of cold air surrounds us as Elian yanks us into the shadows then we're back on top of the cliff. His finger lifts to my cheek as he drags it down my face. "I would break you." His words are always so different from his actions.

"You could never break me, Elian." My traitorous voice comes out breathier than I'd intended and his dark gaze flicks down to my nipples which are hardened to points from the cold. I'm sure they're standing at attention for him through the thin cotton of my t-shirt. I didn't bother throwing on a bra because I didn't think I'd meet anyone out here.

"Are you actually turned on from the exhilaration of us doing that?"

"No," I lie, glancing away from him.

"Liar." He calls my bluff, tapping my chin to bring my gaze back to his and he smiles. It's a vicious sort of smile; the only kind he's good at.

"How do you know?" I taunt.

He taps his head. Duh, he can read my aura and I'm sure it's shining like a bright beacon that says, "I'm fucking horny!" Or maybe it says, "I'm fucking crazy for wanting you!" I'm not entirely certain. Either assessment would be accurate right now.

My chest heaves with every breath I pull in, causing my hardened peaks to brush against his with each inhale. Elian definitely notices and his eyes darken with lust. "I'm tired of fighting my feelings for you."

"Then don't."

His eyes brighten, thawing their normal icy glow. He reaches between us, one hand traveling up my thigh to my tiny shorts. Running his finger over my slit through the fabric, he smirks when he finds the wet spot. "I'm going to devour you, Sadie." His words shouldn't send a thrill straight down to my lady bits, but they do, and he knows it.

In a blur of movement, Elian has my legs wrapped around his waist and my back pressed up against a tree. The rough bark bites into my skin through the thin cotton, sending a white hot jolt down to my clit. I never would've guessed that I'd be one to like the pain but sometimes pain and pleasure go hand in hand.

He readjusts his grip on me, making my back scrape the tree again. My nipples brush his chest once more, adding to the sensations running through me.

My hand travels down his biceps, feeling the muscles as they flex to hold me in place. Little raised bumps capture my attention, and with a start I discover that Elian is covered in a ton of tiny, raised scars but there's no time to dwell on them and if I draw attention to them, he may shut down again.

Elian slides me back to the ground to yank my shorts off and the jolt pulls me back to the moment. My shirt flies off next, leaving me only in my thin cotton panties. Crap, I should've worn the lacey ones to bed.

Wait, this is Elian. Why do I care?

Maybe because subconsciously a part of me enjoys the banter between us. When he's not being a raging douchebag, he can often be nice to be around, but now isn't the time for such thoughts.

He clicks his tongue. "This just won't do." He shreds my panties with his hands, baring me to him and exposing me to the cool air. His finger finds my slit again, eliciting a groan from me when he palms my pussy.

His eyes drink me in, lapping me up like a starving man in the desert. I relish in the feeling for a moment before he lifts my ripped panties in the air to gloat, before shoving them into his sweats pocket.

"Hey!" I protest, coming down from my lust high a bit. "I only have so many pairs of those."

He gives me a careless shrug. "You can go bare every day for all I fucking care."

"Asshole."

"I'll play with that too, don't you worry, pet. But let's see if you'll still be calling me that in a moment." Elian adjusts me once more, raising me up in the air. My brain registers what his plan is as my legs find purchase on his shoulders.

Oh, shit.

A gasp escapes my lips, making him chuckle darkly. "Where has all that fire gone, huh, Little Pet? You're not even fighting me. The asshole who has done nothing but fucking hate you."

That ignites a fire in my belly, making the air crackle with even more tension between us. "I don't have to like you to get off."

"There it is," he growls as he lifts me up and throws me back against the bark.

The stinging bite is quickly replaced by pleasure as he rests one hand on my belly while keeping the other one underneath me and buries his head between my thighs. He laps me up like I'm the most delectable flavor known to man. My hands find his hair as I ride his face. I tug on the strands, making him growl into my pussy, which feels so fucking good. He's sporting a little bit of stubble that scrapes my thighs each time he dips his head further into me, heightening everything.

When he sucks my clit into his mouth, that's when I lose it. I start bucking and grinding against his face, taking my pleasure from him. Owning it. Like I said, I don't have to like him to get off and he's doing a damn good job of keeping me distracted from thoughts of what tomorrow will bring.

In my lust-filled opinion, you really should fuck someone you hate at least once in your life. The sensations should be forbidden, locked up like dirty little secrets. Yet, here Elian and I are exposing them in front of the Night Goddess so she can bear witness.

He pulls back a bit, making me whimper. "Come for me, Pet." His gaze sears into mine, scorching me on the spot as he dives back into my cunt and sucks my clit into his mouth once more. I can't help it. I come hard, screaming, seeing stars, leaving the earth. Hell, I'm pretty sure I see Saturn on my way back down.

"Hmm, you do come on command." He smirks and blows on my sensitive nub to draw out the sensations. I smack his arm, but little good it does. My whole body feels like jelly, like literally putty in his hands as he slides my feet carefully to the ground and I secretly savor our moment.

26

ELIAN

This is not how I expected this to go. Much like Sadie, I have my own demons that plague me each night. Sometimes the pressure weighing me down every single day is too much to bear on my own and tonight, I snapped.

Now I'm going to lose myself in her even though I don't fucking deserve her.

You worry about her, my inner voice says, calling me out. And hell, it's not wrong. Ever since the night we found the blood written across the walls of her friend's old house, I've been diving deep into her past. Since that gut-wrenching memory she accidentally projected into my mind through the others bond. I've been trying to find out as much as I can about this uncle who marred her perfect skin. Unfortunately, the asshole might as well be a ghost. There's no record of him whatsoever.

Shoving all of that away, I refocus on the moment when Sadie says something. "Let me in, Elian," she demands, punctuating her statement with a finger to my chest, then her eyes soften and she lays her hand on my chest. "You're clearly in pain. Talk to me."

"I don't want to talk. I want to rearrange your fucking insides." She gasps at the same time her pupils dilate. She's as fucked in the head as I am. Her darkness calls to mine. "Now, I'm going to rut you right here out in the open. We're going to desecrate this space with our coupling, and I'm going to fuck you against this tree until my come is dripping down your thighs."

Her breathing quickens as my hands find the band of my sweatpants, but she stops me before I can pull them down and turns serious for a moment. "You may be getting my body, but you're going to have to work for my heart. I won't be satisfied until you're on your knees worshipping me like the Goddess I am."

Maybe I'm a coward but I'm not ready for that yet. I haven't come to terms with the fact she might die tomorrow if Savannah gets her way. Rather than give me a chance to respond, she yanks my sweats down herself, freeing my cock. It springs up like it's dying to see her, and the sight of my size visibly distracts her for a moment. I don't know what compels me to speak, but I say, "Are you ready to be the first to take this giant cock, Pet?"

She startles, looking up at me with those wide eyes.

Goddess, she's perfect.

"You've never—"

"Fucked anyone? No. I haven't."

"But Savannah?" She can't keep the jealousy from her eyes and I hate that I'm the one who put it there.

"I wouldn't touch that bitch if my life depended on it," I tell her sincerely.

"Really?" she questions, and there's so much vulnerability in it my heart constricts.

"Yes," I respond, hoping she can see the truth behind my

eyes. She nods and opens her mouth, but I don't give her another chance to speak. Instead, I invade her space again, admiring the toned flesh of her legs and arms sparkling under the moonlight. She looks absolutely divine, and I wasn't lying when I said I was going to enjoy devouring her.

"Turn around and put your hands against the tree," I command.

"No," she says with a defiant grin, flipping the tables on me as she launches herself at me, taking me down to the ground with surprising strength. She's on top of me before I can even blink, aligning my dick at her soaked entrance. I grip her hips and thrust mine up to meet hers, entering her in one long stroke. A strangled gasp-groan leaves her luscious lips as her head tips back, fully seated on my cock, her gorgeous tits heaving in the air.

I take the opportunity to savor being inside her for the first time. She feels like absolute heaven and it makes me regret ever treating her like shit. Eventually, I start rocking inside her, loving the way her pussy grips my dick like it's a glove made for me alone. Although, that's not entirely true, because my brothers have had her before me. They're better men than I.

Sadie recovers quickly, dragging her nails down my chest. Hard. Hard enough that there will likely be her red marks on me tomorrow. Good. She starts to meet me thrust for thrust, taking her pleasure from me. We're both a frenzied blur of movement as we rock into each other, fighting for dominance.

That's the thing with us though. I don't believe one of us will ever outweigh the other. She gives as good as she takes and I think that's partly why I respect her so much, even when I should hate her for ruining my plans. Revenge is a dish best served when no one sees it coming. When there's no one involved to get hurt. Now there is, and I'm going to do my best to protect her from it all.

Although, she's going to have to do all the heavy lifting in the arena tomorrow. Savannah will be absolutely relentless in her pursuit of us and I'm sure the Elders are going to give their little favored bitch an advantage. Yeah, our little mate needs to be on her toes. Not to mention my bastard father will be there— watching me, taunting me…

My pace increases as I ram up into her over and over again. The pleasure starts to blur with the pain. Like a light guiding me out of my darkness, she looks down at me. Not with pity but understanding. "Talk to me," she says between pants, desperately trying to tear my walls to the ground.

"What do you want me to say?" I snarl. "Do you want me to talk about how my father would take his anger out on me? About how he would cut into my flesh with each life lesson he taught? Or do you want to know how you ruined my plans to finally take him down? To earn my revenge? Tell me, Mercedes, what exactly do you want to know? Does any of it make a Godsdamned difference?"

Without warning, I lift my back from the ground, repositioning into a sitting position. Wrapping her around my body, I lift us from the ground, still connected as I slam her back into the tree.

"Of course it does, Elian. You matter! Your fucking story matters!" she screams, gripping the back of my head and slamming my mouth into hers. Our teeth clash, our tongues twirl, all the while I keep my tempo deep in her sweet cunt. She groans, allowing me better access to her mouth and I oblige. It's in this moment that I realize this is not only our first fuck, but also our first kiss.

I'd be lying if I said I wasn't already addicted.

When I pull back, she nips my bottom lip, drawing a tiny amount of blood at the same time she rakes her fingers through my scalp. My whole body shudders as the pleasure and pain explode through me.

"I think you're the first person to ever say that to me, besides my Circle." I hate the admission as soon as it's off my tongue. I grit my teeth, placing my hand on her throat, loving the excited little sound that escapes her mouth when I apply a little bit of pressure, loving when I feel a rush of heat on my dick. "No more talking, Pet. Let me fuck you into oblivion."

And I deliver my promise, staring directly into my Little Pet's eyes with my hand on her throat as I rut into her over and over again.

"Come for me," Sadie whispers, looking entirely too smug for my liking.

Oh, that won't do.

"Get ready to brace your hands against the tree," I tell her, and it's the only warning I give as I lift her off my cock and spin her around. She does as I ask and catches herself against the tree as I enter her from behind once more.

"You like it rough and dirty, don't you?"

"This is what you call rough and dirty?" she taunts. "I thought you were going to fuck me into oblivion. Devour me and all that shit. I don't feel—" She cuts off as I borrow a little stream of icy shadows from the realm and they find her clit.

"Shit," she breathes. "More, Elian."

Who am I to deny her pleasure?

I let more surround her while simultaneously using my Weaver abilities to slam into her faster. "More, Elian. More!"

I spit on her asshole and wet my finger with it thoroughly. Once she's drenched enough, I start swirling around her back entrance, drawing desperate moans from her throat. Her lovely tits bounce from each thrust and our smacking sounds penetrate the forest while our combined scent permeates the air. It's enough to drive me utterly wild.

My finger slips inside her ass at the same moment her

cunt pulses around my cock, pulling a strangled cry from my lips as the pleasure in my spine becomes too much. In a few more rushed thrusts, I'm coming inside of her with a roar. My teeth slam into the back of her neck, leaving my own mark against her beautiful skin.

Yeah, I'm officially addicted.

We stay like that for a while. Both of us are too afraid to move and ruin the moment. I don't want to let her go because I know what tomorrow entails. The Elders, Savannah, my father. The whole fucking farce.

If I could, I'd take her place and let them damn me instead of her.

Something tells me none of us will walk away unscathed.

27

SADIE

Eventually, Elian lets me down. My arms are burning from holding myself up, my shoulder tingles from being bitten, and my pussy is sore from our rough fucking, but I'm not mad about it. When the fucker told me I would be his first, I was shocked at first and then excited. "How did you learn to fuck like that?" I ask, still somewhat out of breath. He definitely delivered on each promise he made me.

The corner of his lip turns up. "I like to watch."

That shouldn't turn me on again. Hell, I've orgasmed twice, but my body still craves more. Elian sees the desire in my eyes and it lights up his cold ones, which seem to have a little less ice in them now. *Yep. I'm finally thawing the bastard out,* I think smugly as he wraps his arms around my waist and carries me back inside.

A glint of silver catches my eye from the moonlight, and I spot a chain dangling from Elian's neck. Upon closer inspection I find the gorgeous pendant I was drawn to at the concert resting above his heart and I jolt. "It was *you?*"

Elian glances down and then back up. "What was me?"

"You bought the pendant I loved at the concert. Why?"

He shrugs. "Honestly, I really don't fucking know..." He trails off. "You can have it, if you want. I don't know what possessed me to buy the thing anyway. Maybe I subconsciously knew you were going to be important before I ever even saw your aura or your face. Too bad I loathed you from the start," he says, but there's no real bite to his tone.

I take a long look at the beautiful moons on the pendant. They still beckon to me like a siren, but... "No, I think you should keep it. Turns out moons look good on you."

Elian's chest vibrates with a silent laugh. He kicks open the door to his room and carries me through, our clothes forgotten. My back bounces in his soft sheets as he descends on me once more, eyes narrowed.

"This is what you want? Because once you have all of me, there's no going back."

"Oh, fuck off, Elian. You'll still be the cold, icy, bastard that you are and have always been tomorrow. I'm not naïve in thinking that you'll suddenly become a teddy bear. But that's the thing. We'll always be opposite magnets pushing away from each other, but sometimes, well, sometimes we're going to spin each other around and find comfort once more. We can push and pull at each other all we want, but in the end, you're fucking mine and I'm not letting you go because of your stupid bullshit."

"Then you're going to have all of me, Sadie. I hope you're ready."

I am. I've never been more sure of anything in my life. I belong with my mates, and Elian is one of them. Though, he still has a metric fuck ton of groveling to do before I let him into my heart or my soul.

"You're going to have to earn this heart. I hope you're up for it."

"Challenge accepted," he says, sliding into my heat once more.

SADIE

As the saying goes, the world waits for no one. The earth is still going to continue spinning on its course no matter what's happening down below, even though there have been many times I wish it did stop, if only for a moment.

Today is the day I finally meet the Elders. I thought I'd wake up feeling the dread of not knowing what's to come. I thought I'd wake up with regrets or feel nervous, but none of that has hit me yet. Even as Ash carefully starts the last stitch in my dress for the appearance I have to make this evening. Everything has to be absolutely perfect, to the Elders standards, or else we risk offending them. As if my appearance should be what fucking matters.

Apparently, it does though. Quite a lot according to Kaos. The Elders require formal attire in their presence and at their dinner parties. Tonight though, it'll just be us and them. My thoughts travel to when Ash and I got ready together like this the last time, albeit for a more exciting reason then. That was the night my world changed irrevocably for the better.

The night that everything turned on its head. The night I met my mates.

As if she can sense the direction of my thoughts, Ash stops stitching. "If you could go back to that night, would you change it? Would you still go, knowing what you know now?"

"Absolutely," I say without hesitation, and my mate marks tingle. I glance at my wrist, admiring Kaos and Dante's symbol. I'm ready to add to it. I wouldn't be the same without them and I'd never go back to living the way that Ash and I were—in a constant battle with ourselves that we didn't even realize we were having. "Is that silly of me? People are at war, my life has been threatened more times than I can count, but when I think of them…" I blow out a breath. "Everything seems worth it."

She looks at me for a long moment before a broad smile comes across her face. "Jesus, babe. When did you become such a sad sap?" We both let loose a laugh at that and I smack her arm. "Careful, I am holding a needle, you know!" she hollers.

I ignore her protests and turn around, wrapping her in a hug. "You know I love you, right?" I ask. "I'd do absolutely anything to keep you safe from this world."

"I know," she says as she steps back from my embrace, swallowing thickly. "But you don't have to face this alone, Sades. I'll be here for you."

I wince, knowing what I have planned for her and also knowing she's not going to like it. It's what has to be done to protect her. She's a distraction I can't afford going into this. I refuse to let the Elders get their grubby paws on her again.

"Enough of the sad shit." She motions for me to turn back around. "I need to finish your dress or else you'll be late!"

Once she's satisfied my dress is up to par and will accommodate my last minute design choice, she takes the time to plait my hair into a braid that is so complicated I can't even follow the motions. The front part curls along the side of my head while the back is neatly twisted and hangs behind me. When she finishes, she walks me over to the mirror.

A gasp escapes me when I catch a glimpse of my appearance for the first time. The fabric hugs my body in all the right ways, trailing to the floor in a flood of black. The front dips between my breasts and the slit runs all the way down to my navel. The bodice gets significantly smaller toward the straps on my shoulders.

Each side of the dress is split, giving me plenty of room to move and to breathe without making me feel trapped and stuffy. Or like my girls are going to fall out for the entire world to see. When my legs are straight, you can't even see the thigh holster I'm wearing with my shadestone dagger.

The fabric is covered with thousands of tiny studs that shine in the light over the black webbing that runs down the length of it—combined with the silver threads woven throughout, it gives it the illusion of star fall. My fingers find the tulle section Ash added in, all different shades of russet yellows, purples, and oranges and it makes me smug. Now I'm representing the Night and the Light and it is, by far, the most elegant, badass dress I've ever seen in my entire life.

It's also more than just a fashion statement. It's a message.

"Ash, this is stunning. Where did you find this?"

"I didn't. I made it."

My mouth pops open. I know she's quite talented with sewing but I never realized how much until now. In our free time back at the duplex, she used to take our drab clothes and turn them into something spectacular like the shirt she made me for the concert. She may not have actual magic, but I'd say this is the closest thing to it. "When the hell did you have the time to do that?" I ask.

CHAPTER 28 | 229

She gives a small shrug. "While you were off with your hotties."

There's no use hiding the tears in my eyes as I run my fingers over the silver studs. "It's so beautiful, thank you."

She makes a noise of objection and smacks my cheeks. "Don't you dare cry and ruin your makeup that we spent ages on." She wipes at the tears staining her own eyes. "I need to go get ready myself. I'll see you in a bit."

Guilt smacks me square in the chest with the knowledge of what I'm about to say, of the look that's going to be in her eyes when I do what needs to be done to keep her safe. "Ash, we need to talk."

She stops her in her tracks and whatever she sees in my face makes hers twist with anger. "Don't you dare, Mer. I know how you are, and I refuse to let you lock me out of this."

I shake my head. "I need you to stay with Bedi. She knows how to keep you safe. I couldn't live with myself if they got ahold of you again."

"Nope. Nuh uh. Absolutely not." She grabs my hand. "We are in this together, like always, remember?"

A lump the size of a watermelon forms in my throat, I have to swallow it down before I can speak again. "It's not up for debate, Ash. I've already made up my mind. Bedi is going to watch over you, Emma, and Vinson until it's safe again. We have no idea what we're going to be walking into tonight. I don't even know if we'll all leave in one piece."

"I need to stand my ground, let them know that I'm not afraid—" Ash starts, but I cut her off.

"And I need to keep you safe!" Softly I add, "Please, don't make this harder than it already is."

When she sees that I'm not going to relent, her expression shutters and she drops my hand, making me feel worse than I thought possible. "I can't believe you're going to ship me off like this." Betrayal dances in those hazel eyes of hers which look dull now.

"It won't be for long, I promise. Only until we figure out what we're dealing with and make a plan. Your go-bag is still packed, correct?"

"You know I'd never be caught somewhere without it ready," she snaps, her tone upset.

I nod, having figured as much considering I'm the same way. Mine is repacked and under the bed with more supplies than before in case of an emergency. I even recommended that my mates pack their own go-bags, which they did without question.

When a stray tear slides down my face, Ash's eyes track it and her face softens. "I'm fucking mad as hell at you for doing this without telling me but I also understand your need to keep us all safe." Her arms go around me once more and it's a strain to hold back further tears. "One of these days you're going to have to realize that you can't protect everyone and that's okay. We all make our own beds, so let us lie in them."

"I know, but this is serious. These are supernatural problems, and I don't want you caught up in them anymore than you have to be."

"You stubborn bitch, you know there's nowhere else in this world or any other I'd rather be than with my best friend."

Hemsworth appears in the doorway with Bedi trailing along behind him. I swear his bottom jaw hits the floor when he sees me. "Hot damn, you do clean up nice, Weaver." He gives my leg a boop with his nose in greeting and I bury my fingers in his fur, loving the calm that washes over me. Hems is my rock.

Bedi glances between us with a knowing eye. "I'm sorry to interrupt your moment but we didn't want you to be late."

"Thank you for doing this," I respond, thinking back to the note I received this morning stating she would be here. Getting a note out of thin air was pretty freaky but also handy. I'll have to remember it for future uses.

"Absolutely, dear." She gives me a meaningful look and gives my shoulder a squeeze. "You need to stay vigilant tonight. Something is blocking my gift of sight and that's never happened before. Even I do not know what you will be walking into tonight."

Wonderful.

"I will, don't worry."

Before anything else can be said, Ash is throwing her arms around me. "Give that bitch hell for me tonight. You do whatever it takes to stay alive, okay?" Her grip tightens with the last of her words.

"As if I'd let that bitch best me," I say, feeling confident in my abilities as a fighter and as a Weaver.

"Hey, we need to get going, we're going to be la—" Dante cuts off when he sees me. "Holy shit." He practically trips over the rug trying to get to me but manages to right himself before he smacks face-first into the ground. "You look absolutely ravishing, Angel."

"Why, thank you, Blondie. You don't look half bad yourself." He's sporting a navy tuxedo that really brings focus to his tousled blond hair. I reach over and try to smooth it out but it does nothing. His hair is just perpetually messy, and I dig it. Ash hands him a silver pocket square that matches the sparkles of my dress which he stuffs into the little pocket of his coat.

Dante leans in, making my vision swim with nothing but his amber eyes. "I'm going to immensely enjoy peeling that off of you tonight." His fingers skim my back, making my breath hitch.

"For Goddess' sake," Hemsworth whines. "Get a fucking room."

"We would, if we weren't on a time crunch," we both say at the same time.

Bedi chuckles at our antics. "Keep her safe, Dante. This world needs her."

"With my life," he responds, crossing his hand over his heart then bows. When he's right side up again, he extends a hand to me like a true gentleman would. My heart flutters in my chest at the adoring expression on his face as I grasp his fingers with mine. "Are you ready?"

"As I'll ever be."

I say one last goodbye to my best friend and Bedi before Hemsworth and Dante lead me out of the room. We make it to the steps to find the others waiting for me at the bottom.

I'm totally about to have one of those cheesy movie moments as I descend the steps to my waiting men. They're all facing the opposite way talking about something in hushed tones. Kaos glances over his shoulder and freezes when he sees me. He taps Reed on the shoulder and then they turn around, jaws dropping.

Dante gives my hand a little squeeze when I pause in my descent, but I can't help it. They've taken my breath away and my legs have become lead, leaving me glued to the spot. I take this small moment to let everything else go, to study them in all their fancy glory fully, trying to commit each piece of them to memory. Just in case things go south tonight. I want their images burned into my brain.

Kaos is wearing a crisp black suit that has thin silver pinstripes that almost seem to move with the light. He shoots me a dashing smile and my heart leaps with all of the devotion in his gaze.

I move on to my next mate and have to do a double take because I've only ever seen him with his glasses on. Reed is standing there, watching me with a smile tipping up the corner of his lips, in contacts instead of glasses for once. He's wearing a gray tux that compliments his fiery red hair well.

My gaze travels to the right, landing on my asshole mate. Even Elian matches me, in an all black suit, perfectly pressed with a silver undershirt beneath his jacket. His mask is firmly in place but even he can't hide the hunger and desire in his gaze as he takes me in. My other mates already know what happened between him and I. Honestly, I'd be surprised if the whole house didn't hear us fucking until the sun rose into the sky.

Facing Vinson at the end of the steps near my other mates is bittersweet. He looks like he always does in the suit he wears during his duties, but tonight somehow seems different. Pale. Weak. Sweat beads across his forehead but the smile he gives me when he sees me is absolutely brilliant.

Until it's not.

His eyes suddenly roll into the back of his head and he starts to collapse. A gasp escapes my lips as I rush forward to catch him before his head smacks the ground. Thankfully, I reach him in time and the others are around us in an instant with Kaos taking the lead to check him over for injuries. When the black glow sluggishly tries to enter Vin's body and then fades back into Kaos, I don't even have to see the grim look on his face to know there's nothing he can do.

"I'm sorry, Little Flame. I know you care for the shifter but there's nothing I can do to help him right now. We've tried everything. Every healing method in the books."

"And we're going to be late if we don't leave now," Elian adds somewhat gently, with as much softness as the man is capable of, anyway.

"Screw the Elders and the challenge!" The frantic tone of my voice startles them and they all do a double take at me. "We have to do something to help him."

Elian scrubs a hand down his face. "The magic binding you and Savannah to this challenge tonight will not allow you to ignore it, I'm afraid." Great. That's exactly what I want to hear. "Soon you will not be able to ignore the pull and we'll only be digging our graves further if we're late."

I stroke Vin's hair back from his face and he stirs. "What happened?" he asks.

"You collapsed. Are you okay?"

"Don't worry about me, I'll be fine. You need to get going before you're late," Vin says to me, and Dante lifts him under his arms to help him stand again. Even though he looks fairly disoriented he keeps his back straight and his smile soft.

"But what if something happens while we're gone?" I ask.

"I'll watch over him," Reed answers, watching me carefully.

Elian shuts his pocket watch with a soft click. "I'm afraid that isn't an option, Reed. You have also been invited and your presence is required."

Reed pales at this news making the fire inside my belly rage a little higher. "After everything they've done to him and his people... he's now *required* to come tonight? To face the people who made him watch them kill his father?"

Elian gives us a grim nod. "Unfortunately."

I grit my teeth, knowing arguing about any of this is mute even though it makes me rage on the inside. "Fine, but first we're going to help Vin get to his room."

Goddess, we need to come out on the other side of this alive. Afterward we can consider our options and regroup when we have better information about the Elders. I may want to murder these bastards more than anything but even I'm not stupid enough to take them on in *their* territory or risk dealing with their army of followers. No, we're going to have to be smart about how we deal with them.

"When we get home," I make sure to say *when* and not *if*

because I absolutely refuse to die tonight, "Kaos and I are hitting the books to find a cure for Vinson. We are going to heal him, no matter the cost. Hell, we'll even get Bedi involved if that's what it takes."

Sadie Sinclair does not give up easily and I'm *not* giving up on Vin.

"You've got it, Little Flame," Kaos says and helps Dante get Vin settled.

Once they return, Reed clears his throat and twists his hands in a nervous sort of gesture. "Uh, before we leave, there's something I need to tell you all."

"What is it?" I ask. I should probably be more patient but it's already been a long night and I'm not looking forward to any more surprises.

He takes a deep breath. "I received word from a small faction of Light Weavers that somehow managed to survive back home. They want me to take over and stop the fights about who gets to rule in my absence."

My mind begins to reel with that revelation. They want him to go back...

Nope. We haven't even bonded yet. There's still so much to learn about him. "What? No, they can't have you. You belong with us." *With me.*

"Regrettably, my people also need me, Love. But that's not all... They know about you and are willing to give you a chance because of the prophecy."

Elian places his hand up to stop anyone from saying anything else. "We have to leave now." He levels an appraising look on Reed. "We'll discuss this in depth later." Well, either he's taking a page out of my book or he believes in me getting us out of this tonight.

I sigh, fighting the urge to fidget. "Fine. Lead the way."

29

SADIE

The longer the night goes on, the stronger the dread eating at me becomes. At this point there's probably a hole the size of Kentucky in my stomach. But thinking negatively and dwelling on what's to come will only make things worse.

I push all of my doubts out of my mind and take a long, deep breath to center myself like Elian taught me during our training. Once I exhale, I place my poker face on and I'm back to my normal. Well, as normal as one can be in this situation. How have I not lost my head yet?

Finding out there's a whole hidden world of magic with corrupt Elders that are power-mongering bastards that also want you dead for some reason would be enough to drive anyone to madness, yeah?

No. No more doubts, Sadie. Fake it till you make it, right?

Right.

"Listen, Sadie," Elian starts. "You need to keep a clear head while we're in their presence. Keep your head down, look as gorgeous as you are, and try to keep the snark to a minimum.

You know they're going to say things to provoke you, but don't let them win."

The limo suddenly turns, pulling us onto a nicely paved road. The familiar feeling of a ward washes over me as we pass through it, but it doesn't feel anything like Elian's. This one is slimy and makes gooseflesh break across my skin. To make matters worse, the rapidly darkening sky turns a sickly shade of green. Lightning streaks across it, splitting off in several directions. The flash lights up the Elders' sprawling mansion, highlighting all of the dark crevices that are likely hiding horrors one couldn't even begin to describe.

Rain pelts the windows, obscuring our view as our driver, a shifter named Will, pulls around the circular driveway, coming to a stop in front of the marble steps leading to the door. Will hops out, getting soaked in the process until he manages to open the umbrella and quickly comes around to open the door for me.

He inclines his head, sticking his hand out for me to take. "My lady."

He puts his arm on my elbow and I allow him to help me from the limo. My mates file out behind me—each with an umbrella they must've pulled out of their asses. Or their crotches. They seem to hide a shit ton of stuff there already.

Will follows me up the steps with the umbrella but when we make it under the safety of the small covered porch, he inclines his head and disappears back toward the limo. I can't say I blame him. The rain is falling even harder now and it's almost certainly an indication of the things to come this evening. Or it may be because of the Elders.

A presence slams into me seconds before someone speaks. "Ah, you've arrived on time. I'm impressed," the dark, sensual voice says. Their power immediately sets off every single alarm bell that I possess in my arsenal.

This man is bad news, but instead of letting him know that he's affecting me, I simply turn and give him a broad smile. Everyone has their part to play tonight if we want to make it out of here alive and this is mine. A hawk in a den of vipers. That's what I am. Powerful enough to take one on, but several at once?

Their poison would likely kill me before I could take them all down.

The man's lips turn up at the corners highlighting a sharp set of teeth or maybe I'm imagining that, but they do seem sharper than normal ones. "Why, you're quite the beauty, Miss Sinclair. I'd heard of your looks but the rumors didn't quite do you justice." His power brushes against me again, trying to burrow into my walls. I don't let it. I rake my mental claws down it, shredding it from my skin, all the while giving him a smile that could revive the dead.

"Thank you," I say as lightning strikes once more, illuminating his haughty features as he returns my smile. This must be Adam's father. He has the same blond hair, defined jawline, and easy way of talking. The evilest of men are often bound by chaotic beauty.

"I'm Elder Reginald. My counterparts are inside already. We've been *dying* to meet you, you know." His emphasis on dying sends a chill skating down my spine.

"Oh, you have?"

"We have. You've thrown quite the wrench into our society." He waves his hand in dismissal. "Come, let's join the others." Without a proper explanation or another word, he spins on his heel. I follow along behind him with Hemsworth at my side and the others flanking me.

Reginald steers us into the expansive foyer, dripping with opulence and wealth. The walls are lined with expensive crown molding. The chandelier hanging from the ceiling puts the King's to shame. It could likely feed a family for a lifetime. My lip curls. Such loaded fucking pricks. As if sensing my anger and the direction of my thoughts, Hemsworth nudges my thigh and I give him a grateful head pat as I clear my thoughts from my face.

The foyer leads into a hallway that's lined with gaudy paintings of the Elders, each of them with a stern jaw and a glare leveled at the painter. I rack my brain for the names of the other two Elders but I don't think I ever asked the guys. Likely a mistake on my part.

Vald is the twins' father. Vogt is the third and his brother, Kaos projects into my mind, likely sensing my confusion.

Always saving my ass. Thanks, Kaos.

"Just a little further." Reginald takes a few more steps and then sweeps his arm into the entrance of what must be the dining room. Immediately, I notice there's not a chair at the head of the table. Hmm... I wonder if they have spats about who gets to sit there and decide to forgo it entirely. I find Savannah seated to the left of the other Elders, talking their ears off by the looks of it. Adam, Nick, and Niall are seated next to her, their expressions borderline disinterested, like they'd rather be anywhere else. They don't even glance at us as we walk in.

Like I said, everyone has a part to play tonight.

Vald, the twins' father, looks downright bored until he spots me lingering in the doorway and perks up at the sight of me, as does Vogt. They're the spitting image of each other with straight black hair and pinched faces, yet all three of them still look quite young. Although right now they're looking quite inquisitive like I'm a bone they want to pluck and gnaw on, then spit out the remains to let rot.

Vald and Vogt stand, motioning for me to sit down to their right. I steel my spine and make my way over to their side. The weight of their power smacks me full force and I have to concentrate on breathing through the onslaught. My spinal cord feels like a firework sprinkler from the insane amount of juice rolling off these guys. No single person should ever have this much power, let alone three of them. When my butt hits the chair it feels like the point of no return, even if this night has been inevitable since Savannah threw down the challenge.

Hemsworth sits behind me and Vald raises an eyebrow. "So, it's true."

I cock my head to the side, studying his long black robes while my mates file in next with Elian in the seat next to me, Kaos and Dante across from me, and Reed next to Elian. "What's true?" I ask.

"You have a familiar. Did you know that those ancient beings haven't been around in a long time? Some would say they are a sign of the Goddesses favored." His lip curls. "But we do not believe in such fairy tales here. To do so would be treason."

I clamp down on my urge to chew him out. Seems I'm going to be doing that quite a lot in their presence. Hemsworth also stays quiet. Moons, no wonder they lost favor with the Goddess. If they only knew... "Ah, yes. I'm extremely lucky to have found Hemsworth," I respond carefully.

Vald makes a noncommittal noise.

"No matter," Reginald says and motions for the servers, standing like silent wraiths in the back of the room to come forward and fill our drinks. I hadn't noticed them until now but that's likely the point. The male shifter filling my glass shakes a bit as he reaches over me, and I catch a glimpse of something around his neck. *Is that... a fucking collar?*

My nostrils flare and Elian subtly kicks me under the table. I rein it in as quickly as possible then dart a glance at the Elders who are all focused on their wine, much to my relief.

A new round of shifters flit through the doorway,

carrying trays on their shoulders piled high with food. Everything looks delicious but I know better than to accept anything. They've been exceptionally welcoming so far and I know it doesn't bode well for us. Probably trying to flatter us into a false sense of security before striking when we least expect it. Or poison us. Yeah, not the way I want to die, thank you.

A thought strikes me, and I glance around the dining room, not seeing someone I think would be fairly important. *Where is the Elders' Link?* I mentally ask my mates.

Dante sighs and covers it up with a cough. *They leave her locked up in her room. No one has ever really met her. From what I can tell she's more of a breeder than a Link.* Anger flutters through me with his admission because no one should be subjected to that kind of life, but I let it slide and ignore the urge to curl my fingers into fists. There's nothing I can do, and who knows, maybe she likes this life.

Actually, I doubt that.

The shifters finish placing the opulent food on the table, which takes quite a while for the overindulgent feast they prepared. No one speaks while they do and I want to ask what the purpose is for so much food, but I bite my tongue. Such a waste. The Elders immediately dive in after the shifters back away, piling food on their plates. Everyone else waits silently until they're done getting their fill and they motion for us to do the same.

None of my Sworn makes a move toward the food, which is a pity honestly, because it does look delicious and it makes my stomach pang with phantom hunger from the days I used to go without. My Sworn and I wait patiently while the rest fill their plates. None of Adam's crew will look at us still, but Savannah on the other hand, is throwing eye daggers my way. Being in the presence of the Elders must be making her hold her tongue though.

Reginald cracks a smile when he sees us sitting in solidarity. "You would dishonor us by not eating this fanciful feast we've prepared for this occasion? It might be your last meal after all." He directs the last part of that at me.

"It is not a dishonor, Elder. We merely ate before we came. Thank you for offering the gracious meal though," Elian says, covering for us quickly. It's a weak excuse if I've ever heard one but it seems to appease them nonetheless.

"Very well." Much like Adam, Reginald seems to do most of the talking. "I see you followed our orders not to bond with her, unlike your fellow Circle member." He levels a dark look on Dante to which Dante smiles then Reginald turns back to Elian with a smile. "I commend you for that, son. You've always followed in the footsteps of your father, haven't you? So obedient and understanding to our cause."

Dante snorts and covers it up with another cough, and they told *me* to behave. Amateurs.

Good thing they can't read auras, huh, bro? They'd be able to see your stain on our dearest Sadie. Dante says, using his Circle bond with Elian to include me in their mental conversation.

Stain? What stain? I ask.

From him fucking you, he responds. Ah, hell.

Elian's fingers curl into fists at his side. Thankfully, out of view of the Elders. "Yes, Elder. My father has taught me many skills that I apply in my everyday life."

"That he has. Speaking of which—" Reginald looks toward the door where a familiar dead eyed man waltzes through. He has the same high cheekbones and emerald eyes as Elian, and I know without a doubt this must be his father. The only difference between them is the scars marring his father's face and his massive build. This is the same man that was in charge of the attack after leaving Bedi's treehouse. The head of the Elite. The bloodhound on my trail, it seems. Or maybe, it's Elian.

"Seems our head of security has finally arrived. Welcome," Reginald says, grinning to himself like a loon as he beckons him inside. Elian's father crosses a hand over his heart and bows low to the Elders before he faces his son who looks slightly paler than before. Fucking hell.

"You must be Elian's father," I interject before things can escalate. Elian is breathing heavily but seems to calm some when he hears my voice. "Sorry, I don't think I caught your name." I could give a fuck less, honestly, but I'm trying to uphold our role.

His dead eyes travel to me but I don't squirm under their scrutiny. Fuck that. I know if I show this man an ounce of fear, he'll scent it. I hold firm as he says, "Elron." His voice is gruff. Exactly what I'd expect from someone like him. He returns his gaze to the Elders, wiping a bead of blood off his sleeve with a handkerchief. "I apologize for being late. Had to finish taking care of business."

"That's quite all right, Elron," Reginald coos. "Take a seat. Things were just getting started." His eyes flick over to me as he runs that same dark magic over me again. It feels like it's trying to burrow into my skin and slide into my defenses. I rake my mental talons through it, slicing it before it can embed in me. His face doesn't give me anything but the tenseness to his next words gives him away. "Tell us, who are you, Mercedes Sinclair?"

"Please, call me Sadie, and I was your average girl back home. Or well, until I met my Sworn, anyway. Now I'd consider myself very lucky." I give my mates an affectionate glance that definitely isn't all for show.

Reginald nods, meticulously cutting into his steak before taking a dainty bite. Once he swallows and dabs his mouth with his cloth napkin he asks, "We are quite curious about your lineage. Who are your parents?"

I hold my hands in my lap to keep from fidgeting. "My

father's name was Mitchell and my mother's name was Scarlett. They're both dead now," I respond flatly. "Besides, I don't know why my lineage matters."

For some reason my response makes Reginald's smile widen further. "Because, my dear, Weavers are born. Not made."

Oh, yeah. "As I've already explained to my mates, that's not possible. There's no way my father was a Weaver. Nor my mother."

"Child," he chides. "One of them must have been or you wouldn't exist, but that's all right. We'll uncover more about your lineage later. We're far more interested in your abilities—"

Elian interrupts before Reginald can speak further. "She cannot reveal that information to you with Savannah sitting at the table. It would violate the rules of the challenge."

Elron levels a dark glare on his son and Elian flinches. "You know better than to interrupt, son. Do not do so again."

"I may not be able to reveal my powers in front of Savannah, but why don't you tell me about yours, Elder? Seems like you know a lot about me, yet I know nothing about you."

Reginald scowls and ignores my statement. "Very well then, let's get this challenge over with, shall we? We tried being friendly but you ignored our hospitality and it's clear we won't be getting further information from you at this table. That means it's a giant waste of our time and we do not like having our time wasted." He stands, taking one last sip of his wine before placing it on the table a little harder than necessary and some of it splashes over the rim of the glass onto the table. A shifter rushes over to clean it immediately. "Once we know the results of the challenge we will reconvene and discuss your *punishments* for defying our orders."

Reginald turns on his heel, leaving the other two Elders and Elron to file out behind him, with Savannah hot on their heels. Nick and Niall go next, each giving me a slight head nod as they pass. Adam is the last to leave and he leans in close to me, almost within kissing range which causes the guys to protest. He waves them off and says to me, "Do not allow her to corner you, Shadowbringer. She is scrappy and will fight dirty."

"Thank you, Adam." He gives me a nod and backs away, catching up to his brothers in a few long strides. They continue on like nothing ever happened.

Hopefully, I can make it through this night in one piece.

There's no room for anything less. Failure is not an option.

30

SADIE

"The challenge will take place in the arena," Reginald announces after he leads us down a tunnel with what seems like a million steps. "We have prepared the area around the arena with special protection wards that will not allow either of you to leave until the challenge is complete."

By that he means they rigged it, Dante projects to me.

We knew they would.

"We've also modified the rules of the challenge a bit."

Each of my mates tense ever so slightly. Even the trio seem surprised at his announcement. Do their fathers know they were involved in getting Ash out for us and no longer trust them?

Kaos clears his throat. "With all due respect, that's not possible, Elder. The challenge has always been the same since the rules were created. Once the initial challenge is decreed, there will be a fight to the death in one months' time underneath the light of the full moon." He watches him carefully, looking for any signs of deceit, I'm sure.

Reginald looks over his shoulder with a creepy smile as he unlocks the door. "You are correct in that, my boy. *But there are no rules stating we cannot modify or add to it.* The council discussed and thought a fight to the death would be awfully boring. Not to mention end far too quickly, don't you think?" He doesn't even give us a chance to respond. "We've added two more parts." His eyes alight with that cunning superiority I've heard so much about—allowing me to see a small piece of the monster lurking beneath his skin. My internal alarm rings, sending a chill straight down my spine.

He glances at my Sworn and the feeling lessens but doesn't dissolve entirely. "And if you are to be mated to one of these women, they must truly be the best, correct?" His eyes move to his head guard. "Since you orchestrated this for us, Elron, why don't you tell them the rest?"

Elron grunts his affirmation. "There will be three parts to this challenge. One to test Savannah and Sadie's instincts and one to test their mental fortitude. Once those are completed, they will fight to the death as the ancient law demands."

Reginald pushes the double doors open with a grandeur flourish of his hands. "This is going to be such a spectacle to watch!" He claps in glee, leaving all of us a little shell-shocked at the entrance to the arena. The feeling intensifies as we step through into an actual gladiator ring. There are hundreds of seats leading down to a pit with what looks like grass at the bottom. Who the hell has all this underneath their fucking house?

Oh yeah, the Elders. Duh. Silly me.

"Well, what are we waiting for?" Reginald asks, watching us check out the arena. "Nick, if you'd be so kind as to lead Sadie to her dressing room? While she looks absolutely *divine* tonight," he sneers, and I have to bite back my smirk because he actually commented on my dress, "she's not in the proper attire for the challenge. Everything she'll need is there."

Nick's back straightens. "Yes, Elder." He turns to the right and leads us around the top circle of the arena. My mates flank my back, watching it for me so I can take in the space. There's a faint green bubble around the whole arena which I assume is the ward they mentioned. Other than that, there's nothing but grass in the large open space at the bottom.

Before I know it, Nick is stopping in front of a door with my name on it. "Once you enter this room, you will only have ten minutes to get ready. Make the most of it and find a way to hide that." He inclines his head toward my shadestone blade at my thigh. Shit, I thought I'd hidden it better but apparently not. "The ward will disintegrate any outside weapons." Great. Definitely don't want to lose my new favorite blade. "You have to be on the field by the end of the countdown or you'll automatically lose. Good luck."

"Thanks." I don't dare say anything else for fear of the Elders listening in. Hopefully he understands what I'm trying to convey through my facial expressions.

"Stay alive, Sadie Sinclair," he responds before he walks away, leaving all of us to stare at the door.

Everyone ready?

Kaos lays a hand on my shoulder, calming me with his reaffirming touch. *You've got this, Little Flame.*

We've got your back, Angel.

"With you every step of the way, Love," Reed agrees, having heard our mental conversation.

Elian sighs, also having heard the entire conversation through the others. We may not be bonded yet but they can project everything to him through their Circle bond. "Let's just get this over with," he says and with a deep, centering breath I push open the door. Immediately, the lights flick on and there's a loud beep as the clock on the wall starts to count down. Ten minutes. I have ten fucking minutes to get ready. Good thing I don't need to primp like some girls, eh?

Kaos takes the lead, and the others fan out around me, checking for anything hostile in the room. Once they're satisfied there's nothing but a clothing rack and a bench, Kaos points toward the suit hanging on the rack. "This is what you'll be wearing but first—" He crosses the space between us and his lips are on mine in the next instant, kissing the absolute fire out of me, like he wants to imprint himself into my soul and me into his. "You're going out there with my fucking scent all over you so that bitch knows I'm all yours." And shit, if that doesn't make every single nerve in my body come alive.

Another hard body presses in on me from behind and I inhale their toasty bonfire scent. *Dante.* He runs his hands down my sides before moving the braid from my shoulder so he can kiss the tender spot on my neck. I gasp into my kiss with Kaos and he dives in with his tongue. *Do we have time for a quickie? Probably not but—*

Elian clears his throat and reluctantly, Dante and Kaos release me. "I've placed a ward around this room. It should keep prying eyes out until it's time. We need to discuss the new parts of the challenge." He levels his emerald gaze on me. "Savannah is cunning but she's not the sharpest tool in the shed. You'll likely beat her in both mental fortitude and instincts, but you need to be ready for the fight. She's dirty as hell." The corner of his lip tilts. "But you're a little scrappy yourself."

Hemsworth chuffs. "You've seen it firsthand, haven't you? I heard she put you on your ass in the training room a few times."

Elian ignores his jab but it makes the others chuckle. "Listen to me, Sadie. Do not hesitate to end her. She is expendable. You are *not.*"

The clock beeps again, signaling the five-minute mark. "Shit. Someone help me out of this dress." Reed immediately steps forward. His fingers trail down my spine to the zipper above my ass.

"I wish the setting for this was a bit different," he says with a sigh as he unzips my beautiful dress and it falls to the floor in a puddle around my feet.

"Yeah, me too," I whisper back.

The weight of my mates stares follow me as I step out of my dress and walk over to the rack. The suit seems to be made of some kind of nylon material and the fabric glides up my legs as I slide it on. *At least it's comfortable and easy to move in, I guess.*

Reed helps me zip it up and then I turn around to face everyone. "I feel like I'm about to step onto a platform and be lifted into the annual fight to the death in the damn Hunger Games or something."

"Not far from it," Kaos responds. "Just less participants than the book."

I grimace. "No kidding."

The clock chimes again. Three minutes remaining. I unstrap the shadestone from my thigh and hand it to Kaos, hoping the blade deems him worthy enough to hold in my stead. "Mind keeping this safe for me?"

"Anything for you, Little Flame."

Elian draws my attention over to him. "Remember what I taught you while you're out there. Stay centered and level-headed. Focus on what your instincts tell you."

"I'm not nervous, Elian." That familiar bloodlust is slowly awakening in my veins, unfurling her need for revenge inside me like a flower blooming in spring.

"I know," he responds, and if I didn't know any better, I'd say *he* is nervous for *me*, but that's insane, right?

I take a seat on the bench and yank off these dreadful

heels they forced me to wear and pull on the boots left for me. Thankfully, they look like regular combat boots, but they're still not my trusty Converse and I miss the feel of them. The leather isn't worn yet and it scrunches my feet. I don't even want to know how they managed to get my size right either.

Hemsworth nudges my leg once I'm finished. "The rules allow familiars to join their Weavers in the actual battle so I will see you on the field when it's time." He shoots me a wink and backs away to give me a moment with my mates.

Time seems to tick by faster in here, a ploy by the Elders, I'm sure.

Kaos gives my shoulder a squeeze. "It's time. Knock her dead, Little Flame."

Dante scoffs. "More like cut her fucking head off!"

I chuckle and take a step toward the other side that leads into the arena. "No goodbyes. I'll see every single one of you after."

They nod.

"No goodbyes," Reed agrees, and everything unsaid between us flickers through his eyes in an instant. I know he's regretting not bonding to me because I feel the same way. I cross the space between us and grab Reed's face, pulling his lips to mine in a bruising kiss. When we're both seeing stars, I break from him.

"We'll complete our bond once this is all over." I'm tired of fighting fate. Each one of these men fill a different aspect of my needs and it's time I start listening to them.

Tears spring to Reed's eyes as he gives me a small smile then I take a deep breath, straighten my spine, and waltz toward the door, confident in my ability to beat this bitch once and for all.

"Hold up, Sadie, there's one more thing," Elian says, grabbing me by the wrist to stop me from walking through the ward. He grips me by the back of the neck and yanks my mouth to his. Unlike Kaos, he seems to try and suck my soul out of my mouth and into his. In these moments it seems like he's taking and not giving, but I know the truth. When he pulls away, we're both breathing hard. "Don't fucking die."

"Trust me. That's the plan."

31

SADIE

The magic of the Elders ward tingles across my skin as soon as I step through it, and the doorway turns solid behind me. The sound of a metal door sliding into place reaches my ears, and I know there's no going back the way I came until the Elders allow it.

Once my eyes adjust to the brightness of the false lights, I find that it is indeed grass covering the bottom. The next thing I do is check for any exits, but it seems there are none. Two doors. One for me and one for Savannah. The only way out is to be the victor, and I sure as shit don't intend to be the loser.

The walls are taller than I initially thought, stretching at least twenty feet high. The surface is as smooth as glass which means there are no handholds to scale with. Yep, there definitely won't be any climbing out that way to escape. I blow out a breath. I'm truly stuck here.

Just as the clock strikes zero, Savannah emerges from her dressing room, adjusting her suit as she goes. There's not a single auburn hair out of place on her head as she levels her determined gaze on me.

There's a crackle above us as someone seemingly turns on a loudspeaker. I search the sky, finding the Elders sitting in a booth overlooking the arena. Their sons and my mates are with them, standing behind their raised dais with three chairs they've parked their haughty asses into.

Gods, I can't wait to knock them down a peg or two. Or five. "This first test will be all about your mental walls. To be a strong Link, you must first be of sound mind," Reginald announces through the speaker. The grass rustles next to me and something that looks like a snake strikes, their fangs pierce the flesh of my ankle making me wince and my thoughts instantly turn sluggish, like I'm wading through mud.

Judging by Savannah's startled squeal from across the arena, a different snake must have bit her as well.

"In approximately forty-five seconds the venom injected into you by our creations will enter your bloodstream. You will then start hallucinating." He pauses for dramatic effect... or to give the venom more time to process, I'm not sure. Probably both, the fucking bastard.

All I know is I don't like this feeling. My limbs are heavy and tingly. My mind is jumbled. Every time a clear thought tries to come to me, it suddenly drifts away, slipping through my grasp. What the hell am I doing?

Why am I here?

Why does my heart feel like butterflies were let loose inside it?

This isn't right. Something is wrong.

"To pass this test, you must ignore your hallucinations and find the antidote hidden somewhere in the arena. Whoever finds it first will be rewarded in the final round."

Colors suddenly burst through my vision as the venom hits me in full force, and everything flares to life. The grass is now a gorgeous shade of purple and seems like the perfect place for a quick nap. That wouldn't hurt anything, right?

Wait, no. That man said something about an antidote. I have to find it. I have to pass this test. This test... Fuck, the first test. I glance over to find Savannah chasing what seems to be a massive butterfly with the head and body of a lion.

Something silver flashes in my peripheral. *Oooh, shiny.* I pinch the skin of my thigh, hard, hoping the pain will keep me somewhat lucid and it works. My thoughts return to me for a moment. *Don't get distracted, Sadie. Find the antidote and end this round.*

Now, where would those bastards hide said antidote?

Taking in my colorful surroundings, I don't see anything but grass and those lion butterflies. Seriously, how is this even possible?

Then again magic is real, and I have a talking familiar, so this is on par really.

One of the lionflies, as I'm dubbing them, flits around me and when it turns its back toward me, I catch a bit of silver strapped to it. Is that a vial?

How did the Elders make the hallucinogens so realistic?

I don't have time to ponder it. I immediately take off after the lionfly, chasing it across the arena all the while hating how weak the venom makes my legs feel. They're like jello jiggling in a pudding cup. I stumble a few times and quickly realize I'll never catch it this way. It's too fast.

When my thoughts start to stray again, I pinch my thigh once more, digging in even harder than before. The venom is really pumping through me now.

I wait for the lionfly to make its way toward me, readying myself to pounce. Once it's close enough, I launch myself at its back and manage to climb on. I avoid the colorful wings, somewhat remembering that pretty things usually mean danger in nature and grip the vial. The lionfly bucks, trying to throw me off but I squeeze my legs around its back and pop open the cork on the vial, downing the contents in one gulp.

A gong sounds in the distance, signaling my win if I had to guess. Slowly, the vivid colors around me begin to fade, muting into what I'm used to. My heartbeat slows to normal and my thoughts stop racing. *Shit, that was awful.*

Taking in my non-colorful surroundings, I find Savannah still running around, having given in completely to the venom. Her door reappears and a shifter comes out holding a second vial of the antidote. He practically shoves the liquid down her throat and then disappears once more. When she's finally lucid again, she trains those livid eyes onto me.

"You fucking bitch!" she seethes. "How did you manage to fight off the venom so quickly? I practiced with it for a month and never could wear it down that fast! Whatever. It doesn't matter. You may have won the first round but you won't win the next one. I can promise you that." Her eyes gleam like she knows something I don't. I should be surprised she so easily admitted to cheating but I'm not.

I ignore her taunting and turn to face the bastards sitting up in their box of safety. The three of them give me four small claps. "Congratulations on winning the first round, Mercedes," Vald says.

"For this next round, we're going to test your instincts. You have two minutes to decide their fate. Choose wisely," Reginald announces, and the clock above their heads starts its countdown. Shit. *What does he mean by that?*

They don't keep us waiting long. Something whirrs behind us, and I turn to find a circular platform rising up through the grass with two shifters on their knees, hands in each other's grip. One male and one female. If I had to take a wild guess, I'd say they're mated. Their hands are tied with bane ropes to prevent them from shifting and they're shaking. There's a lone dagger on the ground in front of them. My stomach churns with disgust as I come to the realization of what they want us to do.

"Will you spare one and fail the challenge or kill one and win? Tick-tock, ladies. Decisions need to be made." Rage burns through me, stoking that flame inside of me that they ignited by taking Ash from me. "Oh, and if you kill one, you get to keep the dagger for the final round."

The woman cries out. "Please, spare us!" she pleads. "We've done nothing wrong." Her mate quiets her by nudging her shoulder with his.

Forty seconds left according to the clock.

I don't make a move. Screw getting to keep the dagger. I may be many things but a killer of innocents, I am not. Nothing about this couple sets any of my built-in alarms off. They're good people and they don't deserve to die like this.

Savannah glances over at me with a deranged glint in her eye, and I stare in absolute horror as she lunges for the dagger. I didn't think the bitch actually had the balls to do it. I chase after her, ready to do whatever it takes to stop her from murdering these shifters in cold blood, but she's already several paces ahead of me and I'm struck with fear, knowing I'm not going to be able to make it in time.

No, no, no, no!

Her fingers curl around the handle. The man straightens his spine. He looks lovingly over to his mate as Savannah plunges the blade directly into his chest. "I'll see you in the Night Goddess' realm, my love." The light leaves his eyes as blood dribbles down his chin, and he slumps over. Dead.

His mate lets out a cry that rattles my very bones, one I'll never forget. It's the sound of absolute heartbreak. She tries to stand but her legs are so weak that she falls to the ground. Savannah laughs, fucking laughs as she grabs her by her beautiful brown hair and plunges the dagger into her chest as well.

The woman's defiant eyes don't leave mine as she takes her last breaths, and in this moment, I pledge to avenge her and everyone else that has ever suffered at the Elders or the Weavers' hands.

They've awakened the monster inside of me and she's fucking *starving.*

32

SADIE

The clapping from the Elders' applause for Savannah is absolutely thunderous, drowning out the roaring in my ears. I stare after the innocent shifters' bodies long after the floor opens up and swallows them whole.

"Fabulous job, my dear!" Reginald preens through the overhead speaker and the grip I have on my power threatens to snap. I don't let it, instead I lock any emotion other than rage into my box. I realize too late that I played directly into the Elders' hands and let them know shifters are a weakness of mine. *Fuck.* "You have won the dagger as an advantage for the next round, but your opponent has also won an advantage for winning the first round." His lip curls with the last sentence. They weren't expecting me to win.

"Tell me what it is so I can get this over with," I snarl. Elian shoots me a pointed look from the booth, telling me to watch my stone. Right. I'm supposed to be cordial. Oh, well. Fuck these guys and manners. I'm over it. They deserve nothing less than utter destruction at this point.

Reginald chuckles. "You have two options, girl. You can

have a weapon of your choice for the battle ahead." He pauses. Gods, and I thought his son was bad. He's definitely worse when it comes to being dramatic. "Or you can choose to absolve your mates of all their infractions and spare them from our wrath."

I tamp down on the vicious smile that wants to curve my lips. Of course they underestimate me like all the rest. Which is to my advantage in this case. When are these idiots going to learn I don't need a weapon?

I am the fucking weapon.

Just to make them squirm, I take a moment and act like I'm debating my options. I glance down at my hands and over to Savannah, fidget with my suit then finally back up at the Elders. "I choose…" a small smirk forms on my lips, "to absolve my mates."

Reginald scowls, but quickly hides it behind a smile that looks more like a snarl. "Very well. Your mates will be cleared of their infractions, *if you win.* Good luck, Miss Sinclair. You're going to need it."

The sky above us starts to flicker and everything around us becomes darker. The empty seats and the Elders disappear as the top of the arena shifts. Once the flickering stops, I stare up at the simulated night sky. The full moon is huge and tinged a shade of red.

A blood moon? Fitting.

Savannah's cackling draws my attention. Other than after she lost the first round, she has been relatively quiet. "You won't leave this arena alive."

You know, the sensible thing for me to do would probably be to try and talk her out of us killing one another, try to convince her to turn her weapon against the Elders instead, but she's after my men. My *mates*. And those poor shifters…

Before watching her kill those innocent people, I

might've tried my hand at swaying her. I would've said she's merely a pawn in the Elders' game, one they're moving around the board of their own making to help push their agenda. A puppet and their master, but now?

She deserves her fate, and I'm going to be the one to dish out justice.

A dark smile graces my lips. "Are you sure about that?"

For once she looks disturbed, but it doesn't stop her from charging me with her dagger and a Gods awful version of a girly dramatic war cry. I'd cover my ears if she wasn't coming directly at me. She swipes and I jump back to avoid the blade, making her huff and charge me again. I sidestep her easily, keeping my eye on the dagger, still glistening with innocent blood.

We circle each other, each looking for an opening. The door I came out of opens and Hemsworth slinks out, decked in the armor we received at the compound. He reaches my side and I bury my hands in his fur.

"Good to see you, Hems."

"You too, Weaver."

Savannah rolls her eyes. "I'll gut your dog after I gut you, don't you worry. Afterward I'll drag your mates to bed with me. Even the red-headed one. I'd bet his abilities would make for quite the tumble."

I jolt in surprise and she takes the opportunity to strike. I grunt as the blade nicks my arm, drawing a line of blood that slides down my skin. How the hell does she know about Reed's mind-reading abilities?

Mentally, I try to reach my mates but the connection is sluggish and I can't pass anything to them. Thankfully, I can still feel them in my chest, so I try not to worry over it too much. They can't steal our connection.

"Come on, Sadie. Stop toying with the bitch and let's end this," Hemsworth growls, nipping at Savannah's ankles. She grits her teeth and aims the dagger at him. He darts out of range before she can land her strike.

"You got it, Hems."

Shoring my defenses, I call Dante's fire to me, wanting to keep my shadows as my secret weapon for later. I have enough wrath pumping through me right now to manage it fairly easily.

"You don't deserve his fire, you whore!" Savannah screams at me, face twisting in anger when the flames lovingly caress my fingers. Ahh, I forgot Dante is her favorite.

"Don't I, though?" I taunt and wait until the fire in my belly is a raging inferno and then let it out through my palm. Savannah isn't fast enough to dodge it fully and it singes her arm, causing her to cry out in pain.

She charges me once more and this time Hemsworth goes for her, he leaps, and they clash. He manages to latch onto the arm holding the dagger with his teeth, but he doesn't move away fast enough to avoid the blow to his side from her fist. She shakes him off but not before he rips off a part of her flesh and blood dribbles down his jaw. He drops it into the grass and bares his teeth at her again.

She cries out in pain, gripping the area that is missing a large chunk of skin. "You're going to pay for that!" she screams in frustration, abandoning the torn flesh and swipes the dagger toward me again. Or that's what I'm expecting at least. Instead, she ducks under my hand and goes after Hemsworth. Oh, hell no.

The shadows pick up on my rage and they slink from every corner of the arena, seeming to thrive under the moonlight. There can't be shadows without a little light after all.

Savannah's eyes widen as I train them on her and rip her

away before she can hurt Hemsworth. Somehow she manages to land on her feet, and she smirks.

I gather my shadows from around us and make them circle her. They congeal into a solid form, striking out but stop short of reaching her. My heart stutters, watching them frozen in place. I try to move them, but nothing happens.

Shock ripples through me as Savannah holds her hands out and they dissipate like they were never there. She throws her palms out wide, flinging my shadows away from her and causing Hemsworth and I to fly backwards. I manage to stop before hitting the wall, but Hemsworth isn't so lucky. He hits it and doesn't get back up. My nostrils flare with my temper.

"I'm taking it that your mates didn't tell you about my power, did they?" She snaps her fingers. "Oh, that's right. They couldn't. Not so powerful against a leech, are you?"

Keep her talking, Sadie. Formulate a plan.

"A leech?" Gods, if that means what I think it does, it's fitting as hell.

"That's right," Savannah confirms. "One of the most powerful abilities ever known. I'm able to suck any person dry of their power in a matter of minutes." She charges me once more, ramming into me with her shoulder. She angles us toward the wall and my internal alarm blasts louder than a fire engine. Adam told me not to let her corner me. I shove against her hold, thanking my lucky stars that she's too close to me for the dagger to do her any good.

The dagger!

I let go of her with one hand and reach for the blade with the other. Savannah guesses what I'm about to do and tears herself away before I can get a hold of it. "Not so fast, bitch. I'm not stupid enough to let you get a blade. I've heard what you did to poor Benjamin. Such a pity about him and Tyler. They were quite the duo if you know what I mean."

I ignore her taunts. "Why don't you put the dagger down and we can go about this like two women on even footing?"

"How about I suck you dry and get this over with? I'm growing tired of stalling you."

Stalling me? Stalling me for what?

That's the distraction she needs. Savannah darts forward with wicked delight in her eyes. Pain explodes through my body. The dagger goes straight through my shoulder, and I cry out from the force. A sticky substance I know well drips down my arm, staining my suit and the ground with red.

I take in the triumph in her eyes and let it settle for a moment before I yank the dagger out of my shoulder, screaming from the excruciating pain. I borrow Kaos' ability of healing, picturing the seams patching themselves together until I know I'm not going to bleed out, but I don't have time for more than that.

"How!" she demands and it's not a question.

"Fun little trick, isn't it? The perks of having a true mate bond. Something *you* will never know." I growl and launch myself at her. We go rolling across the ground and she throws a punch into my ribs. I grunt from the pain but ignore it and manage to put myself on top. I rip the dagger out of her hand and throw it far out of reach then wrap my fingers around her neck, wanting to physically take the life from her with my bare hands.

She bucks and struggles but much like with the lionfly, I squeeze my legs together tighter and keep her beneath me. She wraps her hands around my wrists and tries to free herself, but I don't budge.

When she realizes she's not going to be able to throw me off, she stops struggling. The night grows darker as she pulls her power into her until the light from the twinkling stars and bright moon is extinguished, leaving us in total darkness. She finally unwraps her hands from my wrists and shoves her hand into my shoulder wound. Blinding white pain explodes behind my eyes, and I'm forced to let her go. She pounces on me, sucking all the power from me. I can't even manage one of Dante's flames, not matter how hard I tug on my dwindling well of magic. I'm well and truly screwed.

Once Savannah stops sucking all my power out of the air, the only thing left is my life force. She yanks on it, and I watch my center slowly start to dim. My breathing slows from lack of oxygen as she pulls my essence out of me, draining me like she said she would. As my heart rate drops, I realize... I'm going to die.

I'm sorry we didn't have more time together, I project to my mates even if they can't hear me. I need to say it. *I know it wasn't long, but I feel like I got to know a piece of each of you and for that I'm grateful. Take care of Ash for me, and Hemsworth, will you? They're going to need you.*

A presence niggles in the back of my mind, fighting the sluggishness to reach my consciousness. I let my mental walls down and allow it in. What's the harm now?

The voice reaches for my mind, wrapping around it. *For the love of the Sun, will you give up so easily? Take my light, Sadie!*

There can't be shadows without a little light...

I cough, tasting the tang of blood on the back of my tongue. *But she's a leech.*

And I'm a Light Weaver. She can't absorb my power. Use it. Now!

We're not mated, Red. Tell the others I'm sorry, will you? I'm sorr—

Suns blaze, Sadie! I'm connected with the others right now. Someone sends me the mental image of them holding hands. *We're connecting as a Circle for you, SO USE THE FUCKING LIGHT!*

Maybe it's the franticness of his voice that finally yanks

me back to the present, or maybe him using a curse word, or hell maybe it's my will to fucking live, but either way, I listen.

I close my eyes because they're pointless anyway. Savannah is trying to suffocate me with my own damn shadows. Instead, I picture the threads connecting me to my Sworn. Kaos and Dante's are still there, albeit dimmer than before. Elian and Reed's strings are practically invisible but they're there. Wait, no, Reed's string is starting to grow brighter and brighter. Sadly, I don't have time to be gentle. I jerk on Reed's thread through his connection with the others and call his power to me with all the strength I have left.

Ever so slowly, his light enters me. My skin starts to glow, and I find Savannah looming over me with wild eyes. She shrieks as I let Reed's power loose, and it snaps into her like the last piece of the puzzle clicking into place. I twist my fist by my side, using it to guide the energy and scald her from the inside out until she explodes in a puff of dust, much like the golems from the concert. Her death is quicker than she deserves but I'm exhausted and depleted, and something tells me this night is far from over.

33

SADIE

The power Savannah consumed is expelled back into the air, slamming into me full force. I gasp from the sensation, hating how weak she managed to make me.

The artificial light in the arena snaps back on, blinding me momentarily. The Elders' raucous applause fills my ears as they smile down upon me with eyes brimming with bloodlust.

My lip curls. These bastards live for this sort of thrill, and it makes me sick to my stomach. They don't care about the lives they ruined, that they wiped from this earth like they meant *nothing*. Savannah may have been an awful bitch and the one who dealt the killing blows to the shifters but in my mind, the Elders are just as guilty as if they were the ones wielding the dagger.

"Well done, child," Vald says, glee lacing every syllable of his tone. Those beady eyes of his shine as he looks down his nose at me. "Get yourself cleaned up. We'd like to take you for a victory stroll through the garden." His tone brokers no room for argument, and I want to scream. More than anything though, I want to go home with my mates, burrow into a nest of limbs, fuck, and then sleep for fifty years.

Of course, that's too much to ask for.

I can barely keep my head up, but I rise from the ground with it held high and my back ramrod straight. I know I can't afford to show any more weakness under the Elders' watchful eyes. Showing that those shifters affected me was bad enough.

Even though my side and shoulder protest from the movement, I stare at them head on, allowing them to see the defiance behind my eyes for the first time tonight. A lot of things have tried to break me in this world and these assholes aren't going to be the first to succeed.

Ignoring the pinch in my shoulder, I cross over to the wall and pick Hemsworth up from the ground, sighing in relief when I find him still breathing. My magic enters him instantly, speeding up his healing process.

"We've got to stop meeting like this, pup," I say when he opens his eyes.

He bares his teeth in a small smile and chuffs, then regrets it. "Don't make me laugh until I'm fully healed."

I carry him through the doorway and deposit him on the bench to finish his healing. Each one of my mates meet me in my dressing room, wrapping me in their arms like they're glad to see I'm still standing—still breathing. I wasn't too certain at the end there that I'd be leaving that arena alive and that's saying something.

I should probably feel relieved, or at the very least, glad that I'm still here and that I won. No such feelings surround me. There's only a deep-seated, bone-deep sort of dread that encases me like the very air I breathe.

This night is far from over.

"Moons above, you scared the shit out of us, Sadie!"

Dante growls, putting me at arms length so he can look me over. "Don't ever do that again."

"Trust me, Blondie, I don't plan on it. Unless you have more skeletons hiding in the closest that will come into the light and challenge me to a fucking fight to the death."

His shoulders shake with laughter as he wraps his arms around me, cradling my head to his chest. "There's that fire."

Before I can respond, Kaos jerks me away, running those calloused hands over each and every part of my body. "Left shoulder," I tell him, thinking about Savannah. I can still feel the phantom blade pushing through the bone and cartilage. "I think my ribs are also bruised." I press lightly on the area and wince. "Make that broken."

To his credit, Kaos merely grits his teeth and gets right to work. Instantly, his black healing magic wraps around me and the pain begins to recede, though I'm sure it will take a while for the mental scars from this ordeal to heal.

Maybe this is what people mean when talking about the stain killing leaves on your soul. Maybe it's not so much as the act itself but the *aftereffects.*

Savannah's death is hitting me harder than those faceless Elites. Probably because we're much closer in age and the fact that I almost lost. I almost fucking died and left my mates to that bitch.

Once my shoulder and ribs are mostly healed, Kaos backs away, allowing me to discard the worn and tattered arena clothes. I don't even bother covering myself up. At this point every person in the room has seen me naked at least once.

When Hemsworth is alert and back on his feet, Elian sighs, running a hand through his tuft of hair. "We shouldn't keep them waiting any longer."

"Let's get this over with."

I slide my beautiful black dress up my frame once more and Reed's deft fingers have me zipped up in no time. He looks a little drained, which is likely from me stealing his magic none too gently, but he doesn't look upset about it. "I'm glad you finally listened to me," he says with tears in his eyes.

I lean in and kiss his cheek where the tear falls. "Thanks for saving me, Red."

"Anything for you, Love."

Kaos hands me my shadestone dagger, which brings me a bit of comfort having something familiar and deadly sharp strapped to me once more, and then we're trailing out the way we came in.

Nick meets us at the entrance to the arena with a sad smile tipping up the corner of his lips. "Glad to see you alive, Shadowbringer. I've been tasked with escorting you to the garden."

"I don't suppose we could skip this victory celebration shit and go home?"

"I'm afraid not. They're not done with you yet, Sinclair. Be on your guard."

"As if I'd ever let it down," I mumble, following him back up the stairs. I swear there's an extra flight or two than there was going in and I'm panting by the time we reach the top.

I've been injected with venom, forced to watch a horrific act, kill a girl tonight, and they want me to join them in their fucking garden?

I have half a mind to ignore Nick and head for the front door but that would only make things worse. At least I absolved my mates of their "crimes."

We reach a sliding glass door that leads to the sprawling covered garden. I spot the Elders standing in a semicircle under the gazebo waiting for us with their hands behind their backs through the glass. Niall and Adam are standing beside them with grim faces.

"There you are!" Reginald says, motioning us forward.

"Congratulations on winning the challenge, dear. It's a pity Savannah was too blinded by her lust for your mates to see the threat you truly are. Such a shame to lose a power like hers." His face pinches for a moment before he masks it. "Ah, well, bygones are bygones, right?"

I should be shocked by his utter disregard for human and supernatural life but I'm not, at least not for her. It takes everything in me to hold back my sneer though. "Right. So, what is this place?" I glance at the exotic looking plants lining the walkway. Most of them look like a cross between orchids and Venus flytraps. The ceiling is a dome shape and paned with darkened glass. So much for getting to see the moon and stars.

Reginald notices where my attention strays. "This, my dear, is our garden." No shit, really? *Keep your mouth shut for a little longer, Sadie.* "The lovely Hedge Weavers we employ in our service tend to it daily, but I'm afraid the flowers aren't why we're out here."

"Oh, and why are we out here then?"

"Come, take a walk with us and I'll show you."

My internal alarms blare louder, cautioning me not to move forward but I don't really have a choice, my Sworn and Hemsworth filing in behind me. The Elders lead us around the pebbled walkway until we reach a large opening. There are several stone statues in the center, most of them with their faces pinched in fear like a macabre centerpiece.

Reginald stops and trains his eyes on me. "I'll skip right to the chase, my dear." Gods, I wish he'd stop calling me that. "I can tell you're exhausted from the events that transpired tonight." He pauses, waiting until he knows he has our full attention. "We want you to pledge your undying loyalty to our cause. We can't have you running amuck causing all sorts of chaos now, can we? It's bad for business."

"Why should we join your cause, exactly?"

Thoughts? I project to my mates.

Obviously, we can't join them, Kaos responds.

No shit, Elian says, tugging on Kaos' bond to respond. Then out loud. "We are already on the side of the Weavers, Elder. Do you require something more?"

Follow my lead, I say.

"Pledge yourself to us in a blood oath, or face the consequences," Vald hisses.

"Why?" I ask.

"Your power of course. You're much too powerful to be allowed free rein. A Night Weaver with a Lighter mate who can borrow his power *and* use their own? We could never allow such a thing to exist without it being loyal to us." It. As if I'm not even a person.

"No. I will take no such oath." Fuck the consequences. I'm tired and I'm pissed. Obviously, they're afraid of us or they wouldn't be asking us to do this.

Reginald grins like the Cheshire cat. Unease takes root in my spine and slowly spreads through my back to my neck. "We thought you might say that and planned accordingly."

Vald snaps his fingers and Elron bursts through the other side of the garden, holding two shifters by the back of their necks. One is the shifter that served me at their dinner table. I'm not sure who the other is. Elron unsheathes the dagger at his side and those dead eyes glint as he trains them on us. Unlike Savannah, this man is no stranger to killing, and I have no doubt he'll murder them in cold blood. My jaw grinds.

"How about now?" Vald asks with a slight chuckle in his tone.

What these bastards haven't realized is while they've been stalling me, I've been stalling them. I give my mates a slight nod and Kaos steps forward to grab their attention. I ignore what he's saying and focus on slowly moving my hand toward my shadestone blade strapped to my thigh. Thankfully, their attention is on him.

"How about this?" I ask as I get the hilt into my palm only for Elian to rip it away from me. His corded arm draws back as he readies to throw it—not at an Elder though. No, he's aiming for his father and it's too late to stop him.

With rage in those emerald eyes, Elian throws his arm forward and lets go. Time seems to slow down as the blade sails through the air. My other mate's shock brushes up against the bond. Seems as though none of us expected Elian to do this.

The Elders turn, surprise registering on their faces when they realize what's happening. Even Elron's eyes widen but he's way too big to move out of the way fast enough. That's why you must have balance—being a brute has its advantages, sure—but you're slow, and in this case, it's going to cost him.

The shadestone embeds itself in his neck and blood pours from the wound. Elron abandons the shifters and reaches up to yank the blade out, only for smoke to rise from his skin as it burns his hand.

Of course! The shadestone doesn't deem him worthy enough to wield it. I glance at Elian's still outstretched, unblemished palm. Interesting.

His father grunts and gurgles, placing his other palm to his neck to try and keep the blood from spewing to no avail. He collapses to his knees. Elian disappears into the shadows only to reappear at his father's side. He leans over to whisper something I don't quite catch into his ear and his father's eyes widen. True fear crosses his features before Elron reaches up to take the dagger out. This time he manages to pull it from his neck, and he throws it across the room, only for it to land near the Elders' feet.

Why? I demand through the bond.

I'm sorry. I had to, Elian responds.

Time returns to normal as Elron looks toward the Elders. The red staining the pebbles beneath him creeps toward the flowers. "Heal. Me." His words are garbled and barely understandable because of the blood flowing from his wound. If I had to guess I'd say he has a minute or two left.

Reginald tsks and turns his back on his head of security. "Well, I sure wasn't expecting that." Elron takes his last gasping breath moments later and slumps over on the pebbles. Elian breathes a sigh of relief and shadows back to us. "This night has taken quite the unexpected turn, hasn't it? Good thing we always have a contingency plan!" He claps his hands in glee, startling us and the shifters Elron was holding scramble for the exit.

"If the poor shifters' lives over there weren't enough to motivate you to listen to us, how about a few lives you care dearly for?" Vogt asks.

Someone steps over Elron's body, making the blood in my veins run cold. "My, my, look at the mess you've made, Mercedes," a dark voice says, one that brushes up against my senses, one that I'd hoped to never hear again unless he was at the end of my blade. Every single muscle in my body tenses at the sound of his voice out of fear. A shudder racks through me as I try to block out the onslaught of trauma and memories that want to surge out of my mental box at the mere sight of him. My uncle. Fuck, this is bad.

I laugh to cover my confusion. "If you think I give a shit about this man, then you're dead wrong." His sharp jawline is still covered in stubble, the way he likes to keep it, and he doesn't look a day older than he did when I last saw him. He's wearing a black robe similar to the Elders but the symbol on his chest is different.

"I thought I taught you better than this, niece. Us Sinclair's always clean up our messes." My gaze darts toward my shadestone dagger at the Elders feet. I calculate my odds of reaching it in a millisecond. I'm too far away. "I wouldn't, if I were you," he says. "You see, the Elders sent me and Elron after something important while they kept you all distracted here." Mickey gestures with his hands, a wicked glint in his eye and someone dear to me steps into view behind him.

A gasp works its way up my throat. "Ash, what are you doing with *him?*"

Tears flow freely down her face, dripping onto the ground as they mingle with Elron's blood. "I'm so sorry, Sadie. I had no other choice." And I notice for the first time that her hands are not bound.

Betrayal burns brightly in my gut. I analyze every conversation we've had over the past month in the blink of an eye, and everything clicks into place. She was the only other one who knew about Reed. She knew Hemsworth could talk. She knows all my secrets. This whole time she's known everything because *I fucking told her.*

"What have you *done?*" My voice cracks, giving away the depth of my emotions.

Ash begins to sob even harder. "Please, you have to forgive me. They put some kind of magic on me where I couldn't talk. I'm sorry, Sadie, but I had no choice."

"We always have a choice, Ash. And you chose *wrong.*"

"He has my parents!" she blurts.

I scoff. "Your parents are dead. I went with you to their fucking funeral!"

She shakes her head. "Mickey can—"

My uncle cuts off her sentence by throwing his elbow into her temple and she slumps to the ground. I wince when she smacks her head on the pebbles, even if she is a traitor and kind of deserves it. I still don't understand how my uncle plays into all this.

Mickey's nose wrinkles. "Enough of that. Now you know

your best friend betrayed you. She has been feeding us information this whole time and you gave it to her so easily."

My emotions flicker between hurt, betrayal, and rage. So much rage that the kindling flame inside me bursts to life. Black starts to bleed into my vision as I feel that same presence taking over like the night of Tyler's death.

"Bring in the others," Reginald snaps.

My stomach churns with anxiety as Emma steps through the doorway sporting a black eye. Her hands are bound with a bane rope, her clothes are torn, she's covered in scratches. Adam takes a step toward her, but Nick stops him with a hand to the chest. The trio have been relatively silent until this point but now they look at their fathers with hatred.

Bedi strolls through the door a moment later, hands also bound, looking even worse than Emma. Her red hair is tangled and wild, and her clothes are tattered and bloody. She definitely put up a fight. She glances at me and mouths, *"I'm sorry."*

Mickey laughs upon seeing her. "Fancy seeing you here, Bedisa. Seems as though you didn't do a very good job of being my niece's protector."

My attention strays behind them as Vinson is dragged through the opening by an unknown Weaver. He looks the worst out of all of them. His head hangs down and he can barely walk. The black veins are now all the way up his neck, crawling up his cheek.

"We're going to kill one of your friends until you pledge your loyalty to us or decide to let them all die. Starting with the shifter since you seem to care about them so much." The unknown Weaver drags Vin over to the Elders and dumps him at their feet. "How many will you let die tonight, Sinclair?"

Shit. Shit. *Shit.*

They've got me cornered. I won't be able to take them all

on before they kill Vinson. Will I let my friends die at the expense of staying out of the Elders' servitude?

Vinson's golden eyes plead with me not to do anything stupid, but I refuse to let him die. I open my mouth to speak, but Reginald beats me to the punch.

"You're taking too long to decide," he says, switching positions with the unknown Weaver to hold Vin up under his arms. Reginald flips the shadestone dagger in his hand. *When did he pick that up?*

How is it not burning him?

People say that every action in this world bears a consequence and I never realized exactly how *true* that was until now. I can see it like a fucked up movie in my head how every single thing I've ever done over the course of my life has led me here, to this moment. This gut-wrenching, all encompassing, life altering moment.

Reginald plunges the blade deep into Vinson's chest and he cries out in pain. My heart slams to a halt as a scream tears from my throat, mixing with his cry. Tears begin to flow freely down my face as I feel the jab to my heart like it's my own.

A steel band wraps around my middle, keeping me from rushing forward. I didn't even realize I was moving.

Reginald laughs and leaves the dagger in Vin's chest as he tosses his lifeless body toward us. Hemsworth dives to the ground and catches Vin's head before it can smack the ground.

My entire world tilts on its axis and the ever-building rage inside me settles in my bones. I'd rather die tonight than pledge myself to these assholes, and I don't care to sacrifice myself to do it.

"Bring the girl next," Vald says, watching his sons carefully, and that's when all hell breaks loose. The trio spring into action, diving for Emma. Niall manages to get a hand around her arm, and they connect as a Circle, disappearing into a cloud of black smoke.

Grab onto Hemsworth! Elian shouts through the bond. His hand wraps around my wrist and I dive for Hems. As soon as my fingers connect with his fur, the familiar swirling black abyss that is Elian's magic surrounds us. Bedi dives toward us, wrapping a hand around Dante's arm just as Elian shadows our Circle out and we escape into the night's sweet embrace leaving my uncle, Ash, and the Elders behind.

A dark, ugly emotion flares to life in my belly, like rot seeping through roots. Anger. Hatred. Resentment. All at the men responsible. All culminating into a toxic concoction in my stomach that churns and broils like acid.

When we pop out of the frigid shadow realm, the familiar walls of the mansion greet us as we all stumble back into reality. Elian grunts, drawing my attention to him as he clutches his side. His wide eyes capture mine as a dribble of blood slides down his nose. So many unspoken things pass between us and then his eyes roll to the back of his head, and he collapses to the ground. Shadowing this many people must have taken it out of him. Shit. Thankfully, Kaos lunges for him and keeps his head from smacking the floor.

I glance over to Vinson who's laying on top of Hemsworth. His body is still on the floor of the mansion. Too fucking still. Blood soaks into Hems' fur and I drop to my knees beside my two fallen mates. Vinson may not be mine, but he wormed his way into my heart, and I don't plan on letting him die.

I take in the harrowed looks in my Sworn's eyes around me and then I know without a shadow of a doubt what my purpose in this life is.

It's time to go after the Elders and anyone else who dares stand in my way. At this point, if you're not with me, then you're against me. It's time to kick ass and take names. I tried to do this the right way and now I'm going to do it my way. This whole world is going to burn until I purge the evil from the very surface. But first, I need to rally the forces because these worlds have been divided for far too long.

My name is Sadie Sinclair, and I'm not going down without one hell of a fight.

34

VINSON

My heart stutters and comes to a full stop as I find Sadie descending the stairs in her evening attire.

She looks absolutely divine with her hair braided into an intricate design and in her beautiful star-fall dress with the different color accents flowing off of it. I wish she had a shifter element on her as well, even if it's selfish of me to want. I wish *my* mark was on her too.

Seeing her like this is bittersweet because I can't go with her... and there's no time to tell her how I feel about her. There's not a single doubt in my mind that she's my mate. The pull between us is too great to be anything else. Alpha Darren teaches us from a young age what to expect and it's everything I thought it would be, but also different because Sadie isn't a shifter. That doesn't matter though, not really. She's always been and forever will be perfect for me.

My wolf prances inside my head like he's punctuating that thought. It's strange to be able to feel him, and even see thoughts and flashes of him, but know that he can never materialize without finding our mate. He nods his head in

Sadie's direction, and I have to tamp down my urge to smile or risk looking like a loon.

The rhythm of my heart kicks back up again as she levels those gorgeous green eyes on me and stops at the edge of the stairs. Suddenly, my whole body starts tingling like there's the weight of a million pounds on me at once, and I lose consciousness.

When I awaken, it's to the soft feeling of someone brushing the hair back from my face. My mother used to do that to wake me every morning when I was a pup, but this is someone different. Someone who makes my skin tingle in a much different way.

My eyes open to find Sadie above me, worry clear in her eyes, and her hands cradling my head in her lap. "What happened?"

"You collapsed. Are you okay?"

"Yeah, don't worry about me, I'll be fine," I tell her, hoping she believes me. "You need to get going before you're late." I try to stand, but it's like my legs don't want to hold me up. Thankfully, Dante lifts me up under my arms to help me stand again. I make sure to keep my back as straight as possible and a soft smile on my lips. She has so much on her plate tonight, I'm the last thing she needs to worry about.

Dante and Kaos help get me settled in the room I'm borrowing in their estate on the twin sized bed. Kaos runs his hands over me and tries to heal me once more to no avail. "I'm sorry, Vinson," he says to me, pain reflected in his eyes.

I wave him on. "Go, protect Sadie at all costs tonight. She's the most important thing."

"That we agree on," Dante says.

They each give me a nod and then leave me alone with my thoughts. I sigh, running a hand across my chin. They really have tried everything for me, and this isn't their fault.

Hell, I wouldn't change taking that hit for Sadie for anything either.

My eyelids begin to droop, and I lay my head against the pillow, promising myself I'm only going to take a short nap. I should know that's a lie, I think as I fall into a deep sleep with Sadie's beautiful image imprinted in my brain.

My mind jolts awake sometime later, but my body is still sluggish, and I have absolutely no idea how much time has passed. It could've been hours or minutes for all I know. Whatever these black veins are doing to me is getting worse. Way worse. I can barely manage to lift my head and when I do, everything is spinning. "Fuck, this is bad," I say out loud.

When the room finally stops its swirling, I glance around, trying and failing to figure out what woke me. I'm almost ready to give up and lay back down when I hear a disturbance downstairs and a crash. I'm on my feet, bracing myself against the wall before I can even think. My headache pounds against my skull behind my eyelids. I don't have time to worry about it.

Shit, is Sadie back already?

Did something happen?

With my adrenaline pumping the fogginess in my limbs seems to dissipate, and I bound down the steps, coming to a halt when I find Bedi and Elian's father fighting against one another with an unknown man standing to the side, watching the spectacle.

Emma's on the ground, with her hands tied behind her back, completely down for the count, and Sadie's friend, Ashley, is sobbing next to her while Bedi fights. She tries to reach for Bedi, to help, I guess, but Elron strikes her down with ease, sending her flying back. She lands on the ground in a heap and sobs. "You weren't supposed to hurt us! Sadie was never supposed to know what I've done!"

The unknown man chuckles. "We lied to you that day, sweetheart. You see, you lead my niece right into a trap of my own design. Now I'll get to bring her, this wretched seer, and her mates down, all thanks to you." He stalks over to her and grips her chin, hauling her from the floor by it. That's when I lose it. Even if she's a fucking traitor, no one hurts a woman around me.

The asshole doesn't see me coming until my fist connects with his face. He rubs his jaw, turns to me, smirks, and raises his fist. I manage to block his first blow with my own, but he reaches under me with his other and gut punches me. As I'm wheezing, he clocks me in the face, and with the poison in my system weakening me, I'm not at full strength.

I'm forced to back up to avoid his next hit and out of the corner of my eye, I watch as Bedi loses her fight with Elron. She collapses to the ground like a sack of potatoes. Shit, we are totally screwed if Bedi went down so easily. The seer is extremely powerful. Shifters have a built-in magic detector, and that woman made the top of my chart, right up there with Sadie. I want nothing more in this moment than to morph into my wolf and let him take charge of the fight, but I can't and it's infuriating.

Elron laughs. "Hurry up, Mickey. We've got a show to get to. Dispose of the shifter quickly."

Mickey looks me up and down and laughs. "No, I think this one is special to my little niece. Why else would he be here with the others? He's coming with us. You go on ahead, they'll notice if you're gone too long."

Fuck, I can't let them take me. I know Sadie and she'd never let them kill me, even to save the greater good. I attempt to fight back but my odds are not good. Mickey may not be a beefy dude, but he's fairly strong and with one well-aimed hit to the temple from him, I go out like a light, hating myself for being too weak to stop them.

Consciousness returns to me sometime later, but I'm barely able to comprehend anything around me other than the feeling of my body sliding across the ground. Someone is dragging me, but to where I have no clue.

"Get up, you filthy shifter," the person holding onto me snarls. "I hope they kill your flea ridden ass first."

With all my might, I pull myself to my feet, realizing my hands are bound with bane rope. Little good that does as I can't call on my wolf anyway.

We emerge into a garden, and I catch a glimpse of Bedi and Ash for the first time since they knocked me out. The Elders, Sadie, and her Sworn seem to be having a standoff in the garden. I jolt when I find Elron's body on the ground.

Fuck, this is so bad.

Words are exchanged but my mind is so foggy I can hardly follow any of it until Reginald motions for the Weaver holding me to bring me forward. "We're going to kill one of your friends until you pledge your loyalty to us or decide to let them all die. Starting with the shifter since you seem to care about them so much." As they're dragging me over, I implore Sadie with my eyes not to do anything stupid, but she's far too stubborn to listen. "How many will you let die tonight, Sinclair?" Reginald asks with glee.

The unknown Weaver practically tosses me into Reginald's arms and it takes my sheer force of will to keep standing. "You're taking too long to decide."

The glistening blood on the blade in Reginald's hand catches my attention seconds before he plunges it into my chest. My entire body tenses with absolute blinding pain, and

I cry out. I'm fairly certain Sadie screams but I can't hear anything over the roar in my ears.

The only thing in my mind besides the agony, is her.

Sadie. My moon.

I'm never going to get to tell her she's *mine*. Even if this world doesn't allow it. Even if we'd be breaking every law in the book. Even if it's only for a little while.

I guess that will always be my biggest regret.

There's some kind of commotion and then a blast of cold air surrounds me, trying to cool my feverish flesh, but there's no use. Is this the afterlife finally coming to claim me?

No, I'm not ready yet.

But, my heart rate is slowing, each thud growing fainter and fainter...

"Godsdammit, Vinson! *STAY WITH ME!*" my mate screams into my ear and another round of anguish flares through my body. Every inch of it is in unrelenting torment. "You can't die, I refuse for you to take him!" she weeps as my heart stops.

"You can't have him, death! Goddess, if you're listening, I will seek vengeance. You do not get to take him from me. Vinson is fucking *MINE!*"

There's a bright flare of light around me, both black and white that blinds me from behind my eyelids. The pain in my chest returns, and then I gasp.

ALSO BY DEMI WARRIK

Thank you so much for sticking with me and reading! I fucking love each and every one of you. If you enjoyed this story, I'd really be forever grateful if you left a review, even if it's only a few words. They mean so much to me. <3

FATES MARK SERIES (COMPLETE):

Called by Fate: (Fates Mark Book Three)

Marked by Night: (Fates Mark Book One)

Bound by Light: (Fates Mark Book Two)

BLOOD CURSED DUET:

Burning Chance: (Blood Cursed Book One)

Blurb: My name is Rue Delacroix, and my life went to hell in a hand basket faster than you can say *destiny sucks.* Starting with getting bit by a feral vampire, which is a death sentence for a witch. Thankfully, three dashing wolf shifters jump in and save my life.

Turns out there's something special about my blood and it cures feral vampires. Yeah. Once that cats out of the bag? Everyone will want to use me or kill me.

Good thing I have those three shifters hell-bent on protecting me, right?

I've also managed to capture the eye of the notorious vampire leader. I shouldn't want him—not when I'm nothing more than an irresistible blood bag to his kind. But I'm drawn to him all the same.

Will we be able to stop the feral fangs from tearing me apart? Or am I doomed to spill every last drop of my blood?

Co-Write with Leah Steele:

Knot a Clue: (Heat Paradise Murder Mystery Omegaverse)

Blurb: After finding out I'm the only omega to emerge in this year's ceremony, I'm whisked away to a hidden resort nestled in the mountains.

What might sound like a nice vacation is anything but. I'm here with twenty hand-selected alphas who are competing for a spot in my pack on live television.

The downside? The public chooses who stays and who goes.

Even worse? Someone is murdered.

Everyone is suspect, aside from the dashing doctor, and the rugged twin contestants who were with me when I found the body.

Can we solve this mystery before the killer strikes again? And more importantly, can I do it without falling for the men I may not be able to keep?

STAY CONNECTED

Do you want to see content like cover reveals, teasers, and exclusive content before anyone else? Then join my reader group! We post lots of bookish related things, sexy men, host giveaways, release parties, and have an overall amazing time. I'd love to have you join the dark side—oops, I mean me.
Demi Warrik's Facebook Reader Group

ACKNOWLEDGMENTS

First, I'd like to thank my readers because without your support, I wouldn't be able to do this. I'm grateful for all of you. From the messages I have received, to the amazing mood boards and reviews, to the comments I have seen rec'ing me. Seriously, you all are the best and I absolutely love the RH indie community. Keep on rockin' badasses. You all are fucking phenomenal.

Next, I'd like to thank my husband because without his unending love, this book likely wouldn't have happened. From doing small things around the house to tolerating my antics when I zone off thinking about a particularly awesome scene. You're the best, boo! I love you to the moon.

I also need to thank some very special people in my life.

Persephone, without your gauntlet idea, I probably never would have met my deadline and even though your need for blood and these punishments suck, I still flove you and I'm glad you're a part of my life.

Luna, oh, Luna. Girl, you're like the balance to keep the scales aligned. Not to mention the voice of reason to Persephone and I's "burn the world down." Without you, the Shire would not be the same. Thanks for always being the sweet one, dork!

Lysanne, my badass PA, our meeting was an act of fate, I swear. I wouldn't be able to keep my damn head on straight without you and I will forever be grateful for you taking me under your wing. Thanks for not laughing at my stupid questions and random mini anxiety attacks. And the dad jokes.

Life wouldn't be the same without them. You're kind of a big dill. *insert pickle meme*

Del, you stuck with me after MBN and are a force to be reckoned with, I tell you. Thanks for letting me bounce ideas off you and being one of the best friends a girl could ask for. Life is so much brighter with you in it.

Rory, where to even begin? You are so amazing and came into my life at exactly the right time to give me that little push I needed. Thank you for listening to me, for the random TikTok's that are fucking hilarious and just—heh, I know—being the best author friend. The world needs more people like you in it, stabby.

To my Mooners, my kick-fucking-ass betas, wow, you ladies definitely took this job seriously and ran with it. Thank you for helping me whip these characters into shape. I appreciate every single one of you. #Mooners4eva!

To Raven and Polly, my beautiful editing tag team, thank you for everything that you do. I seriously could not appreciate you both more!

Wow, that was a lot of thank you's! Haha I'm sure I'm probably missing someone but just know that if you're in my life, I'm so happy you are. Thank you from the bottom of my heart.

ABOUT THE AUTHOR

Demi Warrik is an emerging romance author dedicated to giving you stories you can ditch reality with. She loves animals of all kinds, the smell of books and coffee, which she prefers. In her free time she enjoys writing romantic shenanigans that you'll be laughing about for days. Most of the time you can find her with her nose shoved in a book or plotting someone's demise. In a story, of course! Join Demi on her journey to finally write down the plethora of characters swirling around in her brain demanding to have their stories told. She'd love it if you would.

Join my newsletter:
http://www.demiwarrik.com

Printed in Great Britain
by Amazon